SHADOWS & BRIMSTONE

A MYSTIC INVESTIGATORS OMNIBUS

PATRICK THOMAS & JOHN L. FRENCH

PADWOLF PULP

PADWOLF PULP

an imprint of Padwolf Publishing Inc.

PADWOLF PUBLISHING INC.
WWW.PADWOLF.COM
www.facebook.com/Padwolf

WWW.PATTHOMAS.NET
www.facebook.com/PatrickThomasAuthor

WWW.MYSTICINVESTIGATORS.COM

ISBN 10 digit 1-890096-66-0   ISBN 13 digit 978-1-890096-66-3

First Printing. Printed in the USA.

Contents

MYSTIC
INVESTIGATORS™
From The
SHADOWS

Murphy's Noir™
Pulp Adventure featuring

The Nightmare™

Nemesis™

The Pink Reaper™

Praise for Bullets &
Brimstone
"If paranormal
that mocks the
darkness is your
cup of tea, check
this out."-Wendy
S. Delmater,
Abyss & Apex

Patrick Thomas & John L. French

From The Shadows

The woman in black who, before now, had little memory of who and what she was suddenly remembered. She was not just a woman. She was something of myth and legend, a force of nature with a mission and a purpose. She was the daughter of Nyx, a child of the night. She was the enforcer for the Council of Thrones. She was the agent of retribution. She was Vengeance. She was Nemesis.

And she had awakened.

Bullets & Brimstone

Police officer Tim Blake was himself watching the fire and waiting for his tour of duty to end. He hoped his relief would not be long in coming. He'd pulled OT three shifts running and all he wanted tonight was to go home and be with his wife and kids. He had just checked his watch for the third time in ten minutes when there came the sound of a building coming down.

Looking up, Blake was amazed to see a man walk from the cascade of falling brick and lumber. He thought at first it was a firefighter or detective who had gotten just a bit too close, but no, he decided, the man had come from inside the house.

No freaking way, the logical part of his mind told him.

Way, argued that part that believed what he'd just seen. And that's when Blake noticed something else.

The guy looked like Bogart. No so much in the normal way. His face was different, but it took effort to realize that. He was Bogart in how he moved and dressed. The cut of his jib as they used to say. In much the same way a short, overweight woman could still be an effective Elvis impersonator, this guy aped Bogie. In fact, watching him the tough guy bit didn't seem like it was an act.

Amidst the flames and the water and the organized commotion that followed the collapse, Blake realized that no one else seemed to have seen the man. Knowing it was his duty, Blake moved to confront the stranger.

"Good evening, Officer," the man said as Blake approached him (Rick in Casablanca, that's who he sounds like, the cop thought, even as he prepared to take the guy into custody) "My name is Negral. I'd like to talk to Detective Bianca Jones, please."

FROM THE SHADOWS

A MYSTIC INVESTIGATORS BOOK

PATRICK THOMAS & JOHN L. FRENCH

PADWOLF PULP

This one's for
the Brooklyn nephews
Joel, Timothy, and Luke
[and Valerie for good measure]
-PT

To Tom and Ginger Johnson -
Thanks for keeping Pulp alive
-JLF

THE WOMAN IN BLACK

An adventure of Nemesis and Nightmare

When the woman in black woke in the dark alley she had little memory, save that of an ocean voyage. The things she did, the things that were done to her, she barely recalled. There was a man – no, someone more than a man. Lightning danced in his eyes and fingertips. He offered her a cup and she took it from his hands and drank it all. After that, there was the ship and the journey across the great ocean. She worked for her passage as a servant, almost a slave, with little food and less rest. There were those in the crew who saw a very beautiful woman and wanted more from her than she was willing to give. So they tried to take it, to take her. She remembers screaming, but none of it came from her. She doesn't know why they made those horrible noises of pain and agony, nor does she want to. The shadows of the memories were enough to haunt her. The real thing…She could never have done the things. They were many, she only one woman. After the screaming, however, she was left alone with her empty mind and the fear of what she had done. The terror of what she might be to be able to do. And the remembrance that vengeance felt good.

The rest of the voyage was nothing but shadows, but the darkness made the woman in black comfortable. It was like she belonged to the night, not that she could explain it beyond that. When the ship finally docked, after passing the Great Lady of the Harbor by the island city, she was put off. They came for her in the bright light of day, which is when she felt weakest. Denied of all but the dark clothes she wore and what little she could carry, two friends of those who had screamed carried her off and abandoned her in the light of day. They spit on her and called her witch and other names that would have been appropriate if she had willingly encouraged the men and let them do what they wanted. Had the two men not remembered the screams of their friends that continued throughout the night and started anew the next night, they might have done worse. They were lucky they did not. Her horror at what she had done kept her from fighting back against an eviction, but not another attack. The men left her alone in the alley where she slept and dreamt of what she once knew until the night welcomed and awoke her.

*

For the fifth time in a half hour, Michael Shaw looked at his watch. The only thing worse than the Bolero, he thought, was the Bolero played poorly on an out of tune piano. But Mrs. Rittenhouse had served a very nice dinner, and if listening to her daughter play was the price of the meal then her guests gladly paid it.

Finally, the crescendo came and went and the group suffering was over. Shaw joined in with the polite applause and got in line to congratulate the young girl and her no doubt tone-deaf mother.

A vision in pink came up beside him. "Michael?" it asked.

"Kaye, Kaye Chandler. I didn't expect to see you tonight, not so soon anyway."

"Father insisted I get out of the house. Said two weeks was long enough to hide from the world." Kaye looked at the now empty piano. "After hearing that, perhaps I should have stayed hidden."

"Now, Kaye, as I recall we all went to your dance recitals."

"I was good."

"You were six; you only thought you were good."

"Thought?" said Kaye with a grin that hadn't been on her face in far too long. "Watch this." The pretty blonde kicked her leg straight up so her foot was up above her head, then did a pirouette, spinning several times on her right foot before ending in a full split. The moves were not done with the grace of a ballerina, but that of an athlete.

She rose to the impolite stares of some of the other guests. Kaye smiled and curtseyed to them.

"There will be gossip by tomorrow that I've lost my mind after the murder," she said. "And maybe I have."

"I don't know about that. I was very sorry to hear about your uncle. Do the police have any leads?"

"According to the detective on the case, one Lieutenant Easton, 'progress is being made.'"

"That sounds like police talk for 'we're stumped.'"

"That's what I think, too, Michael." There was a glint in her eye. "But something tells me that somehow justice will find my uncle's killer."

Maybe it will, thought Shaw. Especially if The Nightmare gives justice a hand. Of course, he had no way of knowing that justice was already holding hands with Kaye Chandler. Sadly she didn't know that justice was not a cheap date.

*

It was late when Shaw got home. After heaping the required compliments on the proud mother and embarrassed-to-be-the-center-of attention daughter, he had spent some more time talking to Kaye Chandler, finding out what he could about her uncle's murder, trying to sound sympathetic and not nosy. When Kaye finally pleaded fatigue he offered to drive her home, but she had her own roadster and so they parted when their cars were brought around.

Given his nocturnal activities, Shaw was not one to insist that his house staff stay up until his return. Leaving his LaSalle in the front drive, he let himself into the stately mansion that his family had called home ever since his great-grandfather had won it in a crooked poker game.

The house was dark and quiet, with only enough lighting so one could make his way without mishap. Not that Shaw needed the lights. Since starting his nightly adventures he had become quite at home in the dark and had come to rely on his other senses to see him safely through it.

Shaw made it to his room and was removing the evening

clothes that were *de rigueur* for society's social events when he saw the envelope. It was lying on his dresser, the dresser whose lowest drawer contained a false bottom, under which was a different set of evening wear. The envelope was plain white, letter-sized and addressed in a fluid hand to "The Nightmare."

His first thoughts were *Who?* and *How?* These he quickly dismissed. He knew how. He would have no trouble getting into a house this size with its multiple points of entry so neither would anyone else. As to who – Shaw knew that there were others like him, stalkers of the night who devoted themselves to the cause of justice, taking action when the law could not or would not act. He had no doubt it was one of them.

Opening the envelope, Shaw took out a sheet of paper on which was printed a time, a date, and a single word, "Moran's." It was an obvious invitation, one which Shaw was eager to accept.

*

Moran's was a bar on the city's east side. Nothing fancy, just well-poured drinks at a fair price. When Shaw arrived it was closed – doors locked and windows shuttered. Unusual for a Thursday before midnight.

"I guess finding my way in is part of the initiation," Shaw said to himself. Then he remembered that the invitation was to The Nightmare and not idle millionaire Michael Shaw. Fortunately, he had come dressed for the part – dark suit, black trench coat, gloves, and hat. All that was needed for the costume to be complete was the full face mask. This he donned and so became The Nightmare.

The Nightmare, Shaw thought. One idle comment to a crook whose life he spared and he was stuck with the name. "I'm your worst nightmare." *What was I thinking? Maybe those inside could suggest a better name. But first I have to get inside.*

A fire escape in the rear of a building two houses down. Short leaps across roofs. An open skylight and The Nightmare was inside. When he found the stairs that led to the floors below he saw a note tacked to the open door.

"You could have just knocked," it read. It was signed with a symbol he later learned was Sanskrit.

The bar on the first floor was dark with no lights on save one over a table in the back of the room. This light was arranged so that only the hands of the three men at the table were visible.

The Nightmare approached. A spectral voice stopped him.

"Michael Shaw," the ghostly tones came from everywhere and nowhere.

"Yes." Shaw wondered which of the men were speaking.

"Also known as The Nightmare. You would join our society?"

"I wasn't aware I needed your permission."

Another voice, just as eerie, answered him. "To fight crime, to seek Justice, you do not. No one does. But you may need our help. And to earn that, you must prove yourself worthy."

"And how do I do that?"

"Johnny the Dip is dead," the third man's voice was milder, as if he were more at peace with himself.

"I'd heard that," The Nightmare said. "He was gunned down in an alley off Wall Street."

"What you may not know was that Johnny the Dip was also The Whispering Monk." The first man again, still no way of telling which of the three was speaking. "His death must be avenged. Do that and you will be one of us."

Sure that they could somehow see him, The Nightmare nodded his acceptance of the mission. "And how will you know I've done what you asked?"

He was answered by two different sets of laughter. As they faded out the third man said in a calm voice, "They'll know."

The lights suddenly came on and The Nightmare was alone in the bar.

I'll have to get them to teach me to do that, he thought as a very short man came in from the back. He seemed unfazed by Shaw's appearance.

Stepping behind the bar, the man grew taller. "A ramp," he explained, then added, "You must be the new one. I'm Moran. I own the place."

Taking the extended hand in his, Shaw replied, "I'm The Nightmare."

Moran shrugged. "I've heard worse. Now, if you're willing to raise that mask of yours enough to have a taste, what can I get you? The first drink's on the house, family tradition."

*

In the months since she was abandoned, left alone and friendless, the woman in black learned to survive the streets and alleys. She found where there was shelter from the rain and warm places to sleep, where to find food when hungry and drink when thirsty and how to avoid the predators who stalked people like her. She found others like herself, and they found her. Some offered help, others asked for it, and there were those who just wanted to be left alone in their solitude, misery, or guilt. The woman in black took what she needed and offered what she could, but mostly kept to herself.

At times it seemed that the streets called to her, that the alleys almost spoke her name. "Be one with us. Be our mother, care for us and for those who call us home." The summons nearly woke the memories inside her, brought them to just below the surface of consciousness. The offer was tempting and for all she didn't know, she knew that she could become the protector that was needed. But somehow she also knew that this was not for her, that the Mother of the Streets was someone yet to be and that her own destiny was a different one.

So the woman endured and did what was needed. She ate and drank and slept. Mostly she waited but for what she did not know.

*

The bar known as Dago Mike's was very different than Moran's. For one thing, Moran swept the floor at least twice daily and kept the counters and tables reasonably clean. In Mike's, however, it seemed that the only time a surface felt clean water, a mop, or a rag was when blood needed to be wiped up or sluiced away. And the first drink was not on the house. It was instead as highly priced as any that followed it and at least fifty percent water.

Dago Mike's was one of many seedy taverns Shaw had been in that week. He had the visits down to a science. Order a drink, take a back table, and sit and listen. Shaw listened especially for the names "Johnny the Dip" and "The Whispering Monk." The underworld was a society of rumor and story, of reputation based on deeds both true and imagined. Someone like the Nightmare depended on his feats being exaggerated by those that got away. It added to the mystic and helped instill the fear that sometimes gave him a needed edge. The death of someone like the Monk would not go unremarked for long. Sooner or later a whisper would reach his ears.

The whispers had led him to Mike's, where the word was that this was the last place anyone had seen Johnny. He had ordered his bottle, sat in his corner, and left just before midnight. When dawn came his body was found floating in the harbor.

The whispers also spoke of the occasional disappearance of one of the fair ladies of the streets that offered her body for money. That in itself was not unusual. It was a hard life and not a safe one. But lately, those that disappeared were the newest and the youngest, the ones who had not yet become hardened to the practice of letting men use them.

Maybe a new house had opened. If so, word had not reached the street and no recruiters had been seen. The girls were there one night and gone the next, never to be seen again, except those few whose bodies were found in alleys, dumpsters, and in the water of the river that surrounded the city. But that too was not unusual, and no one remarked on it. It was a tough city and it was a rare night that at least one body was not found. If no one had known the missing, it didn't rate as a topic of conversation.

Maybe, Shaw thought, as he drank his drink and listened to the talk, that the Monk had learned something about the girls, that he knew why they were missing, where they were going and who was leaving bodies in alleys and dumpsters.

If so, somehow the Monk had gotten careless, had said the wrong thing to the wrong person in this very bar and had left unaware of his mistake. And in the life they had both chosen, that was the kind of mistake one made only once.

Enough waiting, Shaw decided. Time to do something stupid and reckless. Picking up his coat and hat, he left his mostly unfinished drink on the table and walked up the bartender.

"I'm looking for a friend of mine," Shaw said in a voice loud enough to be heard by all. "He goes by Johnny the Dip. He used to hang out here sometimes. You seen him lately?"

The bartender shook his head. "He ain't been here for a week or so. Sorry."

Shaw shrugged. "No matter. I'm sure he's floating around someplace. I'll meet up with him sooner or later."

"I'm sure you will," the bartender said, turning to serve another customer.

Shaw pivoted and headed for the front door. As he did the bartender nodded solemnly to two hard men sitting in a corner near the back room.

Like half the bar, Blackie Rogers and Stoner Dance had heard the stranger's question about Johnny the Dip. Unlike the others, Blackie and Stoner could have answered him. They had been present the night Johnny had made his last visit to Dago Mike's. Stoner had made the phone call to let a certain someone know that Johnny was there. Then he and Blackie had carried out that someone's orders.

Now they had new orders. Having been given the nod by the barkeep, they followed the stranger when he left the bar and watched as he cut down the alley.

Shaw knew he was being followed, had counted on it in fact. If they were smart, they would have just let him be. But, he mused, if they were smart, they wouldn't be crooks in the first place. Shaw ducked into the alley's first shadow, putting on his dark coat and hat.

Time, he thought, *to play.*

*

"Where's dat alley lead?" Blackie asked Stoner as their quarry disappeared into its mouth.

"For that guy, a watery grave. Same as we did for the Dip. Let's make this quick."

The two were not that deep into the alley when they heard the laugh, the laugh that told them that they were not alone, the laugh that echoed off the alley walls and came back to them as a sentence of death.

Reaching for their rods, the two men turned a minute too late. The Nightmare was already stepping out of the shadows, his .45s drawn and ready. He fired, striking them in the shoulders and legs, dropping them alive to the alley floor.

The laughter, the roar of guns, sudden pain, and the cold hardness of the alley surface. This was Blackie Rogers's immediate world. Then he felt the warmth of a gun barrel under his jaw, the smell of spent bullets wafting up to his nostrils.

"Who told you to kill Johnny the Dip?"

Until that night, Blackie would have sworn he would never turn yellow or play the rat. That was before the madman with a gun, before the agony in his shoulder and legs, before he was threatened with eternal darkness. He gave up the name as quickly as a frightened child.

As did Stoner. "This guy Marcus had the word out on Johnny. I called him and he said to do the job. He dropped off a grand the next night."

There was one more question. "What was the number?" Stoner gave that up as readily as he did the name.

A name and a number. The Nightmare had gotten what he needed, the next link in the chain. But he also had two men on the ground before him, men whose wounds were not necessarily fatal. But if they lived they would talk and so warn this Marcus. And the Whispering Monk might go unavenged. The only choice was no choice at all. Two .45s sounded as one. There was no laughter as The Nightmare left two dead men in the alley.

*

She was a Pennsylvania girl on her own for the first time. She was a dancer in a city of dancers who was learning that she was not as good as she thought she was. She was a waitress who hated her job. She was behind on her rent and desperate enough to try anything – almost.

There were some things she would not do, not for money, not with strangers. But the blonde man who always left a big tip wasn't asking her to do that. The first day he ate at one of her tables he had noticed that she was, had been, a dancer.

"You've got the legs for it," he said and his smile was warm, not lecherous.

He was tall and good-looking and she was pleased he had noticed her legs.

A few weeks and several dinners later he mentioned the job.

"Nothing unseemly," he assured her. "A club for gentlemen, gentlemen who like watching pretty girls in brief outfits dance while they enjoy some after dinner drinks. And dance is all you would have to do. The rules of the club, you know. No fraternizing with the staff."

"How brief are the costumes?"

He smiled, looked her over and smiled again. "Brief enough and tight enough to display your, ah, attributes, but everything would be covered. Your modesty would be preserved."

It was the way he spoke that convinced her, his concern for her modesty, his use of language. She liked how he had said "unseemly" when he could have used so many other words. He made it sound so sincere and civilized. Like a novel almost.

So she agreed and he gave her the address of the club and told her to be there the night after next. And then with a "see you then" he left, giving her a twenty-dollar bill for a five dollar meal.

Things, the girl thought, *are finally going my way.*

She was, of course, wrong. The man, as men often do when they talk to pretty girls, had lied to her.

*

The club had no name. No sign was on the door. There was nothing to advertise its presence. If you did not know of it, you were not meant to. If you did, you were one of the chosen, and you did not speak of it. Within its walls, society's customs and laws were suspended. Behind its doors, there were only the few rules the club imposed to keep a certain kind of order.

The wait staff was well paid for their service and silence. A harsher payment was promised to anyone who even hinted as to where he worked or what he saw. It was made clear that this payment would be extended to their families as well.

The club was equally generous to its girls, the "fallen flowers" brought in from the streets to satisfy the carnal appetites of its members. Give us six months, the blonde man and a few others like him told them, half a year of doing what you'd be doing anyway and you'll have enough money to quit the life entirely. Then you're just a bus ticket away from a new life, a clean life.

The girls bought the line and most did retire after the six months, taking the bus ticket with the understanding that it was a one-way ride and that a return to the city would be bad for their health.

Some girls did not last the half-year. Some quit and were escorted far away and told of the consequences of their return. A few others fell victim to the darker appetites of some of the club's members. While this kind of behavior was discouraged it was recognized that mistakes were made and accidents happen. The offending member was given a warning and advised that his dues were going to be increased. He was also assured that his "indiscretion" would never come out and never be mentioned again. If he was foolish enough to believe this, so much the better.

*

The man whom everyone believed to be the owner of the club was at his desk when the blonde man came in.

"Excuse me, Mr. Giles."

"What is it, Marcus?"

"Just wanted to let you know that Councilman Pike has finished for the evening. He was most pleased with our selection."

"It wasn't one of our regulars, wasn't it?"

"No, sir. It's the waitress I brought in the other day. You know how the councilman likes them young, fresh, and unwilling."

"Well, he pays for the privilege. About the girl?"

Marcus shook his head. "Pike was … overly enthusiastic. I doubt if she'll last until morning."

"What a waste," Giles sighed. "There are other members who might have enjoyed a bit of recreational rape. Still, it's a big city. It's not like we can't get more when needed."

"Yes, sir. And the waitress?"

"Take care of her in the usual way. Someplace not too close this time."

*

The girl was not quite dead. Marcus could hear her moans from the back seat. It was a sound he enjoyed. He also enjoyed the feeling of anticipation from what he knew was coming next.

Marcus found the alley he had chosen weeks ago for just such an occasion. L-shaped, the back of it was hidden from the street. There was a light at the bend, just bright enough for him to see the girl as he vented his lust while choking off what life she still had in her. He did not know that a door at the end of the alley opened into a vacant storehouse where a woman with not much memory took shelter from the world she only vaguely remembered.

The girl who wanted nothing more than to be a dancer, who had been a waitress, who thought that she had finally caught a lucky break, came back to consciousness as Marcus began to remove what little clothing she still had on.

The horror all came back to her – being seized as soon as she entered the club and locked in a small bedroom. The man who came in, the one who told her to call him "Daddy." She fought as best she could but he overpowered her, ripped off her clothes, and used her in the worst possible ways. And when he was done, he blamed her and called her names. And he beat her until moving was too much effort and breathing only continued because she didn't know how to stop.

And now the would-be dancer was face down in an alley, the odors of garbage and waste overpowering her senses and it was all happening again. This assault, the pain from the last one, the shame and humiliation and the knowledge that she was going to die. In her despair and agony, she called out to the night, "Help me, make them stop, make them pay!"

And she was heard.

The woman in black who, before now, had little memory of who and what she was suddenly remembered. She was not just a woman. She was something of myth and legend, a force of nature with a mission and a purpose. She was the daughter of Nyx, a child of the night. She was the enforcer for the Council of Thrones. She was the agent of retribution. She was Vengeance. She was Nemesis.

And she had awakened.

Nemesis ran from her hiding place and into the alley only to find that she was too late. The young woman who had called for help and vengeance had passed from this world and her abuser was gone. No matter, he might flee the site of his crime but he could not flee Retribution, not once it had been invoked. Pausing a moment to wish the soul of the deceased a safe and happy journey to whatever reward awaited it, Nemesis left the now empty shell of the victim and began her hunt.

Murder leaves a trail. No matter how many lives one has taken, no matter what other horrors one has committed, the act of ending a life leaves a psychic residue that can be followed by those that know how. Nemesis knew how and followed the path left behind by the young woman's killer. It led her uptown – past the mighty cathedral, past the statue of the fire thief, around the great park. She was stopped at the doors of a tall building by a uniformed man who saw only a dirty woman in dark ragged clothes who greatly needed a bath. But then his mind told him that he had sent her away while his eyes failed to see her enter the lobby and mount the stairs in pursuit of her quarry.

Unaware of his impending doom, Marcus was taking a shower. As much as he enjoyed his little "encounters," they always left him feeling dirty. Which, he admitted to himself, was part of their appeal. But now he wished to be clean. He'd had a busy day and tomorrow he would sleep in. When he woke there was that sales girl in Gimbels the judge had mentioned. He might as well start making her acquaintance.

Marcus was almost finished, was just about to step out of the shower when the water became hot, blistering hot, scalding hot. He tried to scream but the heat stole the air from his lungs. With every inch of his body in agony, he somehow stumbled out of the bath and into his bedroom.

Only to be met by a dark force of nature. A tramp of a woman grabbed him and threw him into a wall. He fell but before he could move the toe of a shoe kicked him in his most sensitive area. The pain of his burns now forgotten, Marcus again tried to cry out. Before he could, he was again airborne, this time his face smashing into and breaking the glass of a large mirror.

"Your good looks are gone," he heard a voice that could not possibly be coming from the woman in the black rags. It was too big. It seemed to come from all around him. "And now your manhood as well."

A strong hand reached between Marcus's legs, grabbed and pulled, forever separating him from that which he thought defined him as a man. This time he did scream, but a kick to his stomach cut the yell short. There were still memories that would not return no matter how hard she pulled. One was of a rape, her own by a man who was more lightning than flesh. The woman in black did not know that the father of the gods had drugged her with waters from the underworld that stole her memories and her life time and again. She could not remember his face, only that he chased her whenever she started to remember. The woman in black knew she would never be whole until those memories were hers again. Her own feelings of helplessness at the attack on herself made her response to others who committed the same crime extreme.

"You will go into the afterlife ugly and unmanned. And in the hell I have chosen for you that is not a good thing. Demons will mock you, the damned will pity you, and all will abuse you."

Her fury spent, her vengeance complete, Nemesis watched Marcus bleed out. When he was almost dead, when he was beyond mortal help, she prepared to leave when she heard,

"I really wish you hadn't done that."

Nemesis turned. A man in black stepped from the shadows, holding two very large pistols. *How*, she thought *had he …*

As if reading her mind, the dark clad man said, "I slipped in while you were teaching Mr. Marcus what was no doubt a well-earned lesson. But I wish you'd been a bit more restrained."

"Mortal, how dare you question my judgment?"

The man shook his head. "Not your judgment, simply your timing, Miss …"

"I am Nemesis and I answer to no man."

There was a pause as the man in black considered her answer. Finally, he put his guns away and extended his hand in greeting. "Nemesis. Good name that. I am The Nightmare and I think we're in the same line of work."

Nemesis ignored the hand. Instead, she studied the man in front of her.

"You've caused many deaths, some coldly, some in anger. All were in the cause of justice." She nodded as if in approval. "What did you seek from this man?"

Despite her appearance, there was something about this Nemesis that compelled The Nightmare to answer, something more than having seen her beat a man to death.

"An … associate of mine may have been investigating things with which this man was involved. This man had him killed. I finally traced him here through his phone number. Too late it seems to question him."

"This friend of yours, was he investigating the deaths of young women?"

The Nightmare thought back to the whispers he had heard on the street. "He may have been."

Nemesis now held out her hand. "Then we are allies."

The Nightmare was nearly overwhelmed by the sense of power and authority that came from this seemingly poor and dirty woman. It filled him with a sense of dread and awe he had never before experienced. Somehow he knew that she wasn't human or mortal for that matter. *Being her ally is a good thing*, he thought, knowing he would rather fight an army of the city's worst criminals all armed with Tommy Guns than face this woman unarmed as she was. He'd stand a better chance of surviving the Tommys.

"Then we should search this room. I asked around about this guy Marcus. According to a gun named Cliff, Marcus was high-end muscle. Always worked for someone higher up. No word who his current boss was, but maybe something in this room will tell us."

"No need," said Nemesis. "When the soul of the last woman this Marcus killed cried out to me, I sensed that someone other than he had caused her pain. If her body is still where I left it …"

"In this city, it will be."

"Then that is where we need to go."

"Lead the way, Nemesis but …"

"Yes?"

The Nightmare looked toward the bathroom. "No offense, but would you take a shower first?"

With the sound of running water behind a closed door, The Nightmare searched furniture drawers for something that might be appropriate for one such as Nemesis. She was a tall woman, close to Marcus's size, so his clothing might fit her. He made his choice just as Nemesis stepped from the bath.

He turned and she stood there nude before him. She was proud and beautiful and seemingly unconcerned as to what effect her naked body would have on him.

"Black?" asked Nemesis as she looked at the pants and shirt he had out. She had already tied the scarf he had selected around her breasts and slipped on the briefs that would serve until she could get decent underthings of her own.

"We are creatures of the night. We need to blend in."

"Creatures of Night. You have no idea how right you are." Shaw watched as the shadows seemed to dance around her and hoped it was just a trick his eyes were playing on him.

*

"So now what?" The Nightmare asked as the two stood near the body of what had once been a beautiful young woman.

"The essence of the men who abused this one is still on her body. The one from the man you called 'Marcus' is the strongest, but there is another. From it, I sense a man of some importance, someone of authority. There is not enough for me to trace this man as I did Marcus, but there is an image, a sense of him. A weapon of sorts, a long spear maybe."

The Nightmare thought as to who this might be. He had searched Marcus's room while Nemesis was showering and had not found much, just some discarded notes that seemed to be reminders of past days' activities. One of them had said, "Waitress for C-man."

"It could be," he decided. "Nemesis, if you met this man, would you know for sure?"

"Certainly."

"Then let's go."

*

"I do not like it."

"Trust me; this is a much more fitting punishment than simply killing him."

"There would be nothing simple about this one's death."

What Nemesis did not like was The Nightmare's insistence on letting Councilman Pike live.

It had taken little effort to find and break into Stanley Pike's unguarded house. A widower, he lived alone in a community just west of the city proper. He was asleep when the two broke in and neither woke him up, not at first.

"He is the one," Nemesis assured Shaw.

When Pike did wake, it was to the feel of a gun barrel against his neck. His eyes opened and slowly focused on the sight of a tall woman in black standing over him. There was the look of doom in her eyes.

It was all the councilman could do to keep from soiling his sheets.

A voice whispered in his ear. "You are seconds away from death, Pike – a messy, prolonged death. I suggest you answer this lady's questions." The Nightmare was careful not to make any promises Nemesis would not let him keep.

"There was a girl," said the woman above him with her voice all around him, seemingly coming from the very shadows around him, "one you beat and raped. Tell me of this girl."

Pike shook his head. Even now, with the specter of Retribution looming over him, he remembered the warnings from the Club, what would be done to him should he talk. "I can't, they'll kill me."

"So will we," came the whisper from in front, behind and the side, all at once. "So how long do you want to live? How painful do you want your last hours on earth to be?"

The woman above him reached down, did something to his feet and pain more intense than any he had ever had raced through Pike's body.

The woman in black spoke. "Imagine an hour of that, a day of it. Even after you have told us all we want to know, the pain would continue until your body could no longer feel. Only then would you be granted the brief release of death."

"I would tell the lady about the girl, Pike," The Nightmare advised. "You should have seen what she did to Marcus."

"Marcus!" Pike exclaimed. "Then you know about The Club?"

"Marcus told us all," The Nightmare lied soothingly, "we just need you to confirm a few things. Start with the girl."

Pike was not a brave man. He told them about The Club, and the services it offered, and of what he had done to the girl and to the others like her. When he was done, Nemesis touched his head. Shadows flowed from her finger and he dropped into a deep sleep.

Shaw was too impressed to mention what he saw. "He'll stay that way?"

Nemesis nodded. "For several hours, or until I wake him. It is something I learned from my mother. Now, what is your plan and how is it better than my killing this one slowly?"

The Nightmare smiled and told her. Nemesis approved. He could always die later.

*

"Extra, extra! Councilman arrested in love nest murder. Get your copy now. Extra, extra!"

The next afternoon the papers were filled with the story of how Councilman Stanley Pike was found in a makeshift room in the rear of a dead-end alley–naked, passed out drunk, and covered in the blood of the dead girl who wanted to be a dancer lying beside him.

*

"You'll need a name," Shaw said on the drive back to his mansion.

"I have a name. It is Nemesis."

"Then you need an alias, something by which I can introduce you."

For a few minutes, the woman in black sat in silence.

"I was called 'Leda' once."

"As in 'Leda, the mother of Helen."

There was a wistfulness in her voice when Nemesis replied, "Yes, the very same."

"Then how about 'Leda Troy?'"

"It will do."

Just then Shaw pulled into his front drive. "Home sweet home."

Nemesis looked at him. "This is your home?" At Shaw's nod, she said, "Do you expect us to…"

The question caused Shaw to think back to Nemesis stepping out of the shower. This memory raised hopes and dreams (among other things) but he was above all a gentleman.

"It's a big house. There's more than one bedroom." But he began to imagine what might happen if there was only the one.

"Tomorrow I'll have my chauffeur drive you into the city so you can shop for the necessities," Shaw explained over a late night drink. Nemesis had claimed to be the same woman from myth. Shaw was reserving final judgment. "You may be a goddess or something but you're also a woman so I expect that will take most of the day." He grinned as if to say that this remark was a little joke. Her answering smile was one that said it was a very little joke indeed.

"And while you're out spending my great-grandfather's hard earned money, well, to be honest, he didn't exactly earn it because honest was one thing he wasn't, I have an appointment with a Lieutenant Easton of the police about a different matter."

Finishing his drink, Shaw rose. "Miss Troy, I'll bid you goodnight. Sleep as late you want. I always do."

*

Shaw had arranged to meet Easton at Moran's. He liked the place. He had come to like the bartender and the stories he told about the "old country," half of which he was sure were lies and the other half he hoped were because it didn't sound like the man was talking about Ireland.

"Nice place," Jerome Easton said, looking around.

"Order what you like, Lieutenant, the first drink's on the house."

"They're all on the house, Mr. Shaw. It's your party so you're paying. What can I do for you?"

"Lieutenant, you were so very helpful when my chauffer's daughter was killed I thought I'd call on you about another family matter."

"And what is it, Mr. Shaw, that The Nightmare can't help you with?"

Shaw tried to look puzzled. "The Nightmare, Lieutenant? Who

might that be?"

Easton shook his head. "One of those fellows in black that this city seems plagued with. This one gunned the men who killed the little girl. But you wouldn't know anything about that, would you?"

"How would I? But Lieutenant, the reason I invited you for lunch was that my cousin… Actually, she's my sister's husband's niece, but to me she's family…her uncle was murdered and I was wondering if there's been any progress?"

"This wouldn't be the Chandler murder, would it?"

"The very one."

"In that case tell your…friend…The Nightmare to keep his guns in their holsters. The case is closed."

"Very good, Lieutenant. My congratulations."

Easton held up his hand. "Save it. It was another one of those costumed do-gooders. This time it was some dame dressed in a very skimpy outfit. Called herself The Pink Avenger or Pink Reaper or something like that. Left the killer on the front steps of the police station."

"That was damn nice of her."

"I don't know about that. He was babbling in fear of her, offering to confess to anything in order for us to protect him. From a dame." The cop shook his head.

"You'd be amazed at what some women can do," said Shaw. "Well, now that business is over, what say we order and enjoy our meal?"

"In a minute, Mr. Shaw. I'm sure you've heard about Councilman Pike."

Shaw smiled. "Who hasn't?"

"Well, what you haven't heard was that he claims to have been set up by a man and a woman, both dressed in black. But I'm sure you wouldn't know anything about that either."

"Of course not, Lieutenant. But I assure you that if I do hear of anything, you'll be the first to know."

The two men ordered and ate their lunch all the while talking about everything but crime. When they had finished, Shaw paid the check and stood to go. Easton stayed behind with another cup of coffee.

"Good day to you, Lieutenant."

"And to you, Mr. Shaw," Easton said aloud as the millionaire departed. To himself, he said, "And who was that lady you were with last night? Madame Nightmare? And that cousin of yours. Might as well call herself the Pink Nightmare. Ah well, as long as the city keeps paying me, you people can dress however you like and kill all the bad guys. I hate going to court."

*

Nemesis had returned from her shopping trip laden with purchases, all suitable for her age and the times. Still, for their evening activities she had chosen to dress in a black blouse and pants. "They are quite practical," she explained, then added, quite unnecessarily, that she was wearing more appropriate underthings. This, of course, conjured up images that made Shaw again wish that his house did not contain more than one bedroom and that he was not a gentleman.

Pike had given them the location of the club. Driving close to it, their plan was to walk the alleys and shadows until they arrived. Their actions would then be determined by what they found.

That plan changed as soon as Shaw parked the LaSalle.

The sound of sirens was in the air. Fire companies passed them and there was a reddish glow in the direction of their intended destination.

"Leave the cloak," Shaw told his companion and together they walked with the rest of the curious toward the burning building.

"I should have expected this," he said as they watched the fire claim what had been the site of the club. "Whoever did this is smart. He probably assumed that Pike would eventually talk to save his skin, if he hadn't already. No doubt had a new place already picked out in case of just such an emergency. Now we're back at square one."

Nemesis showed no signs of having heard him. Instead, she was staring at the flames. "Not all escaped," she said.

Not bothering to ask how she knew this, Shaw instead asked, "Can you trace their killers?"

"That is the killer." Nemesis pointed to the fire. "They died from heat and smoke. They were left because they had somehow displeased their masters. They were not trusted and now … now their souls call out and demand of me retribution and vengeance. The women who were there, some enjoyed what they did. Others enjoyed the money they received for allowing the degradation of their spirits. Others, others had no choice but to suffer the abuse of their minds and bodies. Come, let us leave this place and plan on how to cause these men great pain."

Turning, Nemesis walked away. Shaw saw no choice but to follow her.

*

"So what do we do now?" Nemesis asked after the two had returned to Shaw's home. "Is there no one else to question?"

Shaw shook his head. "I can't think of anyone. Besides, by now they know Marcus is dead. With Pike being found with the girl, they'll know that someone is investigating them. They'll also know it isn't the police. They'll be more on guard than ever."

"What of that bar you told me about – Dago Mike's? Someone there might know something. We could go there and question them vigorously."

"You mean beat on them until someone talked."

"Is that a problem for you?"

"Things people say to get you to stop the pain cannot always be relied on. There might be a better way. Tomorrow is Friday. Let's spend the weekend making the rounds – the nightclubs, the luncheons, the dinner clubs, the speaks and gambling joints. I'll ask awkward yet pointed questions and you look beautiful and bored."

Nemesis nodded. "That might get us an invitation to the club. But, Michael, what if they suspect something? The invitation might be a trap."

"Of course it will be a trap, Leda," Shaw smiled. "But they won't be expecting us." *Especially you*, he added silently.

*

It was in a casino fronted by an all-night pharmacy that the pair first got the word. One entered through the front and asked for a certain brand of foot powder. The pharmacist then buzzed you into the back where you ascended a flight of stairs to the second floor. The door then opened into a sumptuous room that took up the entire floor. There the elite of the city gathered to lose the money that other people had earned for them.

Shaw, wearing his second best tux, lost a few hands of blackjack and had even worse luck at faro. On the other hand, Nemesis, beautiful in a very revealing black evening gown, did very well at the dice table, the cubes coming up seven and eleven on almost every throw. When they didn't, she immediately made her point.

Seeing her success, Shaw gave up his cards and came over to Nemesis. Putting his arm around her he said, "The goddess of luck must be with you tonight, darling."

"Tyche? We were once on a first name basis, love." Shaw wondered if that was indeed the truth.

As the chips piled higher and higher in front of Nemesis, Shaw noticed a man watching him. He motioned Shaw over.

"Having a good time, Mr. Shaw?"

"She is," Shaw indicated Nemesis who had just rolled another seven. "I'm sorry, but I don't believe we've been introduced."

"We haven't," the man said. "But word is you and the Mrs. might be looking for something, shall we say, less tame than rolling the bones."

Shaw didn't bother to ask how the word had reached the man. He and Nemesis had dropped enough hints around town over the past two nights. That was no doubt why they had been steered to this casino.

Shaw gave a knowing smile. "I'd like to have a bone rolled once or twice, and I'm not talking about dice. My fiancé and I enjoy exotic tastes, ones not usually found in places like this, not even on the floor above."

"The floor above, Mr. Shaw, is not for ladies."

"Really, I heard it was full of them."

"That's true, Mr. Shaw. So let's say it's not for ladies like your fiancé."

"You'd be surprised, Mr.–eh, I didn't catch your name."

"I didn't throw it. But it's Clarke. Call me a messenger. If it's exotic you're looking for, I might have a place to recommend. But it's only for the truly daring, those who appreciate the forbidden."

"How forbidden?"

"Regarding your fiancé, Mr. Shaw, do you believe in sharing?"

"Only if I get to watch."

Shaw was given a phone number and a time to call it. After waiting until Nemesis had won enough to pay for the dress she was wearing and the rest of her purchases, he signaled her that it was time to leave.

*

Nemesis wanted to charge in at once, go directly to the address and turn it to rubble. The woman in black never once mentioned using explosives to do it. Shaw convinced her to wait. He had plans to make and he spent the next day getting ready. After a trip to Moran's he declared himself ready.

Leda Troy and Michael Shaw dropped away a few blocks from the supposed location of the club. Nemesis and The Nightmare continued on. While The Nightmare slipped around back, the woman in black, somehow more invisible in the darkness than her dark clothes alone should make her, watched the front of the club.

"What did you find?" she asked as The Nightmare returned from his recon.

"No guards in sight, fire escape to the roof, easy upper access from the other houses. It shouldn't be a problem. What did you see?"

"It's been a busy night. Several expensive cars have pulled up and let out wealthy looking men. A few women, none of them came alone."

We have been given the right address then, thought The Nightmare. *Now if we've only made enough noise.* "What else did you see?" he asked his companion.

"Only the two men behind you with guns."

One man pulled the mask from The Nightmare's face. "I'm disappointed in you, Mr. Shaw," said the other. It was Clarke, the man he had met the night before, "a man of your standing, playing at dress-up and hide-and-seek."

"Just wanted to make sure we were at the right place," The Nightmare said, not too convincingly. "The mask is so we wouldn't be recognized."

"Nice try, but if that's the case, why isn't the lady wearing one?" Clarke asked. "Now you'll stand for a search and if you move, you'll both be shot. Nothing fatal, just very painful."

With well-acted fear in her voice, Nemesis asked, "What's going to happen to us?"

"To Mr. Shaw, nothing at first. To you, that depends on the imagination and desires of the club members to whom we turn you over." Clarke then turned to The Nightmare. "But don't worry, Mr. Shaw; as promised, you'll get to watch. And when we're done with her, when she's no longer useful or beautiful, you'll get to see her die, right before we kill you."

The search of The Nightmare was very thorough. He was stripped of his both guns and coat before being marched toward the club. And while it was clear from her nearly skin-tight clothing that Nemesis was not carrying any weapons, that did not stop both men from running their hands up and down her lovely body. The men didn't seem to notice the self-control the woman in black employed to not hurt either of them, but Shaw did, thanking her silently.

"It's a shame I'm not a member," Clarke said with a leer, "I'd like a chance at you myself."

Then at gunpoint he led them inside.

The front door opened into a large hall. This, in turn, led to a grand ballroom in which most of the club's guests had been gathered. Nemesis and The Nightmare were taken to the front so they could be seen by all.

Staying close to their captives, Clarke and his partner kept their weapons trained on the pair as a man dressed in evening clothes approached.

"Good evening," he said politely. "I'm called Giles and I manage this club. And you are?"

"Very disappointed in the way you treat your new members."

"How very clever. I like that about your kind. How you masked do-gooders always joke in the face of danger. There was another like you not too long ago. He went for a permanent swim. You'll meet him soon. You two can trade bon mots."

To the assembled crowd Giles announced, "May I have your attention. As promised, a special treat to christen our new location. Some of you will get your chance with this lovely lady here. How many depends on how just how much abuse she can take. And just before dawn, two of you will be afforded the opportunity few are ever offered, the chance to kill a fellow human being in cold blood. Those of you interested please leave your bids with Mr. Sanders, while Mr. Clarke and I take these two to our guest room."

"There's one thing you failed to consider, Giles," The Nightmare said before they could be led away.

"Oh, is this the part where you tell me I'm never going to get away with this. That sooner or later I'll be brought to justice, that you have friends who will avenge you?"

"No, this is the part where I tell you that my friends are already here."

Dark clad men, the city's avengers of the night, suddenly appeared. They entered from the back, off the fire escape, and down through the roof. Sinister laughter from several of them echoed off the walls as a leaden rain fell on those assembled in the room.

Taking advantage of the moment's confusion caused by the arrival of the men Shaw had summoned through Moran, he struck out at the men holding him captive, knocking them down and reclaiming his weapons.

As Nemesis pulled Clarke aside, The Nightmare shot the man

who had stood with him in the chest. To be sure, he shot him again then looked for Giles. But the club manager was gone.

He turned to Nemesis. "Will you be okay?"

The woman in black's smile chilled even The Nightmare. "Here in the midst of those who would have raped me and seen me dead, men against whom countless souls cry out for retribution? I couldn't be better." She bent down to the fallen Clarke. "This is what I was created for."

"And you," Nemesis picked up the man and threw him against a wall as easily as she would have a rag doll. "You wanted a chance with me. You will have it. And when you are no longer useful or beautiful, I'll get to see you die."

Very casually, Nemesis broke Clarke's left arm just below the shoulder. Then she broke it again, this time near the wrist. Then after she broke his elbow she paid similar attention to his right arm, before moving on to his legs. In quick order, working methodically and ignoring the ever-increasing screams, Nemesis fractured most every bone in the man's body. When she was finished she let him drop to the floor – broken, barely breathing, but alive.

"You'll die by morning," she told him, "and suffer greatly every second you remain alive. As you die, know that what you are feeling is mild compared to the agony you will suffer in the special hell reserved for you."

She left him there and went off to her own special mission.

It was not a night for mercy. It was, instead, one of vengeance and harsh justice. The men whose twisted desires had brought them to the club and the ones who saw to it that these lusts were sated – all were guilty. Those who fought back and those who tried to escape – all would pay. The ones who paid to use and abuse women and the men who collected the money, there was no difference between them. They were collectively responsible for all that happened – the rapes, the tortures, the deaths and the murder of Johnny the Dip, who had also been The Whispering Monk. He was one of a fellowship of Dark Justice, the members of which were now assembled. And tonight his death would be avenged.

There were those who tried to fight back, who traded bullets with men in dark cloaks who fought from the shadows. These men were shot down. Some tried to hide, they were hunted and dispatched. Still others tried to flee through open doors and windows. They were met by the agents of the city's vigilantes who dealt with them as harshly as would their masters.

And in the middle of the slaughter, issuing his own laugh amidst the chaos and confusion, was Michael Shaw, he who was The Nightmare. The laughter was a lie, for he did not enjoy what was he was doing. But he knew it was grim work that had to be done, a lesson to be taught. For when morning came and deaths counted he knew that the word would go out as to the dire consequences of striking down one of the night's protectors.

It ended as quickly as it had begun. One minute there was the thundering of great automatics and the next silence. All the foemen were dead. One by one the victors faded back into the shadows from which they had emerged, leaving The Nightmare alone.

Alone? he thought, *where is Nemesis*? And scanning the faces of the dead, he realized someone else was missing.

The Nightmare found Giles hiding in a closet just behind the bar.

"Please," the club manager begged. "I can give you names, pictures, movies. I have files on the city's most important men."

"Not enough," The Nightmare decreed, "not tonight." Shaw then raised his big .45 and ended the man's life.

After leaving Clarke behind, Nemesis saw that her mission of retribution was being well handled by the men in black. She therefore went off to save the innocent.

Men tried to stop her. She was unarmed and thus a seemingly easy victim. Those who thought this did not live to regret their mistake as Nemesis left caved-in chests, twisted necks, and bloodied bodies in her wake.

She went to the kitchens and told the cooks and waiters to flee. She found the maids and cleaners and showed them a safe way out. She then sought the women who serviced the men of the club.

Some had been brought there against their will, others had come willingly but had since regretted their decisions. A few reveled in their position and had even aided in the abuse of their fellows. To these Nemesis showed no more mercy than The Nightmare and his allies granted to the men they fought. And once her grisly task was complete, she led the others to the basement, to await the end of the slaughter above.

When it was over, when the shooting and laughter stopped and quiet ruled the house, Nemesis brought her charges to the first floor.

"See this and remember," she told some of the women, those who had thought to earn an easy living on their backs. "The next time it might be your bodies lying there. Go and seek a better way of life." To the others she offered what words of comfort she had, knowing what they had suffered and wishing there was something she could do to ease their long years of painful memories.

With the women safely out of the house, Nemesis sought out The Nightmare, finding him in the grand ballroom, alone with the dead.

He was a sight. Still maskless, his clothes torn and ripped, he was bleeding from several minor wounds. She imagined that she looked much the same, save that the blood on her clothes belonged to others.

The battle over and won, passion and excitement still ran through her.

"There is something about combat," Nemesis told him, "do you feel it?"

"Yes, I do," admitted The Nightmare. "The police will be here soon. We should go."

"Yes, we should, but not because of the police."

As sirens screamed in the distance, The Nightmare and the Woman in Black went out into the darkness.

There may have been more than one bedroom in the Shaw mansion, but for what was left of the night Michael Shaw and Leda Troy needed only one. In the morning Shaw awoke to find a note where a lover had been.

"There are others who need me and one who pursues me that I still cannot fully remember. If he can harm me, he can do much worse to you. I go to keep you safe and to help those I can. I will remember you for as long as I can. Farewell, my love."

*

Word of the righteous slaughter spread quickly and for a time the streets of the city were quiet. The Nightmare and others like him went out but found little to do. During that time a woman in pink received an invitation to Moran's and was welcomed into a select group. Gradually though, the city resumed its dangerous ways. But while what had happened in the club with no name was forgotten and faded into myth and legend, Michael Shaw never forgot the myth that had come into his life, and from then on, when The Nightmare dreamed, it was of a woman in black.

A NASTY BUSINESS

An adventure of the Nightmare and Pink Reaper

Barry and Suzanne Goldman were a nice young couple, married only a few years but they acted as if their honeymoon had never ended. Thanks to their savings and loans from their parents, they had enough money to open their own business in a quiet neighborhood on the east side of the city. A lunchroom – nothing fancy, just a place to get a sandwich or some soup, maybe even a late breakfast. Suzanne cooked while Barry waited on the customers.

Business was slow for the first month, then it started picking up as one person after another discovered the Eastside Lunchroom and told their friends. Word of mouth helped, but what the couple gave their customers to put in their mouths clinched the deal.

"You're going to need to get some help in here. And soon," Kaye Chandler told Barry as she sat at the counter and finished her hot roast beef on rye.

"I was saying that just last night to Suzanne, Miss Chandler. Someone to help her in the kitchen, a busboy to clear the tables. Maybe a waitress."

Kaye looked around the restaurant. It was half full. With some more help service would get better and then it would be packed.

"Better make that two waitresses, Mr. Goldman. I think you'll soon need them. If you're looking to hire…" Kaye thought of the servants in her father's mansion. Maybe they could recommend some people. These days, everyone knew someone who was out of work.

Barry shook his head. "Thank you, but I have too many relatives. If I were to hire outside the family…" He sighed. "Let's just say that when the Goldmans got together things would not be comfortable for me."

Kaye smiled in understanding. "So your only problem will be which cousins to hire."

"That's easy. The best cook for the kitchen, the youngest as busboy, and the two prettiest for waitresses."

Kaye laughed and finished her sandwich. She would have liked to linger over a piece of pie but she had shopping to do uptown and later she had to meet her cousin. That night, she had some "family business" of her own to take care of as well.

"A nice girl," Barry thought as he watched Kaye Chandler leave. "Not bad looking either. Pink is her color." And not being that long married, he quickly thought of his wife. Suzanne didn't wear pink. Well, there was that nightgown, the one she wore on special nights. That was pink, almost. Mostly it wasn't there.

A warm glow rushed through Barry before he pushed such thoughts aside. There were customers to serve and tables to clear. Miss Chandler was right. He was going to need some help and soon. As he rung up another order he tried to decide which of his cousins were the prettiest.

Lunch was soon over, the last of the diners had finished and paid and then it was time to lock up, clean up and get ready for the next day. Barry could hear Suzanne in the kitchen, singing to herself as she cleaned the dishes. He had just started for the door when the three men walked in.

Barry recognized them. They had been in twice before. They ordered coffee and Danish. As they ate and drank they looked around the lunchroom.

"I'm sorry, gentlemen, but we're closed." Mindful of customer relations Barry added, "But maybe some coffees to go, on the house."

One of the men, the one in the middle, blonde and well dressed, shook his head. "Not today, Mr. Goldman, not today. Or tomorrow, or the next day. Or even the day after that."

"I don't understand."

"I'm sure you don't, Mr. Goldman. But you soon will. You see, I'm starting my own business. Rather, the people I work for are." The blonde man gave Barry an evil smile. "The insurance business."

Barry understood. "Protection." And the blonde man nodded at the word.

He had been told to expect this. This was the city after all and there was no avoiding certain elements. His father and his uncles had told him what to do. "Pay," they had said. "Pay at first, then tell us. We'll make some calls, we know people. They'll make calls. You'll still pay, but not as much, and to the right people, not just the first punks who come through your door."

So armed and comforted with the knowledge of how things worked, Barry asked, "How much?"

The blonde man surprised him. "For you, nothing." Seeming to enjoy the look on Barry's face he went on. "You see, we're new to the neighborhood, but not to the racket. In the past, there's always some like you who know how things are. And then there are others who need a mild lesson before they go along. And then there are those, well, they only pay after an example or two has been made."

The blonde man nodded and the two men with him moved toward the counter, one going behind it, approaching Barry. The other headed for the kitchen where Suzanne, unaware of what was happening, was still singing.

"We're trying something new this time," the blonde man explained as one of his men quickly grabbed Barry and stuffed a towel in his mouth to keep him from crying out and warning his wife. "This time we're making the example first, so that no one thinks to object. Too bad for you there's so many lunchrooms in the area."

Barry tried to fight back, but the man who held him struck him hard twice. Once on the floor, he was kicked in the stomach and in the head. And as consciousness faded, he barely heard the blonde man say, "Do what you like to her then trash the place. When you're finished, well, we only need one of them alive as an example. It might as well be the Jew on the floor."

Barry passed out just as his wife started screaming.

*

There were three of them – Lefty DiPietro, Tony Mullins, and

Slow Georgie Strand. They were holed up in a condemned building in the warehouse district. Two days before they had held up a bank. While they had gotten away with the money, things did not go as planned.

"Why the hell did you have to shoot a cop?" Tony asked Slow Georgie.

"He was right outside," Georgie protested, "drawing down on me. What was I supposed to do, let him shoot me?"

That would have been a good idea, Tony thought then caught a look from Lefty. He could tell the Eye-tie was thinking the same thing. Then it would have been just the two of them with bigger shares for each. Instead, all three were wanted men with little chance of spending any of the loot. Every cop in the city was looking for them. And that wasn't the worst of it. The police could be dodged; even with a fellow officer cooling on the slab, some could be bought.

But there were others.

"Why not wait until it gets dark, then try a sneak outta here. Go down to Philly or Baltimore?"

Georgie just doesn't get it, Tony thought. Maybe they could buy a break if they left his body on some precinct steps. His body and his gun. No, they were all seen, they were in it together.

"The night's too dangerous, Georgie. You know that. It's not only the police we have to worry about. With a dead cop, they're out there. Every one of them. Hiding in the dark, lurking in the shadows, just waiting for word that we've been spotted. Then it's laughter and gunplay and us waking up in Hell."

"Then why not wait until day when they all crawl back in the caves or wherever they live?"

Lefty spoke up. "Because, you dope, then the cops can see us. Plus the other ones, that Doc fellow and those Justice guys."

"So we're trapped. What we gonna do?"

Georgie might not have been the smartest of the three, but his question had the other two stumped. What were they going to do?

"Two ideas," Tony finally said. "One, we make a break for it at dawn. The ones in the dark, they go in when it gets light. And it might be too early for the others to be awake."

"Might work," Lefty allowed. "What's your other idea?"

"We divvy the money now, then we split, each going our own way. Maybe one of us gets caught, maybe two. But one of us might make it. And the way things are in this city, a one-in-three chance is the best we're gonna get."

Maybe they would have chosen to leave at dawn. Maybe they would have split up. And just maybe they would have done both, waiting until the sun was just about to rise over the city then each of them departing in a different direction. But there's no way to know. Because just as Tony had finished talking, they heard it.

Laughter. Laughter coming all around them. Echoing off the walls and coming down from the ceiling. A creature of doom enjoying his own private joke at their expense.

He stepped out of the shadows, a tall man dressed in black, his face covered by a full mask, his hands out of sight.

"Which one are you?" Georgie wanted to know.

"Does it matter?" was the whispered reply.

"Guess not."

"I don't suppose you boys would like to surrender?"

"We're cop killers," said a resigned Lefty. "We give up, we're gonna fry. Might as well finish it now."

"Not this time."

As the man in black spoke, there came a muffled pop, as if from a silenced pistol. This sound was followed by a crackling buzz as Georgie cried out and went down. Two more pops, more buzzing and the other two dropped.

The man in black, who was called the Nightmare, looked past the fallen killers and watched as a woman stepped out of the darkness. Like him she was covered in black, but only briefly.

The woman drew back her hood revealing the masked face of Kaye Chandler beneath beautiful blonde hair. She then revealed much more as she allowed her cloak to fall open.

She was, by that era's standards, shockingly dressed, if "dressed" was the word for the brief outfit she wore. It barely covered her and in the darkness its pink color blended with her skin to give the illusion she was naked.

"Easy, Michael," the Nightmare said to himself as he took in the alluring sight, "she is somewhat of a relation."

Thus reminded, the Nightmare addressed the woman in pink. "We creatures of the night are supposed to blend in with the darkness. This," the Nightmare held up her cloak to reveal its pink lining, "somewhat defeats the purpose."

"It's a dark pink," the woman protested, then she looked at the still unconscious felons. "You didn't need me for this. Tell me again why you didn't just shoot them."

"Because, Kaye, I promised Lieutenant Easton that I'd try to leave them alive, giving the police credit for the arrest. With your gadgets, that's more easily possible. Once they are in custody, they get a show trial followed by a triple burning. Justice is served and the people's faith in the System is restored."

The woman made a rude sound. "That, Michael Shaw, is what I think of the System. If the System worked, if there truly was justice, I would not have had to hunt down my uncle's killer and become, well, this." She indicated her outfit.

"Speaking of which," Shaw said, "did you hear from Benson?"

"Yes. It seems he had some issues about my calling myself 'The Pink Avenger.'"

"Understandable."

"So for now, I'm sticking with The Pink Reaper."

"I'll call Winchell and let him know. Does Clark know you're using his mercy bullets?"

There was that sound again. "This isn't his." Kaye held up a large, bulky looking pistol. "My uncle made this. It uses compressed air to fire an electrically charged dart. As you can see, it's strong enough to knock a man out." Then she added, "I have stronger ones if needed."

Shaw nodded in understanding. "Let's tie these three up and go. I'll stop at a pharmacy on the way and call in an 'anonymous tip.' Thank you very much for your help, Miss Reaper."

"Always glad to help, cousin Nightmare. You can thank me by buying me lunch tomorrow. I know this great place on the Eastside."

As they left, Shaw looked down at the three men who would soon be getting a much greater jolt of electricity than they had received that night.

"When will they learn that vacant buildings in the warehouse district are the first places we look?"

*

Kaye had given Shaw the address to meet her for lunch. He was early and occupied himself watching the police, both plainclothed and uniformed, work behind barriers set up on the opposite sidewalk. Much of their activity was taking place inside a lunchroom and Shaw had the feeling that Kaye was going to have to find a new favorite place to eat.

Kaye noticed her cousin before seeing what was going on across the street. "Michael, why are you standing over here, why aren't you …"

She turned, uttered a very unladylike word and started to rush across the street. Shaw grabbed her arm.

"Easy, Kaye. It's daylight and we're not dressed for what you're thinking. At least I'm not. For all I know, that outfit of yours doubles as underwear. In fact, from what I saw last night, I think it might be underwear."

This earned Shaw a nasty look. "A girl needs some advantage over you big strong men. My outfit is designed to distract my opponents."

"Well, just make sure everything's tied nice and tight so your 'distractions' don't fall out."

Concentrating on what was going on across the street, Kaye let this last comment go without reply. "Do you think it's a robbery or something? No, I think that detective in gray works for Homicide. Maybe someone got killed inside the store. Maybe a gangland slaying. I hear that's how they do it in Chicago. I hope the Goldmans are all right."

As the Nightmare, Shaw had been on the streets somewhat longer than Kaye. He had learned early on that the more cops on a scene, the more serious the crime was likely to be. And there were too many cops across the street for the Goldmans to be all right.

"Michael, can you think of any way for us to find out what's happened."

"I could drop into the newsstand and make a call. No, if that's who I think it is getting out of that car I won't have to. It is. Now, Kaye, just lean against a wall and wait. We'll know soon enough."

Kaye nodded. She too had recognized Lieutenant Jerome Easton. Easton had been the detective who investigated the murder of her uncle. That murder had been solved by the woman now calling herself the Pink Reaper. Back when he was a sergeant he had investigated the killing of a little girl, a girl who had been the daughter of Michael Shaw's chauffeur. That case had ended in gunfire and bloodshed, officially labeled as abated by death, all thanks to a man in black some called the Nightmare.

Jerome Easton was not a stupid man. It hadn't taken him long to make the connection between certain black and pink vigilantes and the pair he spotted across the street from the murder scene. He knew who they were. And they knew he knew. That was enough for him.

Of course, he didn't have proof. He didn't seek it and trusted that they were smart enough not to leave it. If ever he needed it, if ever the two crossed the line, it would be easy enough to find. For now, he was content to let them haunt the shadows and take down the monsters the law couldn't or wouldn't touch.

Easton cast a glance across the street. Shaw and the girl were pretending not to have noticed him. He went inside the lunchroom.

Twenty minutes later he came out, visibly shaken. Again he looked across the street. Good, they were still there. If any crime called out for the vengeance of the street, this one did. Easton's only question was,

"How did you know?"

He hadn't bothered with any preliminary greetings, no wordplay where he would accuse and they would deny. Still shaken from what he had seen, he just blurted out his query.

That's not how this is done, Shaw thought, but on seeing the lieutenant's pale face he decided that maybe today was not the time to play the game.

"How did we know what, Lieutenant?"

"You mean, you two aren't for …" he gestured across the street "… that?"

"What we're here for, Lieutenant," Kaye said, "is to eat. The Goldmans make such a nice lunch."

"Made." And with one word Easton let them know just who the victims were.

Kaye stifled a sob.

"What happened, Lieutenant?" asked Shaw, struggling to keep the Nightmare part of him subdued. "A robbery gone bad?"

"If only. The protection racket, with a new twist. The gang served up an example first. 'Pay up or what happened to the Goldmans will happen to you.'"

"Barry and Suzanne, what did happen to them?"

"It's not pretty, Miss Chandler."

"I can take it, Lieutenant."

"Yeah, I guess you can. All right, and you can pass this information on to whoever helped catch the cop killers last night if you should meet them."

Shaw nodded. Now that the fiction had been established, the game could begin.

"There were three of them. The one in charge was blonde; otherwise average everything – looks, height, complexion. The other two, dark and large. These two beat down Mr. Goldman, then went into the kitchen and…took turns with the wife. From what the coroner says, they each took a couple of turns before gutting her."

"Oh my god!" exclaimed Kaye.

Shaw remained quiet. Not too long ago he had seen worse, when he and a woman in black had quite violently closed down a den of depravity. Inwardly Shaw sighed. He hadn't thought of Leda for a few days now. If what Easton said was true, and Shaw had no reason to believe it wasn't, what happened to Suzanne Goldman was enough to summon her back.

"All I have to do is ask," Shaw said to himself. And he almost did, then thought better of it. Leda had her own problems and he would not willingly put her in harm's way for something he could handle himself. Themselves, he corrected as Kaye spoke up.

"What about Barry, is he …"

"They left him alive, as an example. He's the reason we know what we do."

"Then he can identify the killers?" *Maybe*, Shaw thought, *there'll be no need of the Reaper or Nightmare.*

Easton shook his head. "Goldman wasn't on the scene. He was rushed to the hospital before I got here. But I'm told from the cops who saw him that Goldman will never ID anyone ever again. Hot grease does horrible things to a person's eyes."

*

"Hello, Sampson's Bakery, how can I help you?"

"Is this Mr. Sampson?"

"Yes, it is."

"Mr. Sampson, by now you have no doubt heard about what happened to the Goldmans. It would be a shame if the same thing happened to you, or your wife, or either of your daughters."

"Who is this?"

"Your new partner, the one to whom you'll be paying twenty percent of your weekly gross. A small price for the safety of your family."

"How dare you, I'll call the police."

"Do so, it's a free country. Only, which of your daughters do you want violated first, or should we start with your wife."

"I, I..."

"You'll be contacted about payment. And don't try to cheat us, or your girls will be crippled orphans."

*

"So what do we do now?" Kaye asked over sandwiches and beer at Moran's, a tavern not far from the Goldman's lunchroom.

"What we always do," Shaw replied, "what the life we've chosen demands we do. I put on the black and you the pink. Then it's into the night. We lurk in the shadows, we ask questions, we break heads. We strike terror in the hearts of evildoers until one of them tells us about a blonde man who works with two large, dark men."

Kaye had just asked, "And then what?" when Moran, the not so tall owner of the tavern, came over with another two glasses of the best beer on the Eastside.

"And then, lassie, you find them and make them tell you all about this protection racket that's already ruined the lives of two good folk."

"You've been hanging around my cousin and his friends too long, Mr. Moran."

"That I have, lass, that I have. But they insist on coming here when all decent folk are abed. At least they tip well." Then, as Kaye reached for her beer, he asked her, "Are you sure you're old enough to be drinking that?"

"What does it matter? These days you're not supposed to be selling it."

"Sure I keep forgetting. But I get such a good deal from me cousin Paddy."

"I've been to his place," replied Kaye.

The little man raised an eyebrow. "Then perhaps you've been seeing things many others haven't."

"You have no idea," replied Kaye.

"You'd be surprised, lass." The little man turned to Shaw. "You catch them, Michael, catch them and make them pay."

"I will, Seamus."

"Just how will we make them pay?" Kaye asked after Moran left their table.

"How do you think? This won't be like last night, where we tie the bad guys up in a nice, neat package for the police. You heard Easton, Goldman is beyond identifying anyone. I doubt if any of the three left behind any clues. Any arrest would be a waste of time, any trial a mockery. Justice for the Goldmans will have to come from us and it will be final. If you have a problem with that, let me know and I'll go it alone."

Kaye listened to her cousin talk about killing, not in self-defense as she had once had to do, not in defense of others, but in cold blood, taking it upon himself to sentence men to death. *Can I do that?* she wondered. Then she thought about Barry Goldman, his eyes blind, his face disfigured. She thought about his wife Suzanne and how she had suffered before being cut open and left to die. She felt a part of her heart harden as what was left of her innocence slipped away.

"Let's find these bastards."

*

They went out separately, the Nightmare and the Pink Reaper, so as to cover more ground. As was his habit, Shaw dressed down, in the style of the streets. No black for him, not then. Black was for when the villain had to be surprised and confronted. Instead, Shaw wore tan and brown, a bulky sweater and worn slacks, just a man looking to pass some time in the company of other men.

The bars he frequented were of a lower type than Moran's. They were dirty and dark, and most of their patrons were wanted by the police. Not that any lawman openly set foot in any of them. To do so would only earn their wives a widow's pension.

Shaw knew if any of them even suspected who he was, if they somehow discerned his true intentions, he'd end up in a fight for his life he would have little hope of winning.

"That's why I wear a mask," he said to himself as he slowly sipped his beer and listened to those around him talk of jobs pulled and jobs planned, of who was hiring and who had gone on the lam, and of which would-be crime boss had been gunned down by which crime fighter.

In The Black Ship, the name "Wolf" was mentioned as an up and coming gang leader. In Blind Tom's he caught a rumor of a new racket in town. In Dago Mike's he heard a man whisper a story about a friend of his, a friend who claimed to have abused then cut up "a Jew bitch."

Shaw left before this man did, waited in the shadows and followed him home. Then it was time for the black clothes.

The Pink Reaper did not hide in the shadows. She wanted to be seen, wanted all eyes to be on her.

The Reaper had been on the streets long enough to know which bars were the most likely ones in which to find the criminals she sought. She went there, of course starting with the Pink Rat then moving on to The Junction and then a place called Vic's.

She did the same thing in each bar. On entering, the Reaper would throw back her cloak to reveal the scanty pink costume it covered. Then she'd stand by the door and wait, wait to be seen, wait to be noticed. It never took long.

"I'm looking for three men," she'd announce. "One's blonde, the other two are large and dark. Where are they?"

At first, the replies were predictable. Most of the men were willing to help her, but not in the way she wanted. They were willing to help her in the back, they were willing to help her get on her back. They were willing to help her remove what little clothing she wore.

But the Pink Reaper did not wait to hear most of these crude suggestions. No sooner did she make her demands then she'd spread her cloak wide and let fall pellets which contained a gaseous chemical, one developed by her uncle before his death. He had been collaborating with chemists in Switzerland on the uses of a particular ergot of rye. What he created was a powerful hallucinogenic which when inhaled caused one to experience anything from acute fear to stark terror, oddly enough intensified by the sight of the color pink. Under its influence, which thanks to Kaye's uncle she was quite immune, those exposed saw the Reaper not as a woman in a revealing outfit but as a pink demon from hell to whom they were willing to tell anything.

Kaye did not like to use the gas, not in that way. There was a chance that in the resulting panic someone would be trampled. And should someone be immune to the gas … it hadn't yet happened but if it should…Kaye thought her new cloak bullet-proof but was not anxious to put it to the test.

Kaye had decided that circumstances warranted the risks, and so threw three bars into near bedlam. She did not find the name of the blonde man, but further questioning got her the name of a man who had described to a friend the effects of hot grease on a man's face.

*

"Hollis heard from those men he hired."
"What did they want?"
"What do you think? They want a cut of the action."
"Or what? They'll go to the police?"
"Worse yet, Hollis said they talked about seeing Hopkins."
"We should get rid of them before they do."
"Who should we get?"
"Bringing in more men won't solve the problem, it only changes the names. We'll do it ourselves. Tell Hollis to set up a meeting."

*

"I found out where he lived," Kaye later told Shaw.
"Is that all you did?"
Kaye knew what Shaw was asking. Did she go there? Did she confront him, maybe kill him. She had thought about it, wasn't sure if without the Nightmare standing beside she could go through with it, wasn't sure if that was the kind of heroine she wanted to be. Could she still call herself a heroine if she killed?

To her cousin, all she said was, "Yes, that was all I did, other than find out his name. Teddy Vang."

"Never heard of him. I traced his partner, a guy named Abe Waller. Calls himself 'the Wall,' says no one gets through him."

"And did you ..."

Shaw shook his head. "We still need him, need them both. Now we go play in the shadows. We each follow our own man. With luck, one or both will lead us to their boss. When we find him, when we get the three of them together, we'll put their protection racket out of business for good."

Two nights went by. In those two nights Vang and Waller did

nothing but walk the streets, drink in bars, and go to movies. Vang did stop at a certain red-light establishment, the nature of which the Pink Reaper thankfully recognized before following him inside.

"Why not?" she imagined her cousin asking. "You were certainly dressed for it." She decided he didn't need to know everywhere her quarry had been.

It was on the third night that Vang, followed by the Pink Reaper, was walking east on a street in the Village when he met Waller who had been walking west. Together they went into a small office building.

Two dark shapes separated from the sides of buildings - the Nightmare in a black trenchcoat, hat, and gloves, his face fully covered by an ebony mask; The Pink Reaper, her normally bright clothing concealed by a cloak and hood the color of night. Without a word they followed, entering in time to see the elevator doors close.

They watched the indicator count off the floors. It stopped on 3.

The dark vigilantes were halfway up the stairs when the gunfire started, the booming of a shotgun followed by the rat-tat-tat-tat of a Thompson.

Not one to hesitate in the face of danger, The Nightmare drew a brace of .45s and ran forward up the stairs. The Pink Reaper followed close behind, in her hand her bulky, electric pistol.

The shooting stopped as quickly as it had begun. On reaching the third floor the pair found only the smell of gunpowder and an open door to an office suite.

"An invitation or a trap," the Reaper wondered.

"I think the trap has already been sprung. Let's see if it caught the rats."

Cautiously they entered the suite. There was nothing in the outer rooms but the innermost office was the scene of a slaughter. A shotgun had cut Abe Waller in half just as he entered the room. A Thompson had done the same to Teddy Vang. In a chair behind a desk was a third body, one that had taken two slugs to the chest.

"Hollis Wilder," the Pink Reaper said in recognition.

"I know the name," replied the Nightmare, "if not the face. The senior Wilder was wiped out in the Crash. Locked himself in his penthouse office and took the short way to the street. This would be his …

"Youngest son. The oldest joined the army. His sister married well, okay, not well, but she did marry money. Guess Hollis got tired of sponging off his brother-in-law and went into business for himself."

"Hollis was the bait," the Nightmare said, reading the scene. "He sat in the chair to draw the others' attention. When Waller and Vang came in …" He pointed to an open window. "That leads to the fire escape. That's where the killers stood. This one," he indicated Waller, "didn't have a chance. Vang must have entered last, saw what was going on." The Nightmare nudged a revolver that was on the floor by Vang's body. "He got his gun out and took out Wilder before the Tommy got him."

In the distance came the sound of approaching sirens.

"If we're going to have a chance of escaping," the Reaper said, "we should leave now."

The Nightmare agreed. Taking the elevator to the basement, the pair left by the alley door and were a block away by the time the police arrived in front.

Their masks off, her hood down, Kaye Chandler and Michael Shaw looked like any other couple out for a night's stroll.

"So with those three dead, is our job over?"

"I don't think so, Kaye. I think it just got harder."

"If that's so, what do we do now?"

"I put the mask back on and wait in the shadows. You go home and get some sleep. Tomorrow, after the news breaks, Kaye Chandler can pay her respects to Wilder's sister, and find out all she can about him."

Kaye didn't argue. Although she had seen death before, had even meted it out when there was no other choice, the night's brutal slayings had disturbed her. What was even more disturbing was that but for the killers' interference, it might have been her finger on the trigger. But the line had not been crossed, not this time. She went home and tried to sleep.

There would be no sleep for the Nightmare, not until dawn chased his kind out of the shadows and back indoors. Instead, he made a call, then lurked in an alley across from the murder scene, watching and waiting.

A car pulled up. A tired and somewhat disheveled Lieutenant Easton got out and entered the office building. Ten minutes later he emerged. Standing on the front steps he surveyed the area. Nodding, he descended and crossed the street. His back to the alley, he lit a cigarette.

"You knew I was here?" came a whispered voice.

"Let's see. A mysterious phone call in the middle of the night. Three dead men. A dark alley. Where else would you be? And before we start, is there some kind of rule that says your kind can have only one police contact? I need my sleep, you know." There was a pause. "So, you found the bodies?"

"Yes, we did."

"We? So the girl was with you. I don't care who in her family was killed, she's too young to be dragged into this life. I liked the other one better, the one who dressed darker than you. Nothing happened to her, did it?"

"She happens to other people, Lieutenant."

"I guessed as much. From what little I saw she's more dangerous than the rest of you lot put together. But tell me about our three dead friends. Are the Goldmans avenged?"

"Not by us."

Easton shook his head. "Didn't think so. Shotguns and Tommys aren't your style. How do you see this?"

"Same as you," replied the Nightmare. "Waller and Vang were no longer needed and got the permanent payoff."

"And Wilder?"

"Bad luck and poor planning."

"Amateurs."

"Or beginners. Lieutenant, what's the word about someone called Wolf?"

"Wolf Hopkins. Up and coming gang boss. Brutal as hell. He'll be big one day but not anytime soon. This isn't him. Booze, dames, and drugs, more vice than protection. Nothing to interest your lot – yet."

"Speaking of protection, anything from the Eastside merchants?"

"Not a peep or complaint. It's not surprising, not after what happened to the Goldmans. My guess is that the day after the news hit the paper every one of them got a call. Pay up, go blind, get dead, or have your daughter raped. Most probably paid up. There'll be at least one who didn't. I expect a bombing soon. It's a nasty business."

"Then I'll have to be nastier."

"That's what I'm counting on."

*

The next night, and the nights after that, Michael Shaw went back to the bars and dives. Drinking cheap hooch and avoiding even cheaper floozies, he heard several different stories about how Abe Waller and Teddy Vang met their ends. The best had them taking on a squad of cops and Treasury agents before falling in a hail of bullets. None of the stories mentioned Hollis Wilder. A few mentioned Hopkins. Shaw decided that it was past time he met this "up and comer."

*

Black is not my color, Kaye Chandler thought just before she knocked on the door of the Armstrong residence. She had noted the black wreath on the door. This was a house of mourning. It hadn't been too long ago that things had been more festive. While the wedding of Dorothy Wilder to Boyd Armstrong had not been a high social event – how could it with the bride's father a recent suicide and the groom a stranger from out of town – it had been a happy occasion. Now however …

A properly somber butler opened the door and greeted Kaye. She, in turn, handed him her card and asked to see Mrs. Armstrong. Kaye was ushered into a sitting room where a slightly distracted Dorothy Armstrong greeted her.

"Miss Chandler, forgive me. I know we've met before but my mind's every which way these days."

Kaye smiled. She remembered how it had been. "It was at Mrs. Rittenhouse's last gala. Also at Brook Porter's debut. Plus your family was kind enough to send flowers when my uncle passed. Which is the reason I'm here."

This got Kaye a puzzled "Oh?"

"Like your brother, my uncle was a victim of crime. I thought at this time that maybe you could use a sympathetic and understanding shoulder to cry on, especially coming so soon after your father's death."

Dorothy nodded. "That's very kind of you. But…you'll think this terrible of me…it was not as much of a shock as you'd think. The way Hollis had been acting. Boyd and I know he was up to something. After my father…well, you know…Boyd was kind enough to take my brother in, even give him an allowance, but after a few weeks, Hollis began acting strangely. The police had even come around twice. We didn't suspect, not until we heard the news. Then it all fell into place."

"Do the police have any leads? There was a nice detective who worked my uncle's case. I could make inquiries."

"Don't think me rude, Kaye…I can call you Kaye, can't I…but my brother was killed in a gunfight, shot twice in a dirty office. As hard it is to believe, he was a criminal. I'm sure that the police are doing everything they usually do in cases like this, but the less I know about this matter, the less I have to dwell on what my brother became and how he died, the better."

"I understand." Kaye stood to go. Dorothy rose as well to escort her out. "You have a lovely home," Kaye commented as they walked through the main hall.

"Thanks, but I had little to do with it. Boyd bought it furnished when he got into the city and with all that's happened, we haven't had time to do much with it."

"Your husband, what does he do?"

"A little bit of everything, you know how things are these days."

They seem to be very well, Kaye would have liked to have said as she wondered what little bits of everything could buy the house she'd just visited. By then the two were at the front door, which the butler was holding open.

"You have my number, Dorothy, should you change your mind

about that shoulder."

"Thank you. I suspect I may once the shock wears off."

Shock, maybe, Kaye thought as she drove away in her roadster. But other than the wreath on the door, she hadn't seen any signs of sorrow. Maybe black wasn't Dorothy Armstrong's color either.

*

Eve Webb and her sister Darlene had run a small clothing store just down the street from the Goldman's lunchroom. It was Darlene who had gotten the phone call, the same one Jerome Sampson and the other merchants had received, the one demanding money or else horrible things would happen to them, their store or their loved ones.

The Webb sisters had no loved ones. Neither had ever married. They only had each other and the shop in which they had invested their life savings. And they could not afford twenty percent of the gross if they wanted to keep it open.

"We have to pay, Eve."

"Or else what, Darlene? There's always an 'or else.' There was an 'or else' thirty years ago back in Chi, and another one twenty years ago down in Richmond."

"We paid back then, sister. Now we can't afford to."

"So what was the 'or else?'"

"The man who called threatened our virtue."

Eve laughed. "Big deal, we lost that forty years ago, never missed it. Anyway, we know how to deal with men like that."

Darlene nodded. "Like when we were dancing. Keep a knife handy, let them think we're giving in, then stick them before they can stick us."

"If this man calls back, tell him to stick it. We're not paying."

The night after the Webb sisters got their second phone call, their clothing store was destroyed by a bomb tossed through its front window.

*

Kaye spent the next few days digging. Her shovels were the telephone, the directory, and personal contacts. The object of her search was any information about Boyd Armstrong. She dug long and she dug hard but by week's end, all she had to show for her efforts were lots of empty holes.

"There is no Boyd Armstrong," she complained to her cousin as the two discussed the case in what had been her uncle's workshop.

"Of course there is," Shaw countered, "We went to the wedding, or rather, you did. I had to help Jethro handle that Yeti problem."

Kaye shook her head. "I had the Siberian Countess Caper that weekend. That's when I found out my old cape wasn't as bulletproof as I thought."

"Well, it was in the papers anyway. And if you can't believe what you read …" Shaw's hands wandered toward some five-pointed disks.

"Don't touch those." Kaye's warning came too late as he cut himself on a sharp edge. "Japanese throwing stars."

"Effective weapons," Shaw admitted once he got the bleeding stopped, "With all the stuff you carry they're going to start calling you 'Gadget Girl.' I'm surprised your cape doesn't clink when you move."

Kaye ignored him. "All I'm just saying is that the more 'little bits' Boyd is into, the more there should be some trace of him, some record of his doing business somewhere."

"One would think. Then again, there's very little record of my business transactions."

"Your business, Michael, is spending the money your grandfather stole."

"Great-grandfather" Shaw corrected, "and he didn't steal it, exactly. He may have been a card cheat and a smuggler, but he was not a thief."

"And I bet there was no record of his activities either."

"Just one or two court transcripts, but he was acquitted."

"What, did he bribe the juries?"

"Kaye! What a thing to suggest. Great-grandpa bought the judge, it was cheaper. Anyway, as I about to say, while there is little public record of my financial activities, I do maintain an office at home."

"So this weekend when the Armstrongs are away …"

"And the servants are asleep …"

"The Pink Reaper and The Nightmare should do a little housebreaking."

"The Reaper alone, Kaye. Burglary is at best a solo act. And besides, while you're doing a Raffles, I'll be braving a wolf's lair and hoping not to get bitten."

*

In his room, Michael Shaw dressed for his evening out. Pants, shirt, hat, gloves – unlike his cousin, black was his color. Also black was his trenchcoat, heavy with the weight of .45s in their special holsters. And, finally, the mask that was in its pocket, the mask that covered his features, the mask that was at times his true face.

Dressed to play his part in the game, the Nightmare went out into the darkness.

Finding Wolf Hopkins's headquarters had not been difficult. The gang leader was not yet wanted and so had no reason to hide from the police. No, finding Hopkins had been easy. Getting to see him, however …

"I could try for the bold approach," the Nightmare said to himself as he stood in concealing shadows across from the Brownstone where Hopkins held court. "Kick open the door, guns in hand, demanding to see Hopkins and ready to shoot down any who oppose me. Richard would do that, he actually likes getting shot at. Kent would find a way to sneak in and surprise the wolf at his desk. Nice effect, but that only works once. After that, they're ready for you, and I may have to make a return visit. That leaves only one thing to do."

The Nightmare stepped out of the shadows and into the light of the street lamp in front of the brownstone – and waited.

Hopkins is supposed to be smart. If so, he'll be curious. Of course, he could just have me shot from a window. No, he'll have heard of what happened at that club. No way he'll chance that. None of them will, not yet anyway.

"Go tell the boss there's one of them waiting outside," said the man at the brownstone's front window.

"Them who?"

"One of the dark guys."

"Damn! Which one and what's he doing?"

"Who can tell, and he ain't doing nothing, just standing there. Just tell the boss."

Minutes later the door opened and a man came out. Slowly, like a man sentenced to death, he approached the figure in black, conscious that a black face with cold eyes was watching his every movement.

"The boss sent me out," the man said nervously, expecting at any minute to hear the shot that would send him to eternity. "He wants to know what you want."

The reply came in an icy whisper. "Wolf knows."

"He said you'd say that. He says to come inside."

The Nightmare laughed. Not with a laugh designed to strike fear in the hearts of evildoers, but with a laugh of one enjoying a good joke.

"Inside, in there, anything could happen, to anyone, for any reason. Out here will be fine."

"He said you say something like that, too. He'll be out." The man turned, nodded then, as fast as his dignity would let him, hurried back inside.

Minutes later a different man came out. He was large, clean-shaven and was what some would call handsome. *Not wolf-like at all*, thought the Nightmare, though he did grant that the man moved with a predator's grace.

The man came close and stood before him. "You are Wolf Hopkins?" came the whispered question.

"I am. Which one are you?"

"I'm called the Nightmare."

If Hopkins recognized the name he gave no indication of it.

Instead, he asked, "What do you want?"

"Barry Goldman, scarred and blinded. Suzanne Goldman, violated and killed. Your doing?"

"If you thought that, Nightmare, I'd be dead by now, or you would."

"Abe Waller, Teddy Vang, Hollis Wilder. Killed by your hand or on your orders?"

"Again, no. Although what they did to that dame," Hopkins snorted his disgust, "I would have done it. So would you. What's this about?"

"The protection racket, Hopkins. Four murders and a lot of scared merchants. Are you involved?"

"Let me tell you something, Nightmare, and you can pass it on to your spooky friends. If I'm involved in anything, all you're going to hear is rumor and story. I'm not fool enough to do anything that'll bring you boys in black after me. As for this racket you say is going on, it's brought too much heat. Not our style at all. We like things … quiet."

"We?"

"You know what I mean."

"I do. I also know that you run the Eastside, parts of it anyway. So you no doubt take an interest in what's going on. If not an interest, at least, a percentage."

"Not on this one, Nightmare. This guy's running a lone game. Get him and you'll be doing us all a favor. So if there's nothing else, this conversation is at an end."

"For now, Hopkins."

"Forever, Nightmare. I don't want to see you again."

"Don't worry, next time you won't see me."

*

In her room, Kaye Chandler dressed for her evening out. Standing before her mirror, she liked the way she looked in just her camiknickers (pink of course). Over these, she put on a body stocking close to her own skin tone. *Give them the illusion,* she thought, *not the fact. Michael is right, no sense letting my "distractions" show. Though I do have very nice distractions. If only I had a man to distract.* She then donned the scanty attire that passed for her costume. Finally, the cape, the cape heavy with tools and weapons, the cape that covered her in the night.

Dressed to play her part in the game, the Pink Reaper went out into the darkness.

The Armstrongs were away, Kaye had seen to that. She had suggested to Mrs. Rittenhouse that she invite the couple to dinner to console them in their hour of tragedy. Always one for the big gesture, the grande dame had agreed, at once claiming the idea as her own. And since no one turned down Mrs. Rittenhouse, the Armstrongs were sure to attend.

That left the servants. No problem. With their employers away, most of the help would see this as a night off and likewise disappear. The others would no doubt stay in their rooms and enjoy the quiet. Or else share rooms and enjoy each other.

Kaye just had to be sneaky and stealthy and she was very good at both.

She entered the grounds hooded and cloaked. On her first visit, she had neither seen nor heard any signs of dogs so there was no worry there. Finding a window on the dark side of the house, she oiled its runners, slipped the casement lock, gently raised the sash, and was inside.

Point of entry open or closed, she wondered. Closed, she decided. *If I'm discovered there'd be little chance of getting back. Better not to leave signs of a break-in.*

Using a pocket flash, it took her just a minute to orient herself then five minutes more to find what might be an office. A quick check with her light showed her she was right. Locking the door and lowering the shades, she made herself at home. Knowing she had at least an hour to herself, she then proceeded to ransack Boyd Armstrong's personal papers.

*

"Records of deposits, with no indication of where the money comes from." In the study of his mansion, Michael Shaw looked over the notes Kaye had made from the Armstrong's records. "Methinks that Mr. Armstrong's businesses may not be entirely legitimate. But you say there was no proof of any specific wrongdoing."

Kaye shook her head. "What I saw is what I wrote. Could be he used a different book for each little bit he was involved in."

Shaw turned to a new page of notes. He pointed to an entry. What are these here?"

"Just letters, one or two before each entry."

Shaw sat and thought for a minute. "And you say this was from a new ledger. The first entry date is just a week ago."

"Right after the Goldman's were attacked."

"If that's more than a coincidence, then these letters …"

Kaye picked up on his thought. "B for bakery, L for laundry, DC for dry cleaners, J for jewelers. Quite a list, he almost has the whole alphabet."

"It's certainly suggestive," Shaw cautioned, "and if we're right, that would explain how Hollis got involved. I wonder if Dorothy Armstrong knew her brother was involved in her husband's schemes."

"There's one thing my notes don't show, Michael."

"What's that?"

"The entries from that last ledger were in a woman's handwriting."

All Shaw said to that was "Interesting" then he stared out the window at the rising sun.

Kaye waited for a few minutes but seeing that her cousin was lost in thought and unlikely to find his way back without help she finally said, "What do we do now?"

Shaw took his time answering. "If you mean about the Armstrongs, nothing for now. We have merely a strong suspicion, and while that may be enough for the police, people such as us need to be sure. For all we know, Armstrong may have put his wife on the stroll and the letters stand for the names of the men she's 'entertained.'"

Kaye looked at the amounts listed in her notes. "If so, she's been busy and she comes cheap."

"That was the rumor before she married. But we never dated. But you asked what we do now. Whoever it is, Armstrong or someone else, has to collect the money. We just have to find out how and follow the trail."

*

Like he had every night for the past few days, John Pruitt kept his grocery store open late. He didn't like to, he wanted very much to be at home with his wife and young son. But he didn't have a choice. The two extra hours he stayed open brought in just enough money to pay off the scum who were draining him. And not just him. There William's Dry Cleaning, Sparks and Sons Jewelers, Jerome Sampson's bakery. All of them and more were paying so that their shops wouldn't be bombed, or their employees hurt, or their wives and daughters … but that didn't bear thinking about. If anything happened to Lena …

They had met, most of them anyway, and tried to decide what to do, how to fight this racket. Bill Sparks wanted to go to the police. But he was the only one. The memory of what had happened to the Goldmans was still too fresh. "What if we don't pay?" Saul Williams had asked. The bombing of the Webbs' clothing store had answered that question.

In the end, to protect their families and their livelihoods, they decided to pay and hope against hope that the police would solve Suzanne Goldman's murder and put an end to this nasty business.

It was eight o'clock. Pruitt had just put the "Closed" sign in his window and locked the front door. The day's take, less the protection cut, was in his pocket. He would drop that in the night deposit on the way home. He was about to leave out the back way when …

"John Pruitt."

The voice that came from the darkness was low and cold. It was what Pruitt imagined death sounded like when it was your time.

Maybe it was, he thought.

"Wha…what do you want. I made the first payment; the next one's not due until…"

"I am not one of those who is bleeding you, John Pruitt. My goal is to stop them. And I need your help to do so."

Pruitt suddenly realized who, or rather, what his visitor was. He had read about them in the papers, heard their voices on the radio. But no, their kind fought monsters who threatened the city or fought gangs after rich men's treasures. Never did he think that his problems would be large enough to attract their attention.

And it was their attention that he did not need. What if his new "partner" found out about this visit?

"I …I c-c-can't help you," he managed to stammer out. "Pl-please go."

There was silence. Maybe whoever it was had left. But just as Pruitt thought that the voice in the darkness was back.

"Can't help, or won't. Maybe you think that you are protecting yourself and your family. But what will happen if one week you can't pay? What will you do when brutal men come into your store or break into your home. How will you protect your family then?"

This very thought had kept Pruitt up at night with worry. Now forced to confront this fear, he let go of it and dared to hope.

"What do you need?"

"How is the payment made?"

"Last time, I got a call. A man said to give the money to whoever came to the counter and said, 'Goldman.' It was a boy."

"Did you or anyone follow him?"

"You're joking, right?"

There was laughter in the dark. A reassuring laughter that told Pruitt that his visitor had recognized the absurdity of his question. After the laughter …

"When is the next payment?"

"Two days. Do you want me to signal you, or something?"

"A brave offer, Mr. Pruitt, but that will not be necessary. And trust me; this will be over soon, thanks to you."

"Don't mention it, and I mean that. But what about the next time? And in this city, there will be a next time."

"I will give you a number to call. Give whoever answers your name then say, 'It's the next time.' There will be no time after that."

A phone number was whispered. The hope that Pruitt was feeling grew a little more. "Who are you?" he finally thought to ask. No answer came and it was a few minutes before he realized that he was alone in the dark.

*

Two days after John Pruitt's encounter with the Nightmare, Kaye Chandler was standing at a bus stop across from his grocery store. It was eleven in the morning, it was raining and, just then, she didn't like her cousin very much.

"All you have to do is stand there, Kaye," she said to herself, remembering Shaw's words. "Stand there and pretend to wait on the bus. Keep an eye on the stores and watch for someone, probably a boy, going in and out of all of them. He's the one we want. Follow him and see where he takes the money. That's all. Quite simple really."

"Yeah, right," Kaye muttered. "Just stand there. That's all. Quite simple. Michael didn't mention standing in the rain for two hours. He didn't mention that the temperature would drop five degrees every thirty minutes. Damn him. Next time I need to test a shock dart he's getting one in the ..."

Kaye stopped complaining when what appeared to be a young man or an older boy, come out of Pruitt's Grocery. He immediately went into the Dry Cleaners and from there into the Jeweler's. He made several other stops as well. He was only in each shop for a few minutes and since he wasn't carrying any packages, bags or parcels, it was clear that hadn't done any legitimate business in any of them.

"Damn you, Michael, why must you always be right?" With that final complaint, she followed the young man at a discrete distance. Only to watch him hail a taxi after three blocks.

"How did he find one in the rain?" she asked, then uttered a very unladylike word and looked around for a cab of her own.

She didn't need one. Keeping one eye out for a taxi and the other on her quarry, Kaye was glad that she had taken Michael's advice and worn drab clothes instead of her signature pink. So that she blended in when the "young man" turned in her direction as "he" got into the cab. Even from a distance, recognition was quick.

Well, why not, Kaye thought with a smile, *It worked for Irene Adler*. Then the cab she no longer needed finally answered her hail and she took it back to Shaw's mansion.

*

"Are you sure it was Dorothy?" Shaw asked after Kaye sipped brandy-laced coffee as she tried to warm up. Her clothes were being dried and right then she was sitting in an oversized chair in his study, dressed only in one of his oversized bathrobes. Looking at her like that, Shaw thought, *How young she looks.*

Shaw reminded himself that that "young girl" was really a grown woman, one who played the same dangerous game he did.

Kaye's answer broke his reverie. "Of course I'm sure. My eyesight is excellent."

"I suppose she bound her…" Shaw gestured toward his chest.

"She would have had to. So, do we move tonight or call Easton?"

"There's still no proof the police would accept, so it is up to the Nightmare and Pink Reaper to seek justice for the Goldmans."

"Justice – or vengeance?"

"We seek justice but must be prepared to mete out vengeance. We'll give the Armstrongs a chance, of course. Are you prepared to act if they won't take it?"

For a minute Kaye hesitated, then said, "I'll do what I have to do." Then, "Wouldn't it be easier if we just called this Hopkins and …"

"He'd be far more brutal, and we'd be no less guilty. Kaye, there's more than one reason we wear the black. To blend in, to hide in the darkness, yes. But it also reminds us that in this game we're not the ones wearing the white hats. We're vigilantes, not heroes, and it's a nasty business we've chosen. We are Nightmare and Reaper. We either live up to those names or stay out of the shadows. Now, are you with me or do I go alone? Either way, the Armstrongs may not see the dawn."

Feeling a sudden chill, Kaye Chandler pulled her robe tighter around her. Then she stood. "I better see if my clothes are dry." Slowly she walked to the door of the study. About to leave the room, she turned to her cousin.

"When the Nightmare hunts tonight, the Pink Reaper will walk beside him."

*

"What about the servants?" Kaye asked as she and Shaw rode to the Armstrongs in his LaSalle.

"This time of night they should be asleep. But if you encounter any, remember they're probably not involved in their employers' scheme. Use minimum force."

"And if they're armed?"

"Do what you have to do. And speaking of being armed, don't forget the Armstrongs. They have at least a Tommy and a shotgun."

Kaye was shocked. "You mean, they, alone, but why, it was her own brother?"

"Who was only supposed to set Vang and Waller up to be killed. Who knows why? Maybe they wanted a bigger cut. Maybe it was just to tie up loose ends. Maybe a three-way split sounded better than a five-way. Bad luck for Hollis that Vang got his gun out. Good luck for Dorothy and Boyd. A two-way cut is even better."

"Those guns might make it harder for us."

"And easier."

It wasn't until later that Kaye realized what Shaw meant.

*

The LaSalle pulled up a block away from the Armstrongs' residence. Michael Shaw and Kaye Chandler might have driven up, but it was the Nightmare and Pink Reaper who got out.

"Two lights," came the Nightmare's icy whisper as they approached from the rear.

"Downstairs light is from Boyd's study." The Reaper's voice was as cold as her partner's "Upstairs is probably Dorothy in her bedroom. You take Boyd. Dorothy's mine."

"Agreed. And remember, we offer them the chance. If they turn it down …"

There was little of Kaye Chandler in the Reaper's reply. "They don't see the dawn."

The back door lock yielded to one of the Nightmare's master keys. The dark pair entered silently and split up, the Reaper taking the kitchen stairs to the second floor as The Nightmare made his way to the study.

*

Her form invisible on the narrow, lightless stairway, the Pink Reaper stealthily climbed the back stairs. Like the stairs, the second floor was dark, the only illumination coming from the end of the hall. *The master bedroom*, the Reaper thought and moved toward it, careful to make no sound that would alert her quarry. Drawing her bulky pistol, she set it so that each dart she fired would be more powerful than the last. This would rapidly drain the battery in the grip. She'd only be able to fire five darts. But that wouldn't matter. Her third dart would kill its target.

As the Reaper neared the bedroom door she heard the room's occupant singing. The tune was Barnacle Bill and its lyrics were much bawdier that the version currently playing on the radio. There were, in fact, several verses the Reaper had not heard before. It was not a song that a lady such as Dorothy Armstrong would be singing. And indeed, it was not a woman singing it. The voice belonged to a man – Boyd Armstrong, no doubt.

For a moment, the Pink Reaper gave way to Kaye Chandler, who felt oddly relieved that the opponent she now faced was male. Idly, she wondered what the Nightmare would do when confronted with a woman. Who would win out, the cold avenger or the gentleman she knew Michael Shaw to be? She did not envy him his choice.

The singing having stopped, Kaye gave way to her darker persona and resumed the deadly game.

From the darkness of the hallway, the voice of the Pink Reaper was heard. "Boyd Armstrong, I have come for you." Now that she had his attention, the rose-colored avenger took from her cloak two pellets and threw them into the room. As they broke, their chemicals combined. A bit of tear gas, some smoke, and a sharp noise – all designed to disorient anyone inside.

The Pink Reaper stepped in. "As you've sown, so shall I reap," she intoned in a voice taught her by the man she knew as "Kent."

When the smoke cleared, Armstrong was standing between the bed and a mirrored dresser. His hands weren't raised but they were clearly empty. There was, however, a small revolver on the dresser.

Careful not to make any sudden moves, he asked, "What do you want?"

The Reaper's reply was full of contempt for him and all his kind. "I want you to pay for what was done to Barry and Suzanne Goldman."

There were many ways Armstrong could have responded, from a flat denial to a simple "Who?" It was unfortunate for him that all he saw was a young girl in a revealing outfit, holding a ridiculously large gun. Not sensing the threat, all he said was "Why?"

Far from a denial, the manner of Armstrong's "Why?" was a tacit admission of his guilt.

The Reaper fired her first shot.

A whoosh of air and the dart left the barrel and buried itself in the man's arm. A crackle and the slight smell of ozone as it delivered its charge. A scream of pain and surprise from Armstrong.

He now sensed the threat of the Pink Reaper. Looking at her with a respect born of fear he heard, "Let us not play games. You will write a full confession, detailing your involvement in the protection scheme, the mutilation of Barry Goldman, and the rape and murder of his wife."

"Or?"

The Pink Reaper fired her second shot.

The electric discharge took Armstrong to his knees and nearly caused him to black out. It was only by grasping the edge of the dresser that he was able to remain upright as the Reaper continued.

"Your confession will leave with me. You and your wife will have until the police arrive to seek an escape."

With difficulty, Armstrong straightened. "So that's my choice. Confess and become a wanted man, or you'll keep shocking me until you run out of darts. I think …"

Armstrong moved his head as if looking past the Reaper. An old trick, but one that often works. The Reaper turned as if fooled but kept watch in the mirror. As Armstrong reached for the revolver, she turned back.

And the Pink Reaper fired her third shot.

Boyd Armstrong's back arched as a lethal dose of electricity ran through his body. He fell to the floor, twitched several times then was still.

Looking down at the corpse, the Pink Reaper again briefly gave way to Kaye Chandler. "Thanks for going for the gun," said the woman behind the mask.

*

As the Nightmare entered the study, he found Dorothy Armstrong making entries in a journal. He was about to say something appropriately spooky when the sound of the Pink Reaper's pellets was heard from above.

Startled, Dorothy jumped and in doing so, saw the Nightmare standing in the doorway, .45 in hand.

"My companion is with your husband," he said in a tone that had more Michael Shaw in it than usual. "I'll make you the same offer she's making him. Confess and you'll be given time to escape. Otherwise …" The Nightmare gestured with his heavy automatic.

Seeming to be not at all impressed by the implied threat,

Dorothy smiled. "We both know that you won't pull the trigger. Whatever happens to my husband, I think I'll just sit here and wait for the police. If he confesses, whatever he says about me is a lie. If he dies, I'll be the poor widow who had no idea her husband was a criminal. The police will never get a jury to believe that a woman was involved in such a brutal crime, much less conceived it."

"You?" asked the Nightmare, glad that his full mask would hide the shock on his face.

"Me," Dorothy said with some pride. "The protection racket was Boyd's idea. He'd run one in some other cities before we met. But what was done to the Goldmans, that was mine."

The Nightmare's shock deepened. "Why tell me?"

"It's not like you can testify. And as I said, you won't shoot me. Your kind doesn't kill in cold blood."

There was sorrow in the Nightmare's voice as he said, "That belief, Mrs. Armstrong, was the last of your many mistakes in this whole nasty business."

The Nightmare fired his first shot.

*

Being on the first floor, the Nightmare was already on the lawn when the Pink Reaper emerged from the house.

His shot had awakened the servants and by now the house was ablaze with light. Soon the bodies would be found and the police called. "We'd best be gone," he said.

"No laugh of triumph over evil?"

"I don't feel much like laughing tonight, do you?" When the Pink Reaper shook her head, the Nightmare added, "What of Boyd?"

"He's gone. He made it easy."

The Nightmare looked back at the house and thought of a woman's body on the study floor. "So did she," he said quietly. Then the two dark avengers faded into the night.

DEFYING THE ODDS

An adventure of Nemesis, The Nightmare, and The Pink Reaper

The Woman in Black stood on the sand and looked out over the ocean, staring across the sea toward the land of her birth, the place of her torment.

"What has brought me to this place?" she wondered. "Why here, to the eastern shore of the Great Western Sea?" She had no answer. There was no oracle to guide her path.

So much had happened in the time since her mind had emerged from its ignorant slumber. She had been lost, adrift in a strange country with no money, no friends, not even a sense of self. It took a cry of help from a dying woman to awaken her as to who she was.

She was Nemesis. She was the daughter of the Night. She was the enforcer for the Council of Thrones.

And she was as doomed as the woman whose death she had avenged.

She knew there was more to her power than she could currently call upon. With enough time, she might recover the parts of her missing memory and mind. She had even asked her mother Nyx, but Mother Night would not help her, instead blaming Nemesis for her own foolishness in letting the lord of thunder best her.

He is coming, she thought. *Now that I am awake again, the Thunderer, the Bringer of Lightning will come for me before I gain back all of who I am. He fears that happening. When I was no one, just a homeless wretch with no thought but my next meal and a dry place to sleep, he could not find me. But now that I have again claimed my power, sooner or later he will sense me and seek me out, to vent his lust on me once more then return me to the darkness.*

She could fight him and maybe win. Away from his mountain and in a land where he had few believers he would not be as strong. And she need not fight alone. Nemesis had spent her time helping others and gathering allies. The League of Shadows. Her new trio of agents—Shargrin, the Dead Lady, and the Pink Reaper. Paddy Moran and those at Bulfinche's Pub. Lastly, Nemesis thought of one who, like her, was an avenger and a creature of the night. He had been her friend and ally and together they had fought immense odds to right a great wrong. And on their last night he had become her lover. If summoned, he would stand at her side.

But he who was called The Nightmare was just a mortal and for all his courage, he could not stand against a god. And while not all of her allies were mortal or even alive, they would all likely not last long before the wrath of a god-king.

"Not long," came the unbidden thought. "But maybe long enough to weaken the Thunderer and allow me to strike." And she knew that the Nightmare would do this willingly, just as she would for him. Some of the others would also stand by her side. And if the cause had been anything but her own safety, she might have asked it. But no, she would not trade Shaw's life or any of the others for hers.

Drunken laughter broke into Nemesis's thoughts. Turning away from the ocean, she looked towards the bright lights of the resort that called itself Coast City. Coming from the newly installed boardwalk were three men and a woman, all of whom seemed to have indulged too much at one of the town's many speakeasies. Calling up the darkness that was her birthright as the daughter of the Night, Nemesis hid in the shadows to watch what might happen.

"I told you, I don't want to," the woman protested.

"Then why'd ya come down here?" asked one of the men.

"Wanted ta see the water. You said you'd show me the stars on the water."

"Sure, you can see the stars," said another man, "while you're on your back."

There were more drunken laughs as the last man added, "And then we'll turn you over and you can look at the water."

The three started to undress her.

"But I said no," the woman again complained only to be told,

"Too damned bad. Should have thought of that before you came down here. Now we're gonna come down on you. And there's not a damned thing you can do about it."

There are rules, Nemesis told herself. By her own actions, this woman had put herself in this situation. And she had not yet called for help. And there was not yet anything to avenge. Still, having herself suffered the ordeal the woman was about to endure, the Woman in Black could not idly stand by. The woman finally screamed for help, but her attackers ignored her pleas. Dropping her shadows and calling on a bit of moonlight, Nemesis stood revealed on the sand.

"Let her go." Nemesis's words were soft and almost whispered, but it was clear that all four heard her.

"Who the hell are you?"

"Your Hell, your damnation," she answered the man. "If you persist. Walk away now and live. Stay and you will die."

The warning was lost on the three men, who saw only a woman clad in the sheerest of black.

"Hey, Randy, look at the way this broad is dressed. I think she might be one of those crime-fighting chicks, like the Domino Dame out west."

"Yeah, or that Pink Floozy they got up in New York. Always wondered how one of those gals would feel under me. Guess now's my chance."

The man reached for her.

"Fools," she said, and as quick as thought the Woman in Black was among them. Three blows, all in the right spots and the men were down on the sand.

When on business for the Thrones, she killed. Even when on her own, Nemesis killed those who deserved death for their actions. It had been that way ever since the days of old. Yet, living among mortals like Bulfinche Moran had made her aware of the possibility of redemption. There would be those forever beyond its reach, but there were others who were not. If she killed these men, they would be beyond redemption's reach.

Still, they deserved punishment. Nemesis smiled as an idea came to her. But where to find a shovel at this hour of the night?

It was sometime later when the men awoke to find they seemed paralyzed below the neck. It didn't take but a moment for them to realize they were buried up to their chins in the sand and the tide was coming in. Nemesis had timed it so the first wave smacked them in the face seconds after they realized their predicament.

The trio of would-be rapists started to scream for help, which is when Nemesis who had been standing in front of them allowed the darkness to reveal her.

"Get us out of here!"

"Help us please!"

"We're begging you!"

Nemesis crossed her arms. "Like the woman whom you were going to rape?"

"We were just having some harmless fun," said the one with slicked black hair.

"Me too," she replied. "You can take it up with your maker and see if she cares."

"But we'll drown," Randy said as he realized his coming fate.

"Yes, you will."

"Please, we'll never do anything like this again. We promise," Slick said.

"Well so long as you promised. I'll take my leave of you," said Nemesis, waving her hand. Something dark washed over them and suddenly the sand moved off of them and the men were free. The same dark wave seemed to trip Nemesis, making her fall. Her head snapped back and she lay still.

The men saw. Randy and Slick smiled evilly as they climbed out of the surf toward the fallen woman in black. The third man stood and looked at his companions, his life literally having flashed before his eyes.

"Fellas, maybe we should just leave well enough alone and go," he said,

"The bitch tried to kill us just for having a little fun," said Slick. "I aim to take that fun out of her hide, then bury her up to her neck in the sand and see how she likes it."

"Sounds like a plan," said Randy.

"Just leave her. The cathouse isn't far," he said. "Let's go there instead."

"I ain't paying for it. She is," Slick said.

"Hell yeah," Randy echoed. "I'll get her top, you get her pants."

No sooner did the men's hands touch the woman in black when she sprang into action, her foot connecting with Randy's jaw, knocking him unconscious. At the same time, her hand grabbed hold of Slick's groin and the man fell to his knees as Nemesis rose to hers. From a distance, they may have almost looked like lovers moving to meet each other, at least until Nemesis smashed her forehead into Slick's nose hard enough for him to join his crony in the sleep of the unjust.

The third man put his hands up in front of himself as if the action would ward off the Daughter of Night.

"You made the right choice. You get to live, but know this – I will be watching you. What is your name?"

"Taylor Jones."

"Know this, Taylor Jones, should you ever try to harm another, I will know and I will come for you and you will share the fate of your friends," she said.

"What's going to happen to them?"

"They will be again buried in the sand and this time the tide will claim their lives. I suggest you dedicate your life to making things right, understood?"

"I will," Taylor promised.

"Make sure you do," Nemesis said and pointed back toward the boardwalk. The man got the hint and fled before the woman in black changed her mind.

Nemesis returned the evildoers to their silicone prison and this time the waves drowned out their screams before doing the same to them.

Nemesis returned to the boardwalk to find the woman who had been attacked huddled in a corner crying.

"You," Nemesis pointed to the woman she had just saved. "Are you all right?" The woman nodded numbly, still drunk but not so inebriated that she didn't realize what had almost happened. "Who are you and where are you from?"

"I'm Violet," the woman answered. "I came from up at the place."

"And what place is that?"

Violet pointed further up the boardwalk. "It's a speak and casino in back of Mrs. Foley's hotel. It ain't got a name but everyone calls it after the owner. Some woman named Tycho or something."

Gods below, thought Nemesis. *Could it be?* she asked Violet, "Do you mean 'Tyche?'"

"Yeah, that's the broad. A nice looking chick like you."

Suddenly Nemesis knew what had brought her to this place and that there was a light at the end of her tunnel that might not end in a thunderbolt. But Violet was still badly shaken and very drunk, so she saw the woman home first.

*

The Man in Black stood in the shadows of a darkened hallway and looked out into the street. He was waiting for armed men to arrive. They would come to murder a family hiding in the apartment he was guarding. He was the only one who could stop the killers, the sole chance a husband, wife, and two sons had.

Three weeks ago the Dorseys, tourists on their first day in the city, had gotten lost and driven into the wrong part of town. They had also driven into the middle of a gang rubout. None of them were hurt, but all of them had gotten a good look at the hitmen.

Now their lives were in danger. One try at assassination had already failed. And it was only by chance that the man who was called The Nightmare had heard about the coming attempt.

He had been in a waterfront dive called Dago Mike's. Mike's was a dirty place frequented by the lowest of riffraff. The Nightmare had learned long ago that by ordering a bottle and sitting quietly in a corner he could learn much about the goings on of crime and criminals.

"The Wolf is getting nervous," said one rough looking man to another. "That family's still alive and can finger Jake Green and Charlie Heywood for bumping The Welshman."

"Thought the Dead Man was taking care of them."

"Somebody got the Dead Man – one of them."

"Them" were the city's dark protectors, avengers in black who haunted the night and struck for Justice when the Law failed. The Nightmare was one of their number and had, in fact, stopped the Dead Man.

"Which one?"

"Does it matter? Anyway, Wolf is worried that if Green and Heywood go down, they'll turn yellow and put him in as ordering the hit."

"So why hasn't Wolf tried again?" asked the second mobster.

"Ain't like he hasn't tried. No one knew where the cops had the family holed up until yesterday I hear."

"Somebody squeal?"

"Nah, some janitor at the precinct found a receipt from a boarding house in a trashcan. He's in the know and thought it'd be worth something. It was. Word is the Wolf's sending a team tonight, just in case."

The Nightmare wanted to rush out, find a phone and call his police contact for the Dorseys' current address. He knew better than to try. A sudden departure after hearing such news would give his game away. Instead, he sat patiently and watched the door. When a particularly dangerous looking gunman came in, the disguised Nightmare uttered an oath, did his best to hide his features, and furtively left the bar. Those who saw him leave thought only that he was hiding from the newcomer, a not uncommon occurrence.

A phone call later, The Nightmare was on his way to the Finley Apartments.

As he waited in the darkness, The Nightmare wondered who would arrive first, Wolf Hopkins's mobsmen or the Police Flying Squad that Lieutenant Jerome Easton was supposed to send.

His answer came minutes later when two black touring cars pulled up in front of the building. As he expected, armed men got out, one with a Tommy, two more with shotguns and the others carrying revolvers.

Time to play, thought the Man in Black as he stepped outside to meet his foes.

The laugh froze the gunmen in place. With the Nightmare's challenge coming from nowhere and everywhere the eight men at first did not know which way to turn. It was only when The

Nightmare fired from the doorway with twin .45's that they knew from which direction the attack was coming.

The man with the Tommy went down first, catching two in the chest. A bullet each for those with the shotguns. Then the Nightmare ducked back inside to avoid a hail of revolver slugs.

A moment of silence as the remaining five men wondered what to do. Rushing the door meant death. Remaining there might mean the police. Fleeing would only earn them the wrath of the man who sent them and Wolf Hopkins was not a forgiving boss.

Taking advantage of their hesitation, the Nightmare again emerged from the building. Another rain of death from his guns, three more fallen crooks. And again there was silence.

The Nightmare counted the fallen. "Six," he thought, "not a bad night's work. Maybe the other two …" Whatever thought he had faded when it occurred to him that maybe the other two had been smarter than the six now lying dead or dying on the sidewalk.

The Man in Black rushed into the building to find that one of the two had entered through the back door. Fortunately, there was only one set of stairs and the gunman was only halfway up the first flight when the Nightmare's bullet took him in the back.

That left one remaining foeman. *And if I were he …* thought the Nightmare. Leaping over the body on the steps, he ran up to the third floor in a race against death.

He almost lost. On reaching the top floor the Nightmare heard a gunshot come from the rear apartment. Though winded from his climb, he managed to kick open the front door. Without thinking, without aiming, he loosed shot after shot at the dark figure standing at the fire escape window. A scream, a fall, and the threat was ended.

When he heard the gunfire come from below, Walter Dorsey had been certain that the end had come. *Why did we have to drive? Why didn't we take the train into the city*, he thought, not for the first time. Rushing his family into the bathroom, he prepared to defend them as best he could. A butcher's knife from the kitchen was small protection against guns, but it was all he had.

He wasn't expecting the shot from the window. Somehow it merely grazed his arm. Before a second shot could be fired, the front door burst open and hell was unleashed on his attacker.

Dorsey looked at his savior. A tall man dressed all in the color of night, his face fully covered by a black mask. "Are you all right?" the man asked him.

"Uh, yeah," Dorsey looked at his arm, "just a scratch. I'm okay."

"And your family?"

A quick check in the bathroom found them frightened but unharmed.

"Thank you," said Muriel Dorsey, "Mr. …?"

"I'm called the Nightmare, Ma'am." He looked at the knife Dorsey was still holding. "You're a brave man, sir."

Dorsey dropped the knife, collapsed on the sofa. "I can't be brave anymore. None of us can. Tell them, please, the cops and crooks, they'll listen to you. Tell them that it's over. We won't be testifying, none of us. We want to go home and we want to be safe."

"I'm afraid that won't help, Mr. Dorsey. As long as you and your family are alive, you're a threat to this mob, whether you testify or not."

"Then there's no hope. You saved us tonight, but what about the next time, or the time after that."

"There won't be a next time, Mr. Dorsey. I've thought about this and decided that tonight, I did not arrive in time to save you."

*

The Woman in Pink stood in the stranger's bedroom and looked at the sleeping man. *He looks so peaceful lying there*, she thought, then added, *that's about to change.*

It was two days ago that The Pink Reaper was sitting in a booth in Moran's, a nice little tavern in the east end of the city. She wasn't in her working clothes, that was saved for after hours when she and others like her gathered at the bar to discuss their night's activities. No, this time she had come as her true self, Kaye Chandler, wealthy young heiress and gal about town.

"Miss Chandler."

Kaye looked up to see the rumpled figure of Police Lieutenant

Jerome Easton.

Easton was a rarity in the city, an honest cop and a good man. They had first met when he investigated the murder of her favorite uncle. Despite the lieutenant's best effort, that murder went unsolved until a frustrated Kaye took the law into her own hands and brought the killer to justice as the Pink Reaper.

"You're late, Lieutenant," she said in mock reproof, "I'm not used to being kept waiting."

"I'm sure you're not," Easton said with a smile, "and to make up for it I've taken the liberty of ordering for us."

He sat down just as the waiter brought the drinks. "Coffee for the lieutenant and for you, Miss, a Pink Lady."

"Interesting choice, Lieutenant. You're not drinking."

"I'm on duty. Not that that stops most of my fellow officers, even these days when no one's supposed to. Stupid law that." Easton looked around. "Wonder how this place stays open. Moran must have the luck of the Irish to keep the Feds away."

"You'd be surprised. Now, Lieutenant, why did you need to see me?"

"I need some advice, Miss Chandler. It seems that a fellow officer has a sister, a sister married to a prominent judge."

"Sounds like an ideal situation for a police officer."

"One would think. And to be honest, this judge has helped a bit. The officer's a sergeant now and should soon get his lieutenant's shield."

"So what's the problem?"

Easton sighed. "The sister. My friend has just learned that the judge beats her and, uh, to put it delicately, forces her to do things beyond what a husband should expect of a wife."

Kaye failed to see a problem. "Assault and rape. Arrest him."

"Would it were that simple, Miss Chandler. There is not a jury in the land that would convict a man, any man, of exercising what are considered his rights as a husband."

"That's because juries are made up of men. Put twelve women in that box…"

"And the judge would soon be missing some vital parts, I know, Miss Chandler, and I wouldn't disagree with the verdict. But as things stand today, there's little that can be done. And given that the husband's a judge ..."

"You don't have to finish, Lieutenant. Being a judge he would not even be arrested and would destroy the careers of anyone who tried. He is, in effect, above the law. So, how I can help?"

Kaye knew the answer. Easton, she was sure, was well aware of her nighttime activities, however much he pretended not to be. In turn, Kaye and her cousin Michael Shaw, aka The Nightmare, went along with the game, helping the Lieutenant when they could without admitting anything.

"As I said, Miss Chandler, this judge is beyond the law's reach. I was wondering if you might have any ideas about how to proceed before my friend does something fatally stupid."

"I might, Lieutenant, but don't you usually go to my cousin for this kind of advice."

"Your cousin's 'advice,' Miss Chandler, can at times be extreme. Should anything of a permanent nature happen, given the judge's prominence, who knows where an investigation would lead, what secrets might be revealed."

"I understand, Lieutenant. Let me think about your problem for a few days. Who knows, maybe by then this problem will have resolved itself."

"Thank you, Miss Chandler. Another pink lady?"

"I think one's more than enough."

"Amen to that."

*

"Ulysses Sexton."

The voice brought Sexton from a dreamless sleep. Again he heard it. "Ulysses Sexton."

The judge woke as for a third time the eerie voice spoke.

"Ulysses Sexton."

He looked to see a dark shapeless form standing near the foot of his bed. As he stared pale hands rose up and a black hood dropped back, revealing the head of a beautiful young blonde.

"Who are you?" asked the judge in hope and wonder.

"I'm for you, Your Honor," came the sultry reply. The blonde opened her robe to display a nearly naked body clad in just the briefest of pink lace. "All for you."

Under the covers, the judge felt himself begin to harden. "Who sent you?" he asked. "Was it Burger at the DA's office?"

"No, I came all by myself. I hate coming by myself. Maybe you could come with me."

"Young lady, I think that can be arranged."

As Sexton threw back his covers in invitation, the Pink Reaper drew a large, bulky looking pistol. Aiming for the tent in the judge's pajama bottoms, she fired.

A muffled pop was followed by a crackling buzz and the smell of burning flesh as an electrically charged dart buried itself in a delicate part of the judge's anatomy. Another shot and as the judge again felt intense pain in his most sensitive region the Reaper let drop two capsules containing a gaseous chemical.

The judge in his agony watched as the vision before him slowly changed into a monster from hell. The black cloak with its pink lining became the wings of a great beast as the beauty by his bed became a rose-colored demon.

Sexton screamed, and as he did, he inhaled more of the hallucinatory gas. His mind went away, and while it was gone, the suggestion was made that this dreadful pink creature before was somehow linked to his treatment of women in general and his wife in particular and would be returning night after night. Never again a peaceful night's sleep. Never again the joys of a woman's touch. Never again …

Sexton awoke the next morning convinced he had had the worst dream ever. Until he tried to move and felt the pain in his groin. He shuddered, tried to ignore it and got ready for another day in court.

Before the first hearing was scheduled, he was handed a note. "The lady said it was important," his clerk explained, leaving out the part that the lady had slipped him a five to deliver the message. Sexton looked up from his bench and saw a beautiful young blonde in a dark cloak. Feeling a cold chill he opened the note which read,

"Never again."

He looked again at the woman, who by now had opened her cloak to reveal a tight pink dress beneath it.

The note, the color pink, and a final suggestion made the night before triggered the residual gas in the judge's system. Again his mind went away. This time in public.

"Extra, extra, read all about it! Judge sees pink monsters, goes crazy in court! Paper, Mister?"

Lieutenant Jerome Easton took the late morning edition from the newsie and read how Judge Ulysses Sexton had had a break down in court and was now being treated in a "secure facility." His wife had no comment except that she would now be living with her brother and would be seeking a separation.

So much for Sexton's power and influence, Easton thought, wondering if it would not have been more merciful to have had Kaye Chandler's cousin deal with the judge.

*

She checked in to Foley's Hotel as Leda Troy, using the name The Nightmare had given her. She asked for and was given a room facing the ocean.

"What's there to do at night around here?" Nemesis asked the young desk clerk who simply shrugged.

"Not much, this is kind of a dull town at night."

"Oh, I heard there was some action out back."

Another shrug. "Not for me to say."

Inwardly Nemesis smiled. There were so many ways. Which to choose? She could show him a glimpse into the darkness, not enough to make him mad, just enough to haunt his nights for the rest of his life, but he had done no evil that she knew of. He was a teenaged boy, maybe all of fifteen years old. She was tall and beautiful in tight revealing clothing. A smile, a touch, maybe the hint of a promise she had no intention of keeping and he might tell all he knew. But there was yet an easier way. She took a five from her purse.

The boy eyed the bill as Nemesis asked, "Are you sure you can't say?" He hesitated, then reasoned that if the doll had fins to give away, she was at least a spender and the right sort of dame for the action in the rear. He grabbed the note.

"There's an old house out back, opens after nine. There's a guy at the front door. Word for tonight is 'Fortuna.' That's like fortune but with an 'a.' It's Greek or something. Means luck."

Nemesis smiled, glad for another confirmation of her suspicions. "I've heard the word before. It's Latin, actually." Then she favored the young man with a smile and a touch, both freely given. It made her feel better and him several years older.

*

Kaye Chandler was in her workshop when she heard, "Nice job on the judge. I understand he's still in Bellevue."

Kaye turned to see her cousin standing in the doorway.

"No less than he deserves, Michael. And if he ever gets out …"

"More pink terror? Hey, now that's a name. 'Beware the Pink Terror!'"

"Sound more like a horror flick for the Ethels down in the Village. Besides, I've changed my name enough. So, what brings you by?"

"Just stopped in to see my favorite cousin."

"You don't have any other cousins, and we're not really related. What do you really want, Michael?"

"How'd you like to spend a week or two in an ocean resort with a good-looking millionaire?"

"Sounds like fun. Know any?"

"I meant me."

"Oh, when you said good-looking it confused me. I take it this is not an attempt on my virtue?"

Michael Shaw shook his head at Kaye's question. Not that he hadn't considered it. She was sexy and attractive, a great looking blonde with a swell shape and, despite her youthful appearance, definitely old enough. But she was also the closest to family he had and that was more important than any physical thrills.

With a loud, mock sigh he answered her, "Maybe later. This time, though, you'll have to pack that skimpy thing you call a costume."

"Bad guys on the beach?"

"Not yet, but there will be. Did you read about the shootout at the Finley Apartments?"

"Gang fight? Family caught in the middle and all of them killed? What about it? We going after the ones who did it?"

"No. The papers just have the story Easton fed them. Truth is, the family's alive, for now. They're witnesses against the Hopkins mob and I stopped a rubout. I decided it was safer for them if everyone thought they were dead."

"That won't last. Some cop on the take will talk."

"That's why we're going to Coast City."

"To protect them."

"Not exactly, Kaye. Easton's going to let a few people know that's where the Dorseys are. The hoods will look there and instead ..."

Kaye smiled. "Find us. But what about the Dorseys? Where will they be?"

"Kent's agreed to keep them on his island until the trial. Anyone who finds them there is going to hear a whole lot of laughing before they die."

*

Clad in her finest dress, Nemesis left her room just after nine. Leaving the Foley Hotel by the street door, she crossed over to the unnamed house opposite. It was a medium-sized structure, clearly built as a private residence and not to host countless transient guests. She stood for a few minutes on the sidewalk, watching a number of people approach the door. Some were admitted, others turned away.

"It is time," she decided.

"Fortuna," Nemesis said in perfect Latin to the doorman, using it more as a name than a password. At first, the man seemed as if he were going to challenge her right of entry, but after a look into the darkness in her eyes he stepped aside and let her pass.

A small entry room, more of a large vestibule with a coat check to the right and restrooms to the left. Nemesis had no need for either and so entered the main hall.

Most of the first floor had been gutted to form the casino. Slot machines lined the wall while gaming tables took up the center. At a glance, Nemesis could see people winning and losing at 21, Red Dog, Roulette, and Craps. Extending her senses briefly, she was surprised to find no trace of any trickery. The games were honest, with only luck determining the outcome. Which was no more than Nemesis expected.

If she were correct.

Another glance around the casino floor. There was no sign of the one she sought. How best to attract her attention, if she were indeed present. Nemesis knew of one way for sure.

Walking over to the roulette table, she bought a modest number of chips and placed them all on thirteen black. With a subtle use of power, the ball dropped in the right slot.

When the croupier passed over her winnings, Nemesis made no move to pick them up. "Your chips, Ma'am," he said in an obvious hint.

"I believe the expression is 'Let it ride.'"

Twice more the wheel spun, twice more thirteen black hit. Nemesis now had a small fortune in front of her.

If she's here, that should attract her attention.

Just as she had this thought, Nemesis felt a power enter the room. She turned to see her one-time sister by choice coming toward her.

Dressed in a full-length green gown, Tyche moved with all the grace of the goddess she was even as she quickly moved towards the roulette table.

"I thought I heard someone call my name earlier," she said as she recognized her former companion.

"Greetings, Tyche," replied Nemesis. "Is there somewhere we can talk?"

Moments later, Tyche had led Nemesis to her second-floor office. "What brings you to my temple, sister?" she asked her in Doric Greek.

"Temple?"

"What else would you call a place where people constantly call upon you and throw offerings onto tables in the uncertain hope that their lives will be made better. In this mostly godless land it is more than enough to sustain me."

"And do you at times favor one worshipper over the next?"

"Luck, my dear Invidia, is as blind as Justice. And like Justice, the scales must balance. If someone wins, someone else must lose. Either way, it is their calling on me as Lady Luck that feeds me."

"Which is why I caused the imbalance. I knew you'd seek it out."

"Which leads me again to ask what has brought Vengeance to my door? Certainly, it is no one of my house."

"Rest easy, sister. I come not seeking retribution, but rather shelter. You know my history and what the Thunderer has done to me."

"My father's appetites are infamous. I had heard talk that you were one of his conquests."

"Conquest is apt, for he invaded my body, ravishing me not once but many times. And each time, he has caused me to forget. And now that I have again awakened ..."

"You fear that he will again seek you out and lay you down. But you are Vengeance, why not do for yourself what you have done for so many others?"

"Because Ze... because he owns a piece of my soul, having ripped it from me. It gives him power over me that no other has ever had, power that I may not be able to defeat. I am... not up to full strength yet. Maybe one day I will find the courage to face him and the strength to defeat him. But now ... I seek only to hide from him, to put off the day I know must come until I will make sure he too knows vengeance."

"The only way to hide from my father is to hide from yourself."

"Lethe water?" The idea of water from one of the three rivers in Hades' realm struck a chord within her. "You have some?"

Tyche nodded and pointed to a black vial. "There on that shelf.

I keep it for those who may discover too much about me or my associates. One drop is enough for most bothersome humans. More than that and they forget all."

"Associates? Since when does the Goddess of Fortune partner with mortals?"

"When those mortals have guns and the willingness to use them. A percentage is enough to keep the peace. And they are, at times, useful."

Tyche rose and took the black bottle from the shelf. "Consider the water, sister. Hide from the world for a time. When you return, you may be stronger or he may be weaker."

Nemesis made no move to take up the vial from its place on the desk. It seemed familiar. One of the things that still fled from her thoughts was how he kept stealing her mind. This would explain it.

"The water is one solution, but there is another. Grant me your luck, sister, that he may seek me and never find me."

"And what of the Balance?"

"My good luck would be his ill fortune."

"I will consider it, Nemesis. For the love that was once between us, I will consider it. But for now, if you would return to the casino and lose back the money that you 'won' from me. Just to maintain the Balance."

*

"So where are we staying?" Kaye asked as Shaw turned his rented car on to the long road that led directly into Coast City and nowhere else.

"A room has been reserved at Mrs. Foley's Seaside Hotel."

"Why there? Is that the top spot in Coast City?"

"Far from it. Its main feature is that it has a casino in the back. Casinos mean mob. What better place for a couple on the run to attract attention?"

Kaye sensed that Shaw was not telling her something. "Couple? Room? Michael, are you saying we're checking in as man and wife?"

"I'm about the same size and build as Walter Dorsey and with the right wig you could pass for his wife."

"Where am I going to get 'the right wig?' And what color is it?"

"She's a brunette. And I packed you one. It's a blonde wig by the way."

"But I'm a blonde."

"And Mrs. Dorsey is a brunette. But the wig I packed is so cheap it will be obvious that you're wearing one. We're checking in as the Dorsets. By now Easton has let it slip as to where the Dorseys are hiding."

"So it's a trap and we're bait. But why, if the Dorseys are safe on the island?"

"Wolf Hopkins has twice tried to kill the Dorseys. The first time he lost his best assassin. On the second try, I killed several of his men. This time I hope to kill several more. I want him to understand the cost of killing witnesses. If he believes that any future tip-offs are likely to be traps it might make him think twice about going after them."

"So he goes after their friends and relatives, anyone close to them. What then?"

"Then one night Wolf Hopkins goes to sleep, has a Nightmare, and doesn't wake up."

"Let's get back to us sharing a room. Two beds, I trust."

"Why would we need two beds? We're married."

"Surely you don't expect me to sleep in the same bed as you?"

"I don't expect us to get much sleep at all."

"Michael Shaw!"

"Easy, cousin. I have no designs on whatever virtue you have left. What I meant was that I expect us both to be up all night, in our working clothes, waiting for someone to try and kill us."

By then Shaw had pulled into Coast City proper. It was a quiet little town, with a newly installed boardwalk to help its visitors go from hotel to restaurant to night spot without getting sand in their shoes. Already concession stands had been erected on the wooden walkway, some renting bicycles to those who wanted to cruise the boards and beach chairs and umbrellas for those who just wanted to sit and enjoy the ocean. Other vendors had garish souvenirs for sale, cheap items that sold for three times their value just because they had "Coast City" stamped on them.

Shaw pulled his car up next to the hotel and after Kaye donned what was a very cheap wig, they went in to register.

"Eh, we're the Dorsets," Shaw said diffidently once he was able to attract the desk clerk's attention away from the pulp Western he was reading. "We have a reservation. I believe a Mr. Jerome called it in."

"Oh yeah," said the young man, "we've been expecting you." He handed them a key. "Third-floor front overlooking the beach. And speaking of the beach, if you're thinking of going bathing, maybe you'd like to rent some suits. We have the latest in rubberized swimwear. Only twenty-five cents." The clerk looked right at Kaye as he said, "They're nice and tight. Really shows off your figure."

Thinking of Kaye dressed as the Pink Reaper Shaw thought, *He should see her at night,* as Kaye said indignantly, "Young man, the only man to whom I show my figure is my husband, and that's only at night, with the lights out."

And with that Kaye turned and marched up to her room, leaving Shaw to shoulder their bags up three flights of stairs. When he got to the top, he found Kaye waiting in the hall.

"Forget the key?" he asked.

"I was just thinking."

"About a rubber bathing suit?"

Kaye ignored him. "No, about the way the goof at the desk said that we were expected."

Looking at the room, Shaw asked, "So you think we might have company?"

Kaye nodded. "Maybe a few in the room, some more coming up the stairs behind us."

Shaw carefully put down the bags. "You dressed for work."

"Will be in a minute. You."

"Dressed to kill."

Shaw took a pair of gloves and a black, full-faced mask from his pants pockets. From holsters sewn into his coat came two large .45 semi-automatics. By then Kaye had stripped off her outer clothing to reveal a skimpy pink costume, showing much more of her figure than she would have in any rubber suit. From her purse, she drew several pellets and a small .32 pistol.

"No electric dart gun?" The Nightmare asked.

The Pink Reaper looked at her suitcase. "It's in my bag," she said. "Too bad for them." She looked at the door to their room. "We're going to feel very foolish if I'm wrong."

"Better than feeling dead. You set?" The Reaper nodded. "Ladies first. Go in low at my signal."

The Nightmare's signal was a laugh he had learned from masters of fear. There was no humor in it. Instead, it foretold doom and retribution. It was the sound of Justice about to triumph.

Not bothering with the key, at the sound of the Nightmare's laugh, the Pink Reaper kicked the door at just the right spot. As it flew open, she threw in the pellets. There followed smoke and a loud noise as certain chemicals combined.

The Pink Reaper rolled into the room, came up in a firing stance, saw men with guns choking from the gas and smoke. One of the hoods was holding a chopper. *Too bad for them*, she thought again, but they'd made their choice long ago. She aimed and fired.

Small caliber gunfire. The Reaper's gun. Then the sound of a Thompson. As the Nightmare felt the urge to rush to his comrade's aid she proved right again as three armed men emerged from the stairwell.

Whatever they had been expecting, they were not prepared for the masked figure that greeted them in the hall. Their momentary hesitation cost them their lives. Spending more ammo than necessary, the Nightmare sent leaden hail their way until they fell and moved no more.

One down, thought the Reaper but the other one, the one with the Tommy, was starting to shake off the effect of the gas. He'd already gotten off one burst. The smoke cleared. She saw him clearly now. But that meant he also saw her. They aimed together. He fired first, the Reaper not at all.

Realizing that even a killing shot might not prevent the gunman from loosing a fatal stream of bullets, the Reaper rolled forward, under his aim. Landing on her back in front of him, she kicked out with both legs, catching him in the stomach, forcing him out the window and on to the boardwalk three stories below.

Dressed once again as the Dorsets, Kaye and Shaw joined the rest of the hotel's guests in a mad panic to flee the gunplay. Once in their rented car, Kaye looked at the crowd gathered around the unmoving body of the man she had pushed out the window.

"It's a shame," she said. "It seemed like such a nice quiet place. So where to?"

"The Victorian is just two blocks down. I hear that's a nice place to stay. Separate beds?"

"Separate rooms."

"Are you going to rent a rubber suit?"

"Already have one in my bag."

*

Nemesis was, by nature, a creature of the night. It was when she felt most alive. Sleep was for the day. When the bright sun came out, she most likely was found in bed, waiting for it to sink below the horizon, waiting for her time of the day.

Laughter woke her. It took but a moment for her to identify it. *Gods below*, she thought, *he's followed me here. How*? Then came gunfire from above and she knew that the cruel Fates had once again played their part.

Nemesis fought down her first impulse, to rush to her one-time lover's side, to destroy those who sought to slay him. Then she remembered what he was like in action and smiled. It would not be he who needed help. Still, she extended her senses and found another creature of the dark fighting with him.

This one, though, did not wear the color of night. No, she clothed herself in brightness to defy the dark things. Nemesis recognized her. She shared a kinship with her, this woman who called herself by one of Death's names, but who sought to preserve life. It was why on a number of occasions she had called on Kaye Chandler to act as one of her agents. Her one-time lover had someone very capable watching his back.

The shooting over, Nemesis felt the Reaper and Nightmare pass down the stairs, so close were they that she wondered why they did not sense her, then remembered that they were only mortal. *Which is why Shaw cannot find me here, why I do not dare seek him out.* If he learned of her peril, of the one who was coming for her, he would not leave her side, and so he would die. And that she would not permit. So of all the guests, she was the only one who did not flee the gunfight, the only one who remained in her room. Instead, she followed the pair with her mind until they were a safe distance away. "Goodbye, Michael," she said softly, remembering a night filled with violence and love.

Calm was soon restored. What passed for police in Coast City came by, asked few questions and took away the dead. Nemesis went back to sleep.

Only to wake up in a cold chill. Icy fingers wrapped around her and held her fast. A form emerged from the light.

"I am sorry, sister who was," came Tyche's voice. "As much as I once loved you, I fear my father more. If he were to learn I aided you in any way his wrath could be such that he might take me, his own daughter, in your place. I cannot risk it, I will not hide you."

"Then let me go, release me, and I will be gone from here."

"That cannot be done. Even now Eurus the East Wind flies with my message to him even as Boreas grants me the power of the cold North Wind to bind you. And bound you will stay until released, an offering for my father's favor."

"And how, treacherous one, do your actions maintain your precious Balance?"

"It was ill fate that brought you to my house. Somewhere, good fortune will fall upon a stranger."

"Heed me, you fickle harlot, you who would sell a friend for little gain, that whatever happens to me is on your head. Someday there will be vengeance. So vows Vengeance herself."

"I fear you not. When Father Zeus has finished, you will not remember your name much less your vow." Tyche turned towards the door. "You should have drunk the waters," she said and was gone, leaving Nemesis alone.

There was nothing for her to do but lie there bound and wait for her attacker. That was the worst of it, to endure the assault without the chance of fighting back. Before, even if Zeus found her, she would have had the satisfaction of doing him some damage before suffering the inevitable. Now, in the days before Zeus arrived, she must wait bound and helpless until Zeus had his way then released her.

No, Nemesis realized, those were not the words of Tyche. "Bound you will stay until released," she had said. The words of a god have power and meaning, binding the god as sure as the icy ropes of Boreas bound her. And Tyche had said nothing about Zeus.

Knowing it was her only hope, Nemesis sent out a cry to the only one who could aid her, praying to the Creator of all that his skills were greater than luck.

*

Out on the sand, Michael Shaw, clad in scratchy wool bathing trunks, was watching Kaye Chandler wade in the surf. So was everyone else. *I really should talk to Kaye about her obsession with the color pink*, he thought. *As a costume it's okay, but here on the beach …* Too close to her own skin color, Kaye's pink suit had caused more than one man to stare and stumble, no doubt thinking that Coast City now allowed naturists on their beach.

A dripping Kaye came up to him. "Aren't you going to get wet?"

"No thanks. These trunks itch bad enough. I can't imagine them wet."

"I can," Kaye replied, thinking of how the material might cling to her cousin's strong body. At his shocked look, she said, "Hey, you've ogled me enough, I should get a turn." She made a show of looking him over carefully. "Not bad. Maybe you should get a pink one-piece. We could call you the Pink Terror."

Icelus, my love.

"What was that?" Shaw asked, looking around, not knowing that the voice he heard had been in his head.

"What was what, Michael?"

Icelus, I need you.

"There it is again, someone calling for Icelus."

"Greek avatar for Nightmare. But who …"

"Only one person I know, Kaye. And she only called me that once, when we … well, never mind."

Again Shaw heard, *Icelus, come to me, save me. But beware Tyche, beware the Lady of Luck.*

"Kaye, it's her. It's Nemesis."

"Nemesis?" Michael had told her of their history, but Kaye not shared the name of the woman she had aided on several occasions, referring to her instead as the Mistress of Night. That was at Nemesis' own request for her cousin's own protection. Kaye was not happy with keeping the secret, but she trusted Nemesis with her life, so she had held her tongue in hopes of protecting her cousin from an enemy he could never beat. "The Woman in Black you told me about."

"Yes, she's close, here in Coast City and she needs my help, our help."

"But where is she?"

"Let me think. She mentioned Tyche, told me to beware of her. Called her the Lady of Luck."

"Tyche is the Greek goddess of luck."

"Makes sense, Kaye. It would take god-like power to overcome Nemesis. Tyche must run the casino in back of the Foley Hotel. Leda must have sensed us as we battled. But why didn't she say something then?"

"I'm sure she had her reasons, Michael. But you know we just can't rush in there to her rescue."

"I know, even though every bit of me wants to. We wait, we watch, and we plan. And when we do move we'll have to be extra careful. I have the feeling that this time luck will be against us."

*

In her casino office, Tyche felt Nemesis's use of power. "Call for help as much as you want," she thought. "There is not a god, spirit, or demon who would dare defy Zeus. As for mortal help ..." Tyche made a phone call. "I'm paying for protection," she told the man who answered. "Tonight I expect some."

*

Hidden in the shadows, cloaked in darkness, the Man in Black and the Woman in Pink watched people go and come from the Hotel Foley and the casino in the rear.

"Lots of men in overcoats," the Nightmare observed.

"Overcoats with bulges," remarked the Pink Reaper. "And they're all waiting for us. Half of them in the casino, the other half in the hotel. Fifty-fifty chance."

"No chance at all, Nemesis is in the hotel. This close to her I can feel her."

"So we rush in, take down the bad guys, and save the girl."

"And get ourselves killed. As soon as the shooting starts the thugs from the casino will rush over. We'll be trapped between them and crushed in a vise."

"We'll sneak in. That's what we do."

The Nightmare pictured the Foley in his mind. One set of well-lit stairs, no place to hide in the hallways. Armed men no doubt waiting for them. Maybe Kent could sneak in. Jethro would have some salt to turn himself invisible. But the man who was called the Nightmare was not a lama, nor could he command the shadows. He was just a man who dressed up to play the eternal game of cops and robbers. And as he saw it, he had only one move left to make, possibly his last. *Well*, he thought, *No game lasts forever. And if this one ends with Kaye and Leda both safe, I'll count it as a win.*

"Here's what we'll do," he told the Reaper. "You wait here until the shooting starts. After I draw the mob from the hotel you sneak in and find Nemesis. Get her out and get her safe."

"What about you?" the Reaper asked but found she was talking to empty air. The Nightmare was gone.

How he got inside the casino she didn't know, but from her place in the alley across the street, she heard him. His laugh tonight was defiant, as if daring Chance to do her worse. It was one of a man who goes willingly to his fate in the best of causes. It was one of expected triumph, such was his faith in his plan and in her.

The Nightmare was still laughing when the shooting started and kept laughing when the screaming began. Men with guns rushed from the back door of the Foley only to be met by a stampede of fleeing gamblers.

Sensing that now was the time, the Reaper pulled her cloak around her and made her way around the front.

The young man behind the front desk looked up as the front doors of the Foley burst open. "What the ..." he started to say as a shapeless black form suddenly became a vision in pink. Distracted by the scantily clad woman who wore less than they did on the beach, he did not think to hit the alarm button. Then he thought no more as an electric shock ran through his body and he fell unconscious to the ground.

Shock gun in one hand, pistol in her other, the Pink Reaper raced up the stairs. Twice more she fired, using the pistol on one man who dared to aim a revolver at her and shocking a bellman who got in her way.

Nothing.No one on the first floor but some frightened guests. A shot from the landing above hit her in the back, dropping her to her knees. As she fell, she spun and emptied her pistol into her assailant. Standing, she assessed her condition. She hurt, but the bullet-proof lining of her cloak had held up. She'd be bruised in the morning, but no worse than that. Picking up the man's revolver, she went on.

Cold met her on the second floor. An unearthly chill that came from the front room. As she approached, a frosty mix came from under the door sill and coalesced into an icy form.

Michael didn't say anything about monsters, she thought. But having come this far, she was not going to be deterred by a snowman come to life. As the manifestation of Boreas came forward, bent on carrying out its duty to guard the woman bound in the room behind him, the Pink Reaper turned the dial on her shock gun to the maximum. The frost creature neared, the weapon whined and as it hit its highest pitch, the Reaper slid it along the floor toward her attacker.

"Myth, meet science."

As the weapon overloaded, the heat from the explosion melted her snowy foe.

Armed only with a revolver and what few tricks she had stored in her cloak and gloves, the Woman in Pink entered the room at the end of the hall.

And found the Woman in Black bound to a bed with chains of ice, chains that shattered as the Reaper smashed them with the butt of her gun.

"Hello, Nemesis. We simply have to stop meeting like this."

"Hello, Kaye. I believe the last time I was helping to rescue you. I sensed… the Nightmare. Where is he? I had reached out to him. I thought ..."

"Listen ..."

In the quiet, both women heard distant gunfire. "He was the distraction. Those shots might mean he's still alive. He told me to see you safe, but right now he probably needs my help more than you do, so..."

"No." There was a commanding quality in Nemesis's voice that the Reaper could not ignore. "If he can be saved I will save him. You have done me great service, Kaye ..."

"Nemesis, we're both going and we're wasting time."

The woman in black looked into the eyes of the Pink Reaper. "You have proved your worth to me as a brave and resourceful warrior, but I will go to the Nightmare and save him if I can. We both know I have a better chance." What Nemesis didn't add was that there was a crackle in the air that boded ill of impending destruction. "Instead I must ask yet another service of you. There is something… someone coming that I will have to face, someone more dangerous than a thousand gunmen. Michael and I will be the distraction. You must go to the office on the second floor and look for a small, black vial. Bring it to me here when this is all over."

"Consider it done. Save Michael."

*

Having left the Reaper, the Nightmare approached the casino alone and unmasked. To the man at the door he seemed just another gunman and so entered unchallenged. Once inside, he studied the layout and formed a plan of attack.

The laugh first, he thought. *It might be my last so I'll have to make it a good one. The lights next. Shooting them out will give me the needed darkness and scare away the patrons. They came here to lose money, not their lives. Then it's move quickly and shoot anyone with a gun. And stay alive long enough for Kaye to rescue Leda.* He looked for defensible positions – dark corners and alcoves, gaming tables thick enough to use as shields – anything to reduce the risk.

Time to play, he thought, putting on his mask. The Nightmare laughed and unleashed Hell.

Time stopped. There was nothing for him but the sound of pistols and the smell of gunpowder. The first gunmen, not expecting an attack from within, went down fast and easy. As he'd hoped, reinforcements were delayed by the panic of those trying to escape the shooting. That didn't last. As the entrance cleared, more foemen came in and soon the Nightmare was fighting for his life.

And losing.

He was one against many and though he stayed in the shadows of the darkened room as best he could, bullets still found him. One passed through his leg, slowing him down. Two more struck his left arm, which soon hung uselessly at his side. "A few minutes more," he prayed, knowing that every second he kept the battle raging was another second he gave Kaye to save Leda.

The Man in Black fired the last cartridge from his remaining automatic. A gunman dropped at his feet. As he bent to retrieve the man's revolver, a bullet creased his skull. Blackness fell over the Nightmare and he knew no more.

More scattered shots were fired until the mobsters realized that the invader had fallen. Those who had survived approached his body carefully, mindful of a trick. Some minutes went by, the Nightmare did not move.

"Is he dead?" one asked.

"Let's make sure," said another and, taking careful aim, readied a deadly shot.

Then Vengeance was among them, a woman in black determined to save the man she loved or failing that, avenge him. She had no weapon and needed none. She herself was the most lethal thing in the room.

Chests were caved in, limbs were torn from bodies, heads were smashed. In mere minutes there was no one standing save Nemesis and in the sudden quiet of the room she was relieved to hear the labored breathing of the man she had come to save.

*

Tyche heard the laughter and knew it for what it was, a cry of challenge against her and of the blind chance she personified. She thought to intervene, to bring ill fortune down on the one who dared to defy her in her own temple. Then she thought better of it. Even without her intervention, the odds were against this brave, foolish man. The Balance would be maintained. He would fall and die without even knowing that he had sought his prize in the wrong house.

Then a scream in her mind told her that the avatar of the North Wind she had summoned was no more. Then she felt the icy bonds that had bound Nemesis break. Worse still, the woman who had once called her sister was now the enemy at her gates.

Tyche got up from her desk. She would go down and finish the one in Black, even if it took centuries to restore the Balance.

The Lady of Luck would then have rushed from her office save that at her door she was met by a woman in a black cloak and pink costume, who pointed a revolver at her as if it were a holy talisman.

"Out of my way," she commanded.

"I think not," replied the Reaper. "I'm not one to gamble, but I'm willing to bet that even a goddess would be discomforted by a bullet in the skull."

Tyche moved to strike. The Reaper moved faster, pulling the hammer back with an audible click. Tyche paused.

"We're outside your realm, Lady Luck. In the last few months I've had cause to match my science against magic. You know what? The two aren't that very different. Both have rules. I've learned more than a few from both sides. Whatever happens to me, I will fire this gun. The funny part about you so-called divinities is how much belief affects you. I'm willing to pit my belief in chemistry and physics against yours in yourself. What about you?"

Tyche could feel Nemesis one floor below. Anxious to be rid of her unwanted visitor, she asked, "What do you want?"

"A black vial. Nemesis sent me for it."

The Waters of Lethe. It was too late for that, Tyche knew. *Should Father Zeus arrive and his prize not be here...*She did not want to think of his wrath.

Tyche sprang, trusting in her own luck.

The Pink Reaper fired, depending on science.

Belief is a powerful weapon, especially that of a woman who believes enough in herself and the concept of justice to dress up and fight bad guys she truly had no chance of beating, yet who won time and time again. That belief backed up by a .38 revolver was even more powerful. Combined with Tyche's betrayal of a friend, it was enough to make the goddess' luck fail her and she fell to the floor.

Having found the vial for which she came, The Reaper decided not to return to the Foley to await Nemesis. Instead, she joined the Woman in Black in the casino, where together they took the wounded body of The Nightmare for needed treatment.

*

The Nightmare awoke in a dark room. From the antiseptic smell, he judged that he was in a hospital. "I guessed I lived," he thought, then he heard,

"Good, you're awake." Kaye's voice.

"Were you on time?"

"She's safe, Michael, thanks to you. But for you to stay safe she has to go away again. She hopes you understand."

"I don't. To have come so close to finding her only to lose her once more …"

"At least she's safe, Michael. That's the important thing."

"No, Kaye, it's the only thing."

*

The Lady of Luck awoke on her office floor. Had she been mortal, the Reaper's bullet, fired as it was at point-blank range, would have been fatal. But it is hard to kill a god, especially in her own temple.

Her first thought was to go after Nemesis, to try to retrieve her before she drank the waters and bind her anew. No, the woman in black would be ready for her. It may be hard to kill a god but it is not impossible, not for someone whose very nature was Vengeance. Her next thought was to seek out the mortals who had caused her so much trouble. They had cost her much–her prize was gone, her casino a shambles. It would not take much time to find them and make them pay.

But it was time Tyche did not have. Father Zeus would be here soon. Tyche's final thought was that she should be elsewhere when he arrived, lest he take out his disappointment, anger, and lust on her. There was a town out west of which she'd heard the gamblers speak. Las Vegas they called it. Games of chance were legal there. It would be the first place Zeus looked.

Best to lose oneself among the mortals for a while, Tyche decided. The Balance could maintain itself until Zeus tired of his hunt and went back to his mountain.

*

The Woman in Black looked outward over the ocean. She stared across the sea toward the land of her birth as she held a black vial in her hand.

"You don't have to do this," Kaye Chandler had told her. "I can gather the others. We will stand with you. We, all of us, will fight him together."

"And you will all die. The one who comes, the one who seeks me, is not a minor god such as Tyche, but the father of gods. He is not one to be felled by your belief in science." Nemesis looked at the bottle.

"I'm not going," said Kaye. "And I've got better toys." She held up a new shock gun. "Not properly field tested, but now's as good a time as any."

"Kaye, we will be facing one who controls lightning itself. I doubt your shock gun will do much more than make him laugh," said Nemesis.

"Which is why I made this," said Kaye, gesturing to a metal pole she had placed in the sand. She had buried a cable which connected the rod to what looked like a small cannon. "We'll see if he can take what he dishes out."

"A thunderbolt is magical and electrical in nature…"

"Electrical I got covered. I do have degrees in engineering and chemistry, you know. The rod has a positive charge that will attract the negative charge of the lightning. And I've learned enough from Shargrin and some of the others to build it to compensate for at least some of the magical properties. Heck, Chester Coyle could make him see us as a giant monster and Sarge Winston has a dark god in that gem in his chest that might knock him down a peg or two. Dagonet's magic sword would probably hurt him and isn't Negral a god too? Maybe his fire would be enough to counter the lightning. And Bulfinche would let you hide in her bar. The magic wouldn't work there."

Nemesis sighed. "Negral is practically a forgotten god. At the height of his worship, yes, he would have been an equal, but his believers are long dead. Besides we lost him after he sacrificed his manna to save us.

"And I have killed the guilty, which would surely break Bulfinche Moran's heart. I would rather face the Thunderer than do that. The rest are mortal. I will not ask them to trade their lives for mine."

"You wouldn't have to ask," the Pink Reaper said.

Nemesis' reply was cut off as a sudden wind gust almost knocked the women down as lightning lit the sky.

"It's not hurricane season, is it?" the Pink Reaper asked.

Nemesis shook her head. "He comes."

The Pink Reaper stood a little straighter, making one last cheek of her equipment. "Oh goodie."

"And like a coward, he comes during the day when I am at my weakest," the Daughter of Night said.

"Either way, I say we put his lights out," the woman in pink said.

"Kaye, please go," said Nemesis.

"Nope."

"Then you have my thanks for your friendship," Nemesis said.

Kaye put her hand on the woman in black's shoulder. "You can thank me by buying me dinner when this is all over."

The biggest lightning bolt Kaye Chandler ever witnessed struck the beach in front of them. The sand was transformed into glass as the crackling energies coalesced into a man. Kaye found herself a little disappointed that Zeus was not in a toga, but instead a suit. It felt wrong, despite it being an obviously expensive, custom-tailored suit.

"Okay Zeus, this is your only warning. Nemesis is under my protection. Leave now or I will destroy you," the Pink Reaper said.

Both the Daughter of Night and the ruler of the gods of Olympus looked at the woman in pink as if she were mad.

Then Zeus laughed. "I do not take orders from harlots. I do however enjoy other things with them. You are quite comely and I would be happy to bless you with my attentions."

The idea sickened Kaye, but she was willing to kill or die to protect her friend. This was only a different kind of sacrifice.

"You want me? I'm willing to offer myself freely if you leave Nemesis alone."

Zeus stroked his beard and smiled. "For how long?"

"Forever," Kaye said.

"How about a day?" replied the Thunderer.

"I'm much better than that," the Pink Reaper promised. "Ten

years."

"Two days."

"Eight years."

"Four days."

"A year. My final offer," the Pink Reaper said, thinking that a year might be enough for Nemesis to regain the parts of her that eluded her. Long enough to come up with a plan that would let her win or at least long enough for Kaye to tell the others.

"Tempting, but too long for the goods offered," Zeus said.

"Your loss. Now get lost," Kaye said.

"Speaking to me that way once was amusing. Pity you hadn't the sense to stop while you were ahead."

"Zeus, leave the Reaper out of this," Nemesis said.

"The Reaper is it? I sense no power, no sense of impending death."

"It's the Pink Reaper. Remember it." The Pink Reaper fired a shock dart that took the god in the chest. Sparks jumped and gas poured out into the Thunderer's face and he laughed some more.

"Leave this place and never return," said Kaye, hoping the gas would have some effect on the god.

Zeus watched as the woman in pink twisted into a monster. The sight made him take a step back as the fear effects of the gas kicked in. Then he looked at Nemesis, the one of whom he was truly afraid. Nothing. Which meant it was a trick. Zeus called on the lightning and his body surged with power, burning away any trace of the gas.

"Nemesis, I tire of your pet harlot." Zeus' right hand began to crackle with electricity. The god pulled his arm back like he was winding up to pitch a baseball. When he threw, lightning flew from his fingers toward the Pink Reaper. The god appeared shocked when it curved away from its target, striking the lightning rod instead.

Kaye quickly turned the cannon at the god and fired. Her science had managed to amplify the bolt's power and it knocked Zeus onto his ass.

Nemesis didn't waste the chance, rushing at the fallen god, hitting him with everything she had. Zeus was battered and bleeding in moments and got worse as the Daughter of Night pressed her attack.

The upper hand hers, Nemesis allowed herself the hope that she would be the victor. The Daughter of Night saw the energy gather in Zeus's hands, but did not give any quarter or even flinch. The Thunderer managed to get his hands around the woman in black's throat and lifted her off the sand. He squeezed and let the power flow, first from one hand into Nemesis and back into the other hand. Then he repeated the circuit with the opposite hand. The deadly process repeated itself again and again as Zeus let loose his power until Nemesis convulsed from the electric energies coursing through her body. Still, she managed to strike and kick the god, but with each jolt of lightning her blows weakened.

The Pink Reaper unloaded two guns into the god's back, an automatic in her left hand and a revolver in her right. The bullets penetrated Zeus' skin but went no further. Unwilling to let go of his prey, Zeus merely turned, his eyes aglow. Lightning leapt to the Pink Reaper, knocking her to the ground. If not for her rubber boots, Kaye Chandler would have died. Instead, she found herself laying on glass that had been sand before the god had made his appearance on the beach. As her cheek rubbed against the smooth surface an idea came to her. The god's power had made the glass, which likely gave it unique properties. Using the automatic as a hammer, she smashed the glass into knife size slivers, picking up one in each gloved hand.

Rising to her feet, the Pink Reaper rushed at the god and stabbed him in the back with one of the slivers. It plunged deep into his chest making the god scream in agony. Kaye stabbed the next into his right shoulder, which made Zeus drop Nemesis.

The Pink Reaper was already back at the shattered glass and tossed Nemesis a pair of the silicone blades. Having once witnessed the Daughter of Night pluck throwing knives from the air, she knew Nemesis would easily catch them.

As soon as the woman in black caught them she turned their points on Zeus, one at his throat and the other at his godhood.

"So much as twitch and it will be to your regret, Zeus," Nemesis promised, a dark smile on her face.

The god paled, then looked at Nemesis. "You have changed. Almost what you were, but not quite." His body transformed into a bolt of lightning which shot away down the beach. When electricity again became flesh, the wounds were already starting to heal. "Your umbra shines. There is one you care about. I watched Tyche's place of power before my arrival. You attacked many there to save one man. You and your harlot have hurt me. I go now to hurt him."

"Zeus, no!" Nemesis shouted too late as a thunderbolt struck the clouds. "We need to get to the hospital."

"Not without more glass," the Reaper said, grabbing more shards and putting them in her cape pouch.

The pair raced in Michael Shaw's borrowed car. The hospital was only blocks away, but they could not outrun the storm. They got to the hospital just in time to see a lightning bolt take out a window on the third floor.

"That's Michael's room!" Kaye shouted.

Nemesis was already moving, her power instinctively letting her feet find patches of shadow that allowed her to run up the side of the wall as easily as climbing stairs. The Daughter of Night placed herself between Michael Shaw and the dark cloud just in time to be struck full force by the lightning god becoming flesh.

Michael Shaw woke and turned to see the wall of his hospital room exploding inward. Thinking it was a bomb, the injured Nightmare rolled off his bed, pulling the mattress on top of him as a shield. He quickly grabbed the automatic he had kept beneath his pillow that had fallen with him and got ready for someone to come through the door. Instead, he saw two struggling bodies tumble through the hole in the building.

Noticing one was a woman in black, he whispered "Leda?" then opened fire on the bearded man, ignoring the pain his trip out of bed had caused him.

The bullets caused the god pain and this time there was more blood, but otherwise Zeus seemed barely affected, throwing the woman in black out the hole. Orderlies rushed in. Zeus shot lightning from his fingertips, which sent them packing, slamming the door behind them.

"So you are the mortal Nemesis fancies. Me she refused, but you she gave it up for. I don't see it." Zeus stepped forward and the Nightmare emptied the automatic into the Thunderer, who brought his arms up to protect his face from the bullets.

The Nightmare backed up, swinging the spent gun like a club, but Zeus batted it aside, grabbing the Nightmare by the throat and lifting him off the floor.

The Pink Reaper had managed to climb up the building and into the room. Reaching into her cape, she removed a shard of glass and stabbed deep into his neck. "Let go of him!"

Zeus didn't loosen his grip on the Nightmare's neck, instead swatting backwards and knocking the Pink Reaper into a wall.

The Nightmare's world started to go black around the edges. Shaw reached up and pulled the shard of glass out of the god's neck and slashed at his face, cutting him.

Zeus growled and squeezed harder, until the Nightmare lost consciousness, then dropped the man onto the floor still alive. His death would actually complicate matters greatly. Zeus needed the Daughter of Night to believe he would kill the mortal in order to have her go along with his plans.

Nemesis came back into the room, saw Kaye and Michael down and did a flying double kick into Zeus' chest, knocking him down. Straddling his chest with her legs she held the black vial over his mouth, pulled the stopper and poured some of the dark liquid out. Zeus' eyes went wide and he flung himself away to avoid the water, throwing Nemesis down in the process.

"So you finally figured it out," said Zeus.

"That you have been drugging me with the waters of the Lethe for all these centuries. Why?" Nemesis demanded.

"If I told you…" Zeus stopped. He may have been the king of the Olympians, but if the woman before him ever regained her full remembrance she could make him a memory. And he dared not kill the Daughter of Night or Nyx would destroy even him. The only way to avoid Nyx's wrath would be to somehow forever remain in daylight, impossible even for a god. Drugging Nemesis and destroying her memory was the only option. "It doesn't matter. I give you an option. You drink the water and I'll let them live."

"They are alive?" Nemesis whispered. Zeus nodded as the Pink Reaper stirred.

"I'm still kicking," said Kaye, who crawled to the fallen Nightmare and put his hand on his chest, relieved to find it moving up and down. "Michael's still with us too."

Zeus raised his hand, which glowed even more brightly than it did earlier, and pointed it at the two mortals.

"You drink, they live. Decide."

"You swear by the Styx that they or those they love are never in any way to be touched, harmed, or otherwise be hurt by you in any way."

"I so swear on the Styx," said Zeus.

"Then I will drink," said the woman in black.

"Nemesis, no!" shouted the Pink Reaper, holding another large shard of glass.

"Kaye, it's done."

Tears streaming down her face, she asked, "What should I tell Michael?"

"That I am safe and that he should not seek me out. For all you have done, Kaye Chandler, I thank you. I sense one day that we will meet again. Keep strong, Sister, and protect the weak in my stead."

"I will." The Pink Reaper bent and picked up a cup off the floor. "Let me at least pour it for you."

Nemesis nodded and handed her the vial. Kaye poured some out into the cup.

"All of it, harlot," Zeus ordered. The Pink Reaper flung some of the liquid toward the god who again leapt out of the way. "Are you mad, harlot?"

"That's the Pink Harlot to you. And I'm mad as it gets."

"I'll destroy you."

"No, Zeus you won't. You swore upon the Styx."

The Thunderer balled his hands up into fists but made no move toward the woman in pink.

"Why won't he? He only has to break his word," said Kaye.

"The Styx is the river of death for his pantheon. If he breaks that vow, he will die, lose his power, and become a shade," said the woman in black. "Nobody, especially a god, wants to die."

"Then let him come after me," said the Pink Reaper.

"He will not."

"It was worth a try," said Kaye.

"She will still put the remainder of that bottle in the cup," said Zeus.

Nemesis nodded and Kaye emptied the vial. Nemesis took the cup from her. The women exchanged a glance, each realizing that

Kaye's posturing had spilled more than half the vial. It would not be so long this time until the effects wore off.

Nemesis raised her glass in a toast. "To friends and comrades in arms."

The woman in black drank the contents of the cup. Her eyes rolled back and she collapsed. The Pink Reaper caught her and lowered her to the floor.

Zeus moved closer and stood over the fallen daughter of night.

"Once again I am victorious over the Throne's enforcer."

The Pink Reaper stepped between the gloating god and her friend, her hand holding a shard of glass behind her back.

"Back off, Sparky," the Pink Reaper said.

"Harlot, you had best watch your tone," Zeus said.

"I know you raped her when you first took her memories. I'm not going to let you do it again."

"And how do you plan to stop me as she didn't include herself in the protection?" asked Zeus.

His answer was a blade of glass to his groin. Blood poured out and the king of Olympus fell to his knees.

Nemesis began to wake. With Zeus down, the Pink Reaper guided her out of the room and down the hall. The Pink Reaper entered the stairwell, but it was Kaye Chandler who exited at the bottom, her mask removed and her fuchsia attire covered by a beige trenchcoat.

"Bitch! Vow or no vow I will slay you!" Zeus bellowed as he recovered. He moved to follow.

He was stopped by laughter, laughter directed at him, laughter that could only have come from the man on the floor.

"I think not, oh great and powerful one." There was mockery in the Nightmare's voice.

"You think to stop me, mortal. You can barely rise."

As if to defy the god, Shaw forced himself first to his knees then to his feet. "You've stopped yourself. I was just coming to when you swore on the Styx not to harm me or those I love. So pursue Nemesis at your own risk for she has my love, today and forever."

Looking into the man's heart the god saw that this was true and that his own vow had put Nemesis beyond his reach – for now. With a scream that shook the entire hospital, Zeus transformed into living lightning which shot out the space where there should have been a wall and disappeared into the sky, with a mortal's mocking laughter following him.

The danger passed, the hospital staff rushed in just as Michael Shaw again collapsed.

*

"Was that man okay?" asked the amnesiac woman in black.

"Given time, I think he will be," said Kaye, wondering exactly how she was going to explain this to her cousin. Kaye loaded Nemesis into the borrowed car and took off as much over the speed limit as she could manage without risking attacking police attention.

"I'm so confused. Who am I?" asked the daughter of night.

"You use the name Leda Troy."

"Why can't I remember anything?"

"That's a little harder to explain. I'd rather wait until I get you someplace safe and tell you then." First Kaye knew she needed to get Leda to safety in case Zeus came back for her and that meant getting to Manhattan and Bulfinche's Pub.

After several hours of driving, the sun set and Kaye had to stop to get gas in New Jersey off Route 100. She told the boy manning the pump to fill it up and excused herself to use the restroom, telling Leda to wait in the car and brought a bag with her regular clothes to change into.

Kaye wasn't gone long. In fact, the boy was only just putting the gas hose back on the pump, although the lamp bulb on that side of the island was now out.

"Where did my friend go?" Kaye asked frantically.

The boy looked into the rumble seat, surprised that the woman was gone. "She was there a minute ago. I didn't see or hear her get out, but that bulb blew again and maybe she got out in the dark." Just then the light came back on.

Kaye Chandler searched the rest of the night and into the next morning but found no trace of the amnesiac Nemesis, thinking it was as if the night had swallowed her whole.

MYSTIC
INVESTIGATORS ™
BULLETS &
BRIMSTONE
starring
Bianca Jones &
Hell's Detetective
some partnerships
are made in heaven -
others start out
someplace a
lot warmer
Patrick Thomas & John L. French

BULLETS & BRIMSTONE

A MYSTIC INVESTIGATORS Book

PATRICK THOMAS & JOHN L. FRENCH

PADWOLF PULP

For Colton
-PT

DYSCLAIMER

A Bianca Jones/Hell's Detective adventure

I was born of fire and through it I can come into the mortal world. In ancient days, I could be summoned through a sacrificial blaze. Still could, I suppose, but nobody bothers these days. Doesn't stop me from flame jumping. A lot easier than spending my own power to leave the Pit.

As I stepped from Hell into the burning house, I felt mortals dying around me. They weren't part of my case so I made no move to help them. Wouldn't have mattered if I did. I see burning souls all the time, but this was different than damnation. The humans were past my help. Three were already bound for the Host and the other destined for a hotter place than this. Without even any effort other than a glance around, I knew that the fire had been deliberately set with no purpose other than the joy of the moment.

Time was, eons ago, the arsonist might have been one of my worshipers and this conflagration dedicated to me, set in my honor and kept alive to seek my favor. The heat and flames made me pause, remembering the good old days which always made the present that much bleaker. Nothing mortal could survive this blaze but for me it felt soothing. There was nowhere in Hell like this, the purity of natural burning. In the Pit, there was nothing pure.

Having drawn as much strength as I could from the blaze, it was time to go to work. So fixing the brim of my fedora and tightening the belt of my trench coat, this former and long-forgotten god stepped out into the street.

*

The building was lost. So were those within. Those fighting the fire had been called back. Their mission now was to contain the blaze and make sure it did not spread to the surrounding buildings.

There was mourning for the ones lost inside, both by the neighbors who knew them and by the would-be rescuers who had had no chance to save them. Right now all anyone could do was to watch the flames. Recovery of the remains and the investigation of the crime would have to wait.

There was one in the crowd who watched with excitement, his hand fondling himself through an open pocket of his loose pants. He watched the fire dance and committed its performance to memory. Later, he promised himself, later he would recall the dance that he himself had begun and, once satisfied, sleep soundly.

It was he who first saw the man step from the burning house, the man who had no reason being there, no business surviving the inferno. He saw the man for who he really was and in that instant knew that, finally, there was a god for him. And he followed him.

*

Police officer Tim Blake was himself watching the fire and waiting for his tour of duty to end. He hoped his relief would not be long in coming. He'd pulled OT three shifts running and all he wanted tonight was to go home and be with his wife and kids. He had just checked his watch for the third time in ten minutes when there came the sound of a building coming down.

Looking up, Blake was amazed to see a man walk from the cascade of falling brick and lumber. He thought at first it was a firefighter or detective who had gotten just a bit too close, but no, he decided, the man had come from inside the house.

No freaking way, the logical part of his mind told him.

Way, argued that part that believed what he'd just seen. And that's when Blake noticed something else.

The guy looked like Bogart. No so much in the normal way. His face was different, but it took effort to realize that. He was Bogart in how he moved and dressed. The cut of his jib as they used to say. In much the same way a short, overweight woman could still be an effective Elvis impersonator, this guy aped Bogie. In fact, watching him the tough guy bit didn't seem like it was an act.

Amidst the flames and the water and the organized commotion

that followed the collapse, Blake realized that no one else seemed to have seen the man. Knowing it was his duty, Blake moved to confront the stranger.

"Good evening, Officer," the man said as Blake approached him (Rick in Casablanca, that's who he sounds like, the cop thought, even as he prepared to take the guy into custody) "My name is Negral. I'd like to talk to Detective Bianca Jones, please."

*

Sergeant Bianca Jones was not a happy cop. She had been thirty minutes ago. It was close to the end of her shift, she had the weekend off and she and her husband had made plans to spend it in Ocean City. Then she got word from the fire scene.

Bianca knew about the arson fires that had been plaguing Baltimore's Western District. Five so far, three of them resulting in death. Besides the fact that all the fires had been carefully set, none had any connection with the other. Special Investigations had been called in to help.

Bianca had not expected this help to include her special assignment for the BPD.

Some time ago, purely by accident, Bianca had become involved with the supernatural. After that, she became the Department's unofficial expert on all things occult and extra-normal. She had faced – and beaten – monsters, zombies, vampires, and most recently, Satan himself.

Her status being an open secret in the Department, she was notified of anything spooky, scary, or just plain weird. So when a man who acted like he belonged in an old black and white movie walked from a burning building and asked for her, the man was immediately brought to her office. She stopped only to make a quick phone call.

Of the cities in all the world, Bianca thought when her visitor was described to her, *why did he have to come into mine?* Aloud she said, "Send him in."

*

While cooling my heels outside her office, I had a growing curiosity about a dame who could not only scare my boss but kick his ass three times running. When I was finally admitted, whatever image I had conjured flew out of my mind as I just stood and stared at the real thing.

Small and slender, Bianca Jones looked to be in her mid-teens, maybe early twenties. *This is who Nick is afraid of? She can't be more than …*

"I'm just over five foot," Jones said as if reading my mind. "I'm over twenty-one and quite capable of kicking your ass out of here if you don't sit down and tell me why you're in my city."

I sat. "How do you do, Detective Jones, I'm …"

She ignored my offered hand. "I know who you are. Negral, one-time Sumerian sun god. Now an enforcer for the Prince of Evil."

In Hell I'm used to a certain respect. If not that, at least a politeness born of fear. Even those on Earth who've met me have the sense to be courteous. Jones's attitude was something new. Still, this was her house and I needed her help.

"The way you say it makes it sound worse than it is," I said calmly.

"You work for Satan, how much worse can it be?"

Nick had told me to expect this. Sighing, I very carefully reached into my coat and took out my badge.

"First of all, Detective Jones, I am not an enforcer. I am the Chief of what passes for the police in Hell, charged with maintaining some kind of order amidst eternal chaos. I took the job because the alternative was oblivion. Without worship, a god can fade away and there is a distinct lack of worshippers of Sumerian gods. I like to think that, despite the circumstances, I manage to do some good."

Jones nodded. "That's what the Department of Mystical Affairs told me when I called them. Otherwise, you'd right now be in their custody and on your way to Eastern State Penitentiary for exorcism and deportation."

I chuckled. "Deportation could happen if it didn't violate the latest US-Hell treaty." I can't be kicked out unless convicted of a crime and I wasn't likely to stay around long enough for that to happen. "And exorcism only works on demons, but you're welcome to try."

"Fair enough." Having made her point, Jones's attitude changed. Dropping the hostility but still maintaining some wariness, she smiled. "So, Chief, keeping in mind that I'm not inclined to do your boss any favors, what can I do for you?"

"It's a simple matter, Detective. As you are no doubt aware, my, eh, boss, often makes deals with mortals, offering something they want for something he wants."

"Like their souls."

"If that's what they offer. Sometimes it's simply favor for favor, such as the winning of the lottery in exchange for five years off one's lifespan or the betrayal of a loved one." More often than not, how they handle the deal ends up giving him their souls in the long run anyway. "But to cut things short, this matter involves a standard contract."

"Standard contract?'

"Yes," I nodded. "For her immortal soul, the seller was promised the usual – great wealth, power, as much sex as she wants, and no Earthly consequences for any of her actions."

"For how long?"

"A period not to exceed what would have been her natural lifetime."

Jones shook her head. "She traded her soul for that? Didn't ask for immortality or eternal youth? Damned fool."

"That she is or will be, just as soon as I find her. Which is why I'm here."

Figuring I might as well make myself comfortable, I stood and removed my trench coat, dropping it over the back of a chair. Sitting back down, I explained.

"It's like this —most of these jokers don't realize is that as soon as they sign, they belong to Nick." Jones seemed about to object and I quickly held up my hand to stop her. "Yeah, I know, repentance and all that, but most of them don't think of that before it's too late, then despair sets in and that's another sin. And true repentance? It can't be faked and it's rarer than a virgin in Hollywood. Most marks don't regret the deal, only that they didn't make a better one. The fact is they're Nick's before their blood on the contract has dried. Which means he can find them whenever he wants. He usually doesn't bother until a little before the expiration date."

Jones figured out the problem right away. "But not in this case?"

"No, Detective, not in this case. And for two reasons. The first is that no sooner did the seller sign on the slashed line then she disappeared, literally, right before the agent's eyes."

"Is that unusual?"

"Not in some cases. In this case, the demon involved thought it was part of the bargain. The second problem is, well, you."

Jones looked surprised, although not unpleasantly so. "Me? I admit I've stolen a few souls from your boss ..."

"Three," I reminded her. "And all out from under Nick's nose."

"But none of them involved a signed contract."

"I didn't say they did, Detective Jones. The recent unpleasantness here in Baltimore ..."

"Unpleasantness, Chief? Satan killed a friend and tried to burn my city down."

"But you stopped him, and for the third time. There's power in the number three, Detective Jones. It causes things to happen. Baltimore calls itself 'Charm City.' Well, that means more than it ever did – the charm being that, for a time, Hell has little influence of what goes on here."

"Which means your boss can't find his pigeon and that's why he sent you?"

"That's why he sent me."

"And you want my help?"

"Actually, I need your help."

"What about your boss?"

"He told me to get the job done, whatever it took."

*

Looking across her desk, Bianca studied the cop from Hell. He'd gone to great pains to make himself look harmless – the whole Bogie look – fedora, trench coat, cheap suit needing pressing. Standard 50's PI. That didn't change the fact that he was an agent of the Pit asking her help in sending someone to eternal torment.

Condemning people to Hell is not in my job description, Bianca told herself. She thought about refusing but knew if she did, this Negral would only go off looking on his own and cause who knows how much trouble. Better, she decided, to keep him close and if the opportunity presented itself … well, she'd already stolen three souls from the Devil, why not go for one more?

Choosing her words carefully, Bianca said, "I'll help you find her."

*

"Bianca Jones is no fool," Nick warned me when he gave him this assignment. "I would rather you avoided her."

"Not if you expect me to find the mark. Baltimore's not the biggest city in the world, but finding one person in it without help – impossible. Are you sure this gal is worth it? Why not just wait out the charm?"

"I've lost enough souls in that place!" Nick shouted, slamming a fist down on his desk, causing the damned soul it was carved from excruciating agony. "No more will escape me!"

Then I understood. This was a matter of pride, the boss's original downfall and always a problem for him.

"Is there no one else you can ask?"

I shook my head. "You weren't exactly subtle when you made your big play. Most of the magic users left Baltimore when they sensed your coming. The rest cleared out of Crab Town after Jones … after you did. That dame is our only option."

"Just be wary, Negral. She understands better than most mortals how the game is played."

And Nick should know. His realm is still plagued by a pre-creation monster over which he had no control, courtesy of Detective Jones.

"I'll help you find her." Jones's words brought back Nick's warning. I had no doubt she'd keep her word and do just that. But once the soul was found…

"Just who are we looking for?"

The question broke my reverie. "Rebecca Huntingdon. You may have heard of her."

*

Bianca had. So had most of the citizens of Baltimore as well as anyone in the country with newspaper, Internet, or television access. Huntingdon had been a business genius. Dropping out of high school three months before graduation, she had used her body to get close to a prominent banker. Then she used her brains to slowly take everything he had. By the time she was old enough to legally order a beer, he was penniless and she was on her way to becoming the queen of Baltimore's financial scene. Three years later she owned a good part of the city. Two years after that she disappeared.

Bianca had a hard time believing Negral. "She had everything in the world she needed or wanted. Why would she make a deal with your boss, unless her rise was part of the deal?"

Hell's Detective shook his head. "She did that all on her own. And you are right in that she had everything – money, power, lovers. She also had terminal cancer and only six months to live. That's why she called the boss."

"You said the contract was for her natural lifespan, I take it that's without the cancer?"

"Correct."

Bianca sat back in her chair, thinking about the events of three years ago.

"I don't think I can help you, Negral. Rebecca Huntingdon was a big name in Baltimore. When she disappeared it prompted a huge investigation. And not just locally. The state boys came in. So did more than a few federal agencies. No one could find her. What makes you think we can when the case is more than three years cold?"

Negral smiled. "Because we know something now no one else did. She had infernal help, and she's alive and in the city."

"Because," Bianca continued, "if she were dead she'd be toasting in Hell, and if she were somewhere other than Baltimore ..."

"I wouldn't be here."

Bianca nodded in agreement. Negral had a point. Given the new information, there was a slim chance that Huntingdon could be found. But she needed time to work out a plan, two plans really. But what to do with Negral in the meantime?

Looking at the way Negral was dressed gave the Baltimore cop her answer to that question.

"Like movies?" she asked unnecessarily.

"I think that's obvious."

"I need some time to put things together. There's a theater in north Baltimore called The Senator. This week it's running the old Warner Brothers gangster films – White Heat, Angels with Dirty Faces, Little Caesar, Brother Orchid. Stuff like that. Interested?"

Negral was out the door as soon as Bianca could get him a ride. They agreed to meet later that night for pizza.

"And now," Bianca said to herself once she was alone, "to call Joe and tell him that our trip down the ocean will have to be postponed. And then to figure out how to beat the devil."

Betrayal is the language of Hell. While I'm not as fluent as some of the Pit dwellers, I speak it well enough. You had to if you wanted to endure and thrive in Hell. So as I sat in the dark and watched the rise and fall of a series of gangsters I wondered just how Detective Jones was planning to betray me. Well, maybe betrayal wasn't exactly the right word but she would certainly try a double cross. Not that I blamed her. I'd do the same thing in her place. And I had done the same thing many times down in my place. But I had my own job to do and going back alone was not part of it.

But that was a worry for later. "Little Caesar" was about to start.

When I left The Senator, Jones had a patrol car waiting for me. It took me through a good bit of the city before finally dropping me off in front of a small pizza parlor that could have come from one of the movies I had just seen. "Matthew's Pizzeria – since 1943," said the sign in front.

The inside was perfect. There was such a timeless quality about it that I would not have been surprised if Nick and Nora Charles stepped in after a night of clubbing. Nick would be upset that they served only beer. Nora would order several bottles anyway then try to persuade her husband to take the case everyone already believed he was investigating. The thought made me consider whether I should change my look, start wearing evening dress and get a sexy, smart-talking gal for a partner. Feeling quite at home, I spotted Bianca at a small table along the wall and made my way over to her.

"I've ordered already," she said as I sat down.

"Pizza?"

"What else? But here they're called tomato pies. Best in the city, maybe the country."

"I don't know about that, Jones. I've had a slice or two in New York that would tempt a saint."

"A Matthew's pie would make that saint do things that would cost him his halo. But we'll argue that after dinner. I think I know how to find your lost goat."

"Isn't that my lost sheep?"

Bianca shook her head. "Matthew 25, appropriately enough. Sheep go up. Your boss gets the goats."

"The way I understand it you've been getting Nick's goat for some time now. So what did you come up with?"

Bianca looked around, made sure that none of the other patrons were listening. I cast a small heat confounding just to keep it that way.

"Our working assumption is that Huntingdon is here in Baltimore. Given the nature of this city and the terms of the contract, I have an idea as to where to look. I've started some inquiries but there might be an easier way."

With a dirt-eating grin that could have come from Nick himself, she said, "I'll need the contract."

And there it is, I said to myself, disappointed in Jones for such a transparent attempt. I returned her grin.

"I'll have to see if I can get a hold of it."

"Negral, your boss couldn't lie to me so don't you start. Regardless of your jurisdiction, you're still a cop. That means to extradite a prisoner you need paper on him. That contract is your warrant. No warrant, no prisoner, and you go home with just an 'I went to Baltimore and all I got was Crabs' T-shirt.' Or don't you trust me?"

"I work in Hell, Jones, I don't trust anyone except myself and I keep a close eye on my shadow. Possession of a contract may confer control of the seller's soul. Assuming I have it with me, why should I give it to you? What guarantee would you offer that I'd get it back?'

Then she surprised me. Reaching into her purse, Jones took out a small, black book, one which I recognized right away. It was the Book that would appear on no shelf of any infernal library, the Book which Bianca had recently cited.

Placing her right palm on the cover, Jones said, "I swear to return any document signed in the blood or other body fluid of Rebecca Huntingdon within ten minutes of its receipt by me or any of my agents."

An oath on The Book in reference to a contract from Hell. I was now one step closer to having seen everything. What I didn't see was a loophole in what she'd said. Maybe Jones was on the level. Yeah, and maybe one day I'd get wings and a halo because the Host suddenly needed a detective.

Not sensing any deception I reached into the jacket of my suit coat. Pulling out a parchment, I turned it over.

Jones thanked me then unrolled and read the agreement.

"It's as you described, Negral. Huntingdon's soul in exchange for wealth, power over others, and immunity from consequences, with payment on demand after a period 'not to exceed the seller's natural life expectancy.' It's exactly what I expected."

Why did she smile when she said that? That's what I should have wondered but then Jones called out, "Joe, Tammy." When nobody appeared because they couldn't hear through my confounding, Jones tugged her ear frantically.

Suddenly there were two more people at the table.

Jones was a smart cop. Of course she'd have back-up. And she had mention 'agents' in her oath. I should have expected it, should have been looking for it. The ear tugs were obviously a pre-arranged signal if she got into trouble.

Trying and failing not to appear surprised, I asked, "And these are?"

"Joe Russo, Tammy Dolan," Bianca explained. "There were at another table." At least I wasn't the only surprised one. The pair didn't seem sure if they were joining us or rescuing Jones until her smile told them things were okay. Both relaxed. "Tammy's a criminalist for the BPD Crime Lab. Joe is my husband, a bookseller, and a student of the arcane."

Dolan was an unknown, but Nick had briefed me on Russo. For some reason, he rated him as high a threat as Jones. I didn't see it at first. Then I looked closer and saw about him a goodness that in an earlier century would have made him a saint. Nick was right to be worried. But if that goodness could be corrupted, what an ally he'd make for the Devil. I hoped Jones was keeping close watch over her better half for both their sakes.

Bianca turned the contract toward the newcomers. "Tammy, if you will."

It wasn't until Dolan produced two wet swabs and started dabbing blood from the bottom of the contract that I had the sinking feeling that I'd been played and suckered by an expert. In her oath, Jones had said nothing about erasing the signature. That could have invalidated the contract unless the Devil could get a hold of the client's copy. Oblivion was starting to look like a valid option when, to my great relief, the woman from the Crime Lab took only two small samples, leaving the seller's name intact.

I looked over at Jones. She had that dirt-eating grin again. "Scared you, didn't I?" I acknowledged with a short nod that she had then asked her what she was doing.

"Magic and science, Negral. That's how we're going to find Ms. Huntingdon. Tammy's going to take one sample. She'll analyze it and run the profile through the CODIS DNA database. Joe, here, will take the other sample and use, what's it called again, Joe?"

"Sympathetic magic. Like calling to like. With this," Joe held up his swab, "and a map of the city, I'll be able to trace Ms. Huntingdon's whereabouts. If she's here."

"Where else would she be?" I asked a bit peevishly, somewhat embarrassed that I had not thought of the magic angle. Must be the charm of the city, I told myself. Not wanting to make any more mistakes, I held out my hand. "Detective Jones, your ten minutes are up."

Now let's see what trick she has in mind, I told myself. Again surprising me, as Joe and Tammy left, Jones returned the contract and the rest of the dinners returned their attention to their meals

"And what we will be doing while your experts are at work?"

"Enjoying our pizza," Jones replied as a waitress appeared at the table. "Then we're going hunting."

After what I had to admit was one of the best "tomato pies" I had ever eaten, we drove west, Jones behind the wheel of what was obviously an unmarked police car. Late model Ford, spotlight just outside the driver's window, minor body damage and bad tires. Wherever we were going, Jones wasn't hiding who we were.

After we passed the bright lights of the Inner Harbor, Baltimore got darker and dirtier. The tourists behind us, I could see and smell the desperation of the city's poorer citizens.

"I walked these streets as a rookie, Negral. Command thought it would break me. Cop my size, looking like a little kid; the brass wasn't happy with me on the force. All it did was make me tougher; I learned how to be mean when I had to be. I also learned what drugs did to the people here, what monsters dealers really were. Later I worked sex offense and found out about a whole new breed of monster. Girls and boys, sometimes toddlers, sometimes the elderly – anyone weaker was fair game. So when the supernatural crap hit the fan – the vampires, zombies, incubi and the like – it wasn't anything new, just another level of difficulty."

"And your point, Jones?"

"Where we're going, the people don't fear Hell. They're already there. Where you live is just another level of difficulty."

"And you're taking me to your Hell because ..."

"Think about it. Huntingdon wanted what she was about to lose – money, power, sex. Who in this city can have all that and not have to pay for it? Cops? Not likely? Business people? She'd played that game, knew nothing was certain. Politician? Close but not quite. In this city that only leaves ..."

Jones left it to me to answer.

"The drug dealers. But I'm sure there's more than one. Going to round up the usual suspects?"

"I don't have to. While you were watching Eddie G. I did some research, looked for dealers who started up about three years ago, who are major players and who've never served as much a day locked up. Only one fit the bill, a guy calling himself Dante Daymon. We're going to pay a call on him now."

I wasn't going to bite on the obvious questions. If she already knew about this Dante Daymon, why the bit at Matthews with the blood and contract? Other than to make me sweat, so to speak, it made sense, back-up just in case. As to why the switch from white woman to black man? There was nothing in the contract against it and it sounded like the kind of trick the Boss would play.

We drove north and west in silence. Even though she was cooperating much more than Nick or I thought she would, I was still waiting for Jones to make some kind of move. The last soul she'd snatched from Hell's clutches had done far worse than peddle drugs. He had, in fact, been in league with the Devil and had tried several times to kill Jones. Yet she saved him and forgave him. Would she try any less with this one?

With a growing suspicion that I was missing something, something that Jones had already figured out, we pulled on to a winding street.

"This is where it started." I looked around at blocks of burned out houses. "The fires and riots your boss caused. This is where it started." She slowed down passed one home. "Two cops died in there, ripped apart by an angry mob."

I had to ask. "What happened?"

"Satan tempted them and they fell. They did horrible things and then the same happened to them."

I got the point. The Devil was not a nice person; he was Evil with the big E. I've always known that, but when I signed on I didn't have any other options. Heaven wasn't open to pagan deities and the blackness of non-existence was not appealing.

Jones slowed and pulled into an apartment complex that could have doubled for a WWII concentration camp. It was gated all around with only one way in or out. A sign on the fence would have said "Thorndale Apartments" if it hadn't been shot up and graffiti covered. All the building doors were metal and most sported bullet strikes. The windows that weren't boarded up were covered with grates, even the second story ones. That alone said something about this place.

Stopping the car where everyone could see it, Jones turned to me. "Look familiar?" she asked.

It did. There were places like this down below. They were where the somewhat innocents lived, where there are souls condemned not through any fault of their own but by chance or design. There were those went there regularly and did what they could, including a certain monk who regularly makes my working life miserable. In fact, if not for his actions, they would be constantly tortured instead of always hiding. Unofficially, I may have even have visited a time or ten or more.

Jones was out of the car. Like all good cops in a dangerous situation, she walked through the complex as if she owned the place. Those who saw her knew her for what she was, and no one wanted any part of a cop crazy enough to come alone to a place like this.

But she wasn't alone. I was right behind her. We must have made quite a sight, a small girl and a guy in a trench coat, both of us walking the meanest street this side of Damnation.

It was evening and getting darker every minute. Still, there was enough light to see where we were going. Didn't matter. I hated sunset. Being a sun god, it ebbed my power. People lived here probably only because they had nowhere else to go and that had jaded them. Still, they knew enough to get out of our way. Jones headed for a small group of young men standing in a corner, all of them watching our approach.

I drew on my powers of light and heat, ready to back whatever play Jones was going to make.

One of the pack stepped forward. "What you want, bitch?"

They knew who she was, Jones knew they knew, but she hadn't declared herself, hadn't shown a badge, so the game had to be played, a challenge made to be answered.

"Dante Daymon, where is he?"

"Why for you be bothering Double D?" the pack leader asked.

Double D? My notes didn't include Huntingdon's bra size. The thought occurred to me to ask Jones about it, then I remembered that even in the days of my godhood women were sensitive about such things. Probably best to learn it on my own.

Emboldened by his leader someone else joined in. "Yeah, you buying or selling?" Then the damned fool made a point of looking Jones up and down. "Not that you got that much to sell."

Defiance and hostility was one thing. That was a step over the line.

Jones shook her head. "Now you went and made it personal."

Jones stepped forward, her leg snapped out. There a pop signaling the demise of a healthy knee. As the fool fell she grabbed him and threw him into a wall, twisting at the last minute so he hit it with his back instead of his head. Mercy like that would get her a twenty-one gun salute and a body bag on my beat. Of course, then her killers would dig her up and do it all over again. The joys of the recycled soul.

Hands went for concealed weapons. Jones was faster and had hers out first, the big automatic huge in her small hand. Extending my senses, I sought out the explosive powder in any gun but hers. Let a trigger be pulled and there would be an explosion that would blow the shooter's hand off.

But no one seemed inclined to risk a bullet for their fallen friend. When that became apparent Jones asked without lowering her gat. "Anyone else want to try me?" There were no volunteers. "Then take me to Daymon."

After looking from one to the other, the weakest was picked by intimidating glares from his betters. Our chosen guide broke away with a muttered "follow me" and headed across the way to an open doorway. He stopped and gestured, pointing down. "In there, to your left." He walked away with a "your funeral."

I looked down the lightless stairway. "Abandon all hope."

"Never that, Negral," she said, "never that." Giving me an odd smile she led the way into the darkness. I helped by forming a small fireball that I let float past her to light the way.

Pulse-pounding rap music led to door number one. Didn't take a genius to figure out where Daymon was holding court. Jones made the move to knock, then realized the noise would make that gesture useless. Her hand tried the knob. Locked like a barn after the horses got out.

"Let me," I said. With a finger I guided my floating fireball and had it burn through the lock. It's easier to call up some heat to melt the latch and cylinder, but hardly as impressive. A small kick from my shoe and the door swung open.

The inside of the basement apartment was as rich as the outside was poor. What showed of the living room was tastefully decorated with the finest art and furniture drug money could buy. A sound system that cost more than Jones made in a year took up the better part of one wall and was blaring. The furniture shook with each bass beat. So did the man and the two women on the sofa. They were too involved with their own percussion to notice they weren't alone.

"Negral," Jones all but shouted in my ear, "if you'd do the honors." She pointed to the sound system.

"Gladly," I said. I needed this bozo to leave with me, so a little shock and awe was called for. I poured out a little of the inferno from earlier which blew it up and there was peace and quiet.

"I always did like The Sounds of Silence," Bianca said as it became apparent to the three that were no longer alone.

Jones had her coat back to display her holstered weapon. "Police," she said unnecessarily. To the man, "You Daymon?'

"No, he's not," I said. I'd taken Joe Russo's trick and applied it to the parchment in my pocket. Along with the name in blood, a little bit of one's soul is transferred to every contract. On the drive over I worked it so that that bit of Huntingdon's would heat up when it came near the original.

"He's right. I'm Daymon." A very large black man stepped forward from the rear hall. Daymon was a giant, powerfully built. Bigger than I was, he towered over the much smaller Jones. This was one man she'd not be able to drop easily. Although from the little I knew of Jones I suspected that she'd try if she had to.

The contract warmed up so fast that I thought it might burn a hole in my pocket. I'd found my lost soul, now to bring him in without igniting a major conflict.

"Can I help you, officers?" Daymon asked in a deep voice that suggested he wanted to do anything but.

"Private business, Dante," Jones said, refusing to be intimidated by the large man in front of her. And why should she be? She faced down and beaten worse creatures and she had a sun god backing her up. She looked at the three on the couch. "Your friends should go."

"Wait outside," Daymon said to the three.

"Don't you want extra eyes on the cops, Double D?" one of the women asked.

"S'okay," he replied, "it's cool. I told you, they can't touch me. Now git outside."

Once we were alone, Daymon looked Jones up and down, from his height mostly down.

"You're that little bitch that downed Hector O, ain't you?" He said this with some respect in his voice, so Jones let the slur slide. Daymon looked at me. "You I don't know. You ain't a city cop."

"He's from an … outside jurisdiction, Dante. Way outside. He's got a paper on you."

"Ain't any paper on me. Not in B'more, not anywhere else." Then he got it. With a wide smile, he said, "That time already?"

"It's that time, Dante, or should I call you Rebecca?"

Daymon didn't bother with a denial. "Ain't heard that name in a while. Another lifetime ago. Let's stick with Dante. Name should match a man's equipment, and I must say you folks were awfully generous with the equipment."

He looked at Jones as if inviting a comment, or at least a casual glance at his equipment locker. She shrugged and maintained eye contact.

"The Devil is always generous with his clients, Dante. But now the bill's due. You gonna come quietly or do we do this the hard way?"

Calling up my power, I let it show though, just to avoid any misunderstanding about not being able to back up my threat.

Daymon held up his hands. "No need to get all hot and bothered," he mocked. "I pay my debts." Then to Jones, he said, "Ain't he supposed to serve me with the paper?"

As if she were expecting this, Jones nodded. "Show him the contract, Chief Negral."

I took out the parchment and held it for all to see. "Chief, I'm impressed. Wouldn't want to be arrested by a flunky." He studied the paper in front of him. "Now, Chief, like I said, I pay my debts. Always have, even back when I had tits and a slit. But while that might look like my signature, something tells me that ain't my blood. And don't that make the whole thing invalid?"

Jones was already on her cell. "Joe, heard from Tammy yet. No, I didn't expect the DNA, just the blood types. Yeah, that's what I thought. How about your end? No, try the Thorndales. Anything? Thanks."

She closed the phone.

"The ABO and PGM genetic markers of the blood Tammy took from the contract match the medical records of Rebecca Huntingdon. We also have laughing boy's blood from a bullet he took about thirty months ago. Establishing street cred, Dante?'

"Ain't a player 'til someone tries to cap your ass."

"Anyway, we ran his blood against Tammy's sample. No match."

As I said before, Nick likes to play tricks with his clientele. But it's the nature of his own damnation that he's sometimes too clever for his own purposes.

I suddenly saw myself going back to Hell empty-handed. I wasn't looking forward to explaining to Nick that it was all his fault. That, of course, he wouldn't accept. Maybe he'd blame the agent he sent to finalize the deal. Or maybe he'd blame me.

While trying to figure a way around the dilemma I grasped at the one straw I had left. "What about Joe's test? Anything there?" Maybe, just maybe the blood still matched on a magical level.

This hope was dashed when Jones shook her head.

Damn her. She had this in mind the whole time. She knew or suspected that along with a change in body there'd be a change in the blood. As one cop to another, she should have told me, out of professional courtesy if nothing else. Regardless of jurisdiction, one cop does not make another look foolish in front of a perp.

That decided me.

I shook my head. "As far as I'm concerned the contract's still valid. Looks like the hard way it is."

The problem was that Daymon just might have been right. Intent is important, but it's the blood that seals the deal. I could drag Daymon down to Hell with me, but only as an unwilling soul.

To do that I might have to do the city a favor and burn down the whole complex, Jones and all. And possibly cause a violation of the Host-Horde Treaty.

"Bring it," Daymon growled.

"Hold on, Chief. You too, Dante" Jones interrupted. "Chief Negral," she said formally, "without proper papers I can't let you take this man, whatever he's done. Still, by his own word and past behavior I have to admit that right now he belongs to you, if not now, then when he's brought down by someone who knows how to deal with his kind."

The look she gave Daymon made it clear that he was about to become her new personal project.

"Sooner or later, Dante or Rebecca, you're going to Hell. The only question is how and when – unless ..."

There it was, what Jones had been building to.

"Unless what, bitch?" No respect this time.

"You come clean. Give up the life and give up your crimes. Come in with me and tell it all to the State's Attorney. You'll get some time and a chance to get straight. And once you're straight," Jones looked right at me, "you'll never see this man again."

There was a moment's pause, a moment in which I somehow expected Daymon to take Jones's deal. The actual prospect of going to Hell has scared many a man. When he started laughing I realized that Daymon was not one of those men. Or women.

"Nice try, Detective, but I ain't going nowhere. Your kind can't touch me because of this," he pointed to the contract, "and his kind can't touch me because of that." He pointed the blood.

And that was his mistake. Daymon thought he could have it both ways, and that's something neither Horde nor Host allows. It was time to get nasty.

I let out a dramatic sigh. "He's right, Jones, and so are you. Without a proper signature, this contract is invalid. Are we all in agreement?"

There was a look on Jones's face that suggested she'd caught on. I thought maybe she'd warn him, but she only said, "Agreed."

Secure in his logic, Daymon shrugged. "Okay by me."

That's when I tore the contract in two. The fact that I could told me I'd been right. A valid contract can't be destroyed.

"Let's go, Jones," I said with an air of resignation.

She looked surprised. Nothing had happened on my part. "That's it, we're done?"

"For now. Let's go."

When we emerged into daylight Daymon's crew was assembled by the door. There were more of them then when we went in, but since we didn't have their boss in tow they moved to let us pass.

"Go on ahead," I told Jones. "Start the car. I'll be there in a moment." At her hesitation, I added, "I'm a sun god and a peer of the lords of Hell. I'll be okay."

When she was out of earshot I addressed the crowd. "Double D has left the building. He left you a plaything. He says to party and do whatever you want to her, with his compliments."

Then as they rushed in to see what I meant, I joined Jones in her car.

"What did I miss?" she asked.

"Daymon voided the contract. You saw it yourself. That means, blood or not, I can't claim his soul under its provisions. It also means that he gives up any and all benefits he may have received."

The meaning of my words suddenly hit Jones. I grabbed on to her to keep her cop instinct from rushing out of the car and making a fatal mistake.

"You'd be too late. As soon as I tore up the contract Nick knew the deal was off. Right now, instead of their boss, that group of gangbangers is finding a very vulnerable, very attractive white woman. And right now, Rebecca Huntingdon is getting a small taste of what awaits her when they finally finish with her." Her actions damned her soul and pretty much assured she'd be in Hell thirty minutes before the Devil knows she's dead.

With my enhanced senses, I could hear the woman who had once been Dante Daymon begging and pleading for her life as one after the other of her former crew violently took turns with her. Jones was only human, but maybe she was imaging what was happening.

I waited for her reaction and when it came it surprised me. "She had her chance," Jones said coldly, as she put her car and maneuvered out of the complex. "Two chances really. First when she made your deal, then when she turned down mine. Not that I expected her to take me up on it."

"Then why make it?"

"Because I never abandon hope, Negral."

The job done, it was past time to get back. I had Jones drive me back to where I'd entered this world. Feeling I owed her something, I pointed out a shabby man hiding in the darkness.

"That guy over there, the one staring at where the fire was, he's your arsonist. I felt him when I came through. Right now he's reliving the joy of the dancing flames. Tomorrow he'll start looking for a new target."

As Jones called it in, I moved to get out of the car.

"You don't have to go back, Negral."

"No? The other side doesn't want me."

"Not yet, not like you are. But if you give up the power and the immortality and just be a good cop the gates would swing open. My old partner quit on me. I could use a new one."

I'll be damned, I thought, it wasn't Huntingdon's soul she was after at all. As flattered as I was, I knew I couldn't take the offer. Losing me to Jones might cause Nick to forget that Baltimore was a charmed city. Besides, despite it all, there was some good I could do down below. I thought of Hell's version of the Thorndale Apartments and decided that maybe it was time for a few more innocents to catch a break.

I considered giving Jones the big speech from the end of Casablanca but didn't want to go out on that corny a note. Instead, I just shook my head and said, "It's not in the cards, Bianca."

"Think about it, Negral, and if you ever decide to deal a new deck …"

"I'll whistle."

And with that, I walked into the burned ruins and back into Hell.

DYSCIPLE

A Bianca Jones/Hell's Detective adventure

How does she do it, Colonel Chester Williams thought as he considered the detective sitting in front of him. No more than five foot tall and slender enough to pass as a teenager just months shy of her high school prom; yet she had faced monsters and terrors that most people could not conceive as existing. Vampires, demons, creatures that attacked through dreams and, most recently, the Devil himself – she'd fought and beaten them all. All to keep this city safe. And now …

"So let me get this straight," Williams asked Sergeant Bianca Jones, "The murder victim found in the Thorndale Apartments was Rebecca Huntingdon, the financial wizard who's been missing for the last three years?"

"Yes, sir," Bianca replied "And despite the fact that the several suspects we have in custody all claim that Ms. Huntingdon was a 'gift' from a major drug dealer named Dante Daymon, there's no point in our making a deal for their testimony or even searching for Daymon?"

"None at all, Chief."

"Should I ask why?"

"No, sir."

Given Bianca Jones's unique status in the Baltimore Police Department, Williams was inclined to take her word on this. For her part, Bianca saw no reason to burden the Chief with the knowledge that Rebecca Huntingdon, having made a deal with the devil, had become Dante Daymon and that her extremely violent death had been the result of her trying to renege on the contract.

"What about this Negral fellow, the one who supposedly walked out of a burning building and asked for you?"

Again, Bianca didn't think it wise to relate that "this Negral fellow' was the Devil's Detective, a former sun god now working as head of Hell's security force. It was he who, with Bianca's assistance, had reclaimed Huntingdon's soul. Instead, she said,

"Detective Negral is from an outside agency, someplace far south of here where the weather is very hot and unpleasant. He asked for my help in locating a fugitive."

Contrary to the beliefs of most patrol officers, one does not get to be Chief of Detectives by being dull-witted or slow on the uptake. Colonel Williams considered all that Bianca was and was not telling him and decided that Daymon was now receiving the justice he richly deserved. Changing the subject, he moved on.

"And it was this 'Detective Negral' who identified the arsonist who was setting fires in the Southern District? How did he do that?"

Because, Bianca thought, as a Sumerian sun god he has an affinity for fires and those who start them. Because it was a fire set by this man that allowed Negral to enter this world from Hell. Because Hell's Detective owed me a favor and hated being in anyone's debt.

"I'll ask Negral next time I see him. But it doesn't really matter since I understand the suspect confessed."

"To both arson and murder, Sergeant Jones. In his statement, he claims that God told him to confess. He also claims that God wears a trench coat and looks like Sam Spade."

"This is Baltimore, Chief. On my first night of patrol I once found a man praying to a bleach bottle."

"And I was once told that angels watch us from light sockets. That will be all, Sergeant."

"Thank you, Chief."

After Bianca left his office, Williams let out a sigh of relief. No major problems, then mentally added, not this time.

*

Thurman Reeves no longer felt the heat inside him. Fire did not burn or dance. By court order and common sense, he was denied matches, candles, lighters, and anything else that produced a visible flame. He couldn't even get two sticks to rub together. But that was standard practice for those in his situation – confined to a secure cell while being treated for ongoing psychiatric problems. In Reeves's case, it was homicidal pyromania. He liked to watch buildings burn, preferably with the knowledge that someone inside them was burning as well.

He stopped because his god appeared to him and told him to surrender. He confessed to please his god. And he suffered his confinement because he knew that his god would one day reward his devotion and return to him the ecstasy of heat and light.

Thurman Reeves did not know the name of his god. He had heard it once, but fleetingly and from far away. This lack of knowledge bothered him not. He had faith that all would be revealed to him when it was time for the burning to start anew.

And so he waited and slowly adapted to the routine of his new home at Crown Spring State Hospital. Therapy every day. Group twice a week. Wednesday was meatloaf night. On Sunday they served chicken. Monday evenings were for arts and crafts and on Thursday there was live entertainment. Reeves liked Fridays the best. No therapy for the weekend and Friday was movie night.

There were movies Reeves was not allowed to watch. *The Towering Inferno*, *Backdraft* and *Ladder 49* being just three of them. Old crime dramas, except for White Heat, were considered relatively safe. Which is why he was in the audience the night *The Big Sleep* was screened.

It came back to Reeves slowly. The image of a man coming out of the fire. He was very much like the man in the movie. The clothes could have come from the same tailor. It was not so much the face as the way he moved, the attitude they shared. The name came later, in a dream. "My name is Negral," Reeves finally remembered hearing.

It was Tuesday of the next week when Reeves made his request. His doctor thought it a sign that his condition was improving and readily agreed to it, even went online and ordered the item for him. And so it was that a poster of Humphrey Bogart in a fedora went up in Reeves's room. Thurman Reeves had found his god. Only time would tell what the god would think when he found his new worshipper and Lady Time was a tight-lipped dame. And not even the harshest interrogation would make her spill the beans a moment earlier than she wanted to.

*

My name is Negral. Once in a country now forgotten I was the god of the sun and of fire. But those days are gone and not coming back any more than a teenager's virtue after a vigorous romp in a backseat. New beliefs invaded the land and laid waste worse than any invader had ever done, at least in retrospect. I was too busy ruling an afterlife to care, at least until my ex-wife pulled a coup. By then my worshippers were dead and dust and my powers a matchstick to their former inferno. I watched as most of what remained of my pantheon faded into oblivion. I survived because of a few academics who knew who I had once been, but obscurity was only a layover on the way to oblivion. These days getting worshippers ain't as easy as it used to be. Back in the day, appear in a ball of fire and the people would take care of the rest. Make an appearance every few years and the manna came in. Try it now and folks start looking for the pyrotechnics.

Still, I found a way out. Not a good road despite the type of intentions used in the paving, but better than the alternative. The Devil needed a detective and made me an offer that was better than oblivion.

The deal I made with Satan was a simple one. He needed someone to watch his back, to make sure that the damned and demons under his control stayed that way. Someone to warn him of the inevitable demonic rebellions and to handle any problems that called for an approach more subtle than raining brimstone down upon the transgressor. I needed a purpose and enough manna to fend off oblivion. After some negotiation, we both signed a carefully worded contract and I became the Devil's Detective, the Chief of Hell's Secret Police.

Hell is not a place for feeling good. Sure I like the flames, but the very nature of the Pit was depressing, demoralizing, and destructive of any of the finer virtues and the more uplifting emotions. Even for someone like me who was not condemned for his sins, it can suck away most of the good things in life. In short, cranky was a good day in the Pit.

Yet I was having a good day for no reason at all.

It began when I woke up from a sound sleep. One does not sleep in Hell. The condemned aren't permitted the luxury. Sleep and any ensuing dreams would be an escape from their torment. The keepers of the damned can't allow any of that. The Fallen lost paradise when they rebelled and they know it, remember it every moment. When they sleep and dream of it then wake back in the Pit—well let's say it makes the damnation they inflict even more enthusiastic. That's why demons don't sleep, because a good dream makes their waking even more of a nightmare. It explains why that even on a good day a demon's mood makes my normal cranky look giddy by comparison.

Those of us able to sleep do so fitfully and in secret. First, Hell is an entity unto itself and makes the dreams of those who don't remember paradise into horror shows that are hardly restful. Second, to sleep, perchance to dream, leaves the snoozer vulnerable to attack. And in Hell, there is always someone looking to make your existence more miserable in hopes that it will make theirs less. Hasn't worked yet, but even in Hell hope springs eternal despite the sign on the door. Sadly, it's usually found and bludgeoned to death.

I make a habit of not catching even twenty winks in Hell. I can travel to Earth and do that there. Yet, today I woke up refreshed, my mind untouched by Hell. No night terrors, just several hours of peaceful slumber, having dreamed I was back in Sumer where countless thousands had started fires in my honor.

Even more surprisingly, the good feeling lasted through the day, giving me energy to spare in dealing with the demons, fallen angels, and assorted damned souls who thought they'd found a way around the chaos of rules that Nick has imposed to keep all in line. On some level, it troubled me, but I felt so damn good that I just ran with it, secure in the knowledge that Hell would find a way to crush it before long.

But long came and went and it stayed. The joy in my chest grew each day, fighting off the oppression of the Pit. It was minuscule but I still knew it was there. The best way to describe it was as a match in total darkness that can seem brighter than the sun at high noon. I finally realized that the light was within me, feeding me in a way that the manna the Devil feed me could not. I hadn't felt this good since I got to Hell. Almost as good as it did when I was still worshipped…

I felt like an idiot. It had been so long I hadn't even recognized it. I probably wouldn't have been able to pick it out of a line up even if it smacked me across the face. Fortunately, this was more akin to a knee in the groin.

My mind raced to figure this mystery out. There were still those who worshipped the sun, but most were looking for something to fill an emptiness inside them, making up a religion. None of them used the name Negral so I couldn't even tap into that if I wanted to. Those humans who did know of me were mostly decent sorts, inclined to avoid me as much as possible because of my employer. I doubted Hex or Paddy Moran was about to start a cult in my name. There were some who did believe in my existence but only as an ally and fellow cop. True, Baltimore Detective Bianca Jones had asked me to forswear my allegiance to Hell, give up immortality, and become her partner. But that sort of belief did not lend itself to the power I was feeling.

The case with Jones was my last visit to Earth. I owed her for her help in catching Huntingdon and gave her an arsonist the local cops wouldn't have nailed for months. I had entered the mortal plane through the flames of a burning building, a fire the arsonist Reeves started deliberately. It was child's play to know who had set it and point him out to Jones. Had Reeves somehow been able to sense me for what I was? Firebugs often literally worshipped the fire. If he realized I was a god of the flames, could he have transferred that passion to me? Could Reeves actually be worshipping me?

It had been a very long time, but it was not something any god would forget, just repress so as not to sink into a permanent dark funk. Slowly, carefully, mindful of where I was and the jealousy of my boss, I reached out my mind and sought for my worshipper. I found him staring at a wall, where no doubt some icon representing me was placed.

Somehow he sensed my presence.

"My Lord," he said, getting down on both knees.

I did not reply. No words were needed. As he bathed in what once would have been my glory but these days was simply my presence, I lit up his room and soaked up his worship like a boozehound who had been sober for decades and had just gotten a highball infusion. I had always looked down on junkies but I finally understood their cravings. This was too good to go without ever again. With gods and their followers there is an implied compact, followed at the discretion of the god. Unfortunately, most of us used the worse part of discretion until it was too late and our worshippers drifted away to more attentive gods or simply died off. With only the one follower, I wasn't about to ignore his prayer. Truth be told it was a simple thing, taking a mere fraction of the power that he was feeding me with his fanatical devotion, easily equal to hundreds of half-hearted worshippers. Give me a hundred like him and I would be back to my glory days. No more working for the Devil just to survive. I could go back into Aralu, the afterlife I once ruled. I wouldn't be interested in taking back my ex – or ruling there again. Just a quick visit to rub Ereshkigal's face in the fact that I was a true god again while she was a ghost of one, feeding on the gidem, the shades of our worshippers in the afterlife. Maybe set right a thing or two I should have when I ruled and then it's off to Earth to build up my cult.

But I was getting too far ahead of myself. One worshipper does not a mighty god make. And this one had his issues. Still, I had seen what the Son of the Creator had managed by preaching forgiveness, so I decided to take a page from his playbook and forgive my worshipper. And answered Reeves's prayer by giving him a small portion of the fire he had relit in me.

*

Crown Spring was an old facility. Built on Maryland's Eastern Shore just after the Civil War as a place to house those who minds were shattered by that conflict, it was slowly and not always properly updated. The heating was bad, the plumbing was iffy and the wiring was suspect at best. So when the first of several small fires occurred, no one thought much of it other than to blame management, maintenance or the State Government for cutting the budget yet again.

A mattress fire in the cell three down from Reeves created a bit more excitement and led to an investigation of how the inmate may have started it. Three guards were interviewed but no one thought to question Reeves. How could he have had anything to do with it? They searched his cell and him and found nothing that could make a fire.

Immolated animals – two squirrels, a rabbit and a raccoon – were next found on the grounds. Their deaths were thought to be the result of sick pranks played by local teenagers. That the charred remains were all visible from Reeves's small, barred window was not a concern.

Finally, a fire that seemingly started spontaneously in a bucket of rags somehow spread to the cell directly across from Reeves, who watched with undisguised joy as the man inside it burned. As guards rushed in to fight the blaze and save the trapped inmate, Reeves felt a joy that he had not known since being apprehended.

That night Reeves bowed before the image of his god and most humbly offered worship and thanksgiving. And as his prayers went down to Negral, a grateful and no longer forgotten god returned power in their stead.

*

Being worshipped is intoxicating, more so after not having it for so long. To expand on my boozehound comparison, it was like a drunk who had been following his twelve steps so long he had almost forgotten what top shelf or rotgut tastes like, but still holds on to that memory of a memory. Somehow he stumbles into a Jack Daniels warehouse and manages to get locked inside over a weekend. Right now I was about where the drunk would be by Saturday afternoon and I was craving the rest of the worship bender.

I was still functional, or at least I kept telling myself that, but the premise was truly tested when Nick called me into his office. Of late he'd become obsessed with carpeting, so when I got called on the carpet, it screamed. Oddly this time it did it in four-part disharmony. The latest floor covering was comprised of the skin of four damned souls from an all-girl Goth group. The quartet had bought it in a plane crash on the way to a show. Helped their latest album go platinum, which would give their music immortality. Sadly, that wouldn't help them here. I don't know if there is a rock and roll heaven but I can assure you there are no bands in the Pit. Music lessens torment and so is banned.

These songbirds sang about darkness and extolled the joys of the serving the Devil. But bad lyrics alone wouldn't have landed them here. The fact that they also lived the lifestyle, going so far as to dissect a fan or two, would and did. Oddly they didn't seem too happy now that they got their wish to be up close and personal with Nick. An example of "be careful what you wish for" in action.

"Haven't seen you around lately, Negral." The boss was never one for small talk. "Everything okay?"

The Devil's concern for my well-being set off all my alarms. "Everything's fine," I answered truthfully, a rare event in Hell. "Been keeping busy." I hadn't. I'd been in my room for the past few days soaking up Reeve's adoration.

"No doubt."

It was obvious that Nick sensed there was something wrong. But as it's my habit to keep things from him he didn't sense exactly what was wrong. He has almost ultimate power down in Hell, but also certain blind spots. Pride is his biggest. The Creator would probably take him back if he genuinely asked for forgiveness, or might at least change his lot. Not going to happen any more than a snowball fight in the fire pits. Another is Nick's total belief in himself. If he entertained the occasional self-doubt the likes of Bianca Jones or Hex would have much more difficulty handing him his hat. Nick would never consider someone else in the Pit daring to accept worship without his blessing. I was counting on that to keep him in the dark on my recent change in affairs.

"Just be sure that you're keeping busy on my business and not yours. Now, have you found a replacement for the fire pit overseer that you busted last week?"

Assigning personnel is not one of my stated duties but the fire pit is one of the places where the newly damned are placed for a little roasting. Buys the demons time to come up with a more personalized punishment. It's a sensitive position and requires just the right soul to handle it. I told Nick I was working on it and asked,

"Anything else?"

"There have been some strange power surges lately. Try to trace them, will you?"

I said I would and quickly left, lest he connect the dots and the power surges with my good mood.

Not for the first time I left Nick's office with the thought that I really hated my job. I'm not by nature an evil being. I've done evil, but I always had what I thought was a good reason. Working this beat has taught me the folly of that logic, but didn't stop me from the occasional evil act in my effort to forestall oblivion. I always told myself that if there was another way …

Now there was, and it would be so easy. Thurman had been praying for his release. Odd, I prefer using last names or titles. I couldn't recall exactly when I switched over to using his first name.

This wish I could grant. Once Thurman was free, I would guide his actions. Major fires here and there followed by an Internet pronouncement of why he was setting them. Then a demonstration of my godly abilities, again online. With every download, my powers would increase and soon I would be strong enough to use my escape clause to break my contract with the Devil and carve out my own piece of otherworld real estate.

*

No one heard a thing. No one could explain why the sprinklers, smoke alarms, and newly installed heat detectors didn't go off. What they did know was that there was a man-sized hole in the wall of one of the cells and that Thurman Reeves was missing.

"Who would want to break this guy out?" asked Bret Duncan, Crown Spring's Deputy Security Director.

"Guess he had at least one friend on the outside," replied Detective Richard Welch. "Although how the hell the guy managed to do this without setting off the alarms is something for the crime lab. How about it, White? How'd he do it?"

Maryland State Police Crime Lab Tech Salvatore White had

been examining the hole through which Reeves had escaped for the past thirty minutes. He studied it from the outside going in and the inside going out. He tried to take samples from the parts of the wall that had melted but between the times of escape and discovery they had solidified back into stone. He had just decided to use a hammer and chisel when Welch asked his question.

"Forget the alarms. Try asking how Reeves burned his way through a foot of stone without a lighter, matches or anything else that could cause a flame. And this would require something hot enough to melt stone." White pointed to the burn pattern. "This was done from the inside."

"Oh shit," both Welch and Duncan said simultaneously.

"Oh shit, indeed," thought White, knowing there was only one thing to do in a case like this.

*

Bianca Jones was still in bed. After breakfast, her husband Joe Russo had suggested that it would be a good day to go in late. Despite having just gotten dressed Bianca had agreed with him. She was glad she had and was thinking about taking the rest of the day off when the phone rang.

"That was the MSP Crime Lab," Bianca said as she reluctantly climbed out of bed and started getting dressed. "They've had an escape from Crown Spring." She told Joe who and how.

"I knew it had been too quiet. I was wondering when things would start heating up." At Bianca's look, Joe added, "No pun intended. Want some company? It's an hour drive to the Eastern Shore."

Bianca shook her head. "MSP Crime Lab's on the scene and I'll take Tammy with me. Sal's good but Tammy's used to the weird stuff. I'll need you at the bookstore, looking up what kind of magic can burn through stone."

"Pyromancy," Joe said, kissing Bianca goodbye. Then, as usual, he said several prayers for her quick and safe return.

As Tammy Dolan and Salvatore White discussed what samples

were needed and the best way to collect them, Bianca looked over the crime scene. Like White, she studied the hole from both sides. Not finding any answers, she turned her attention to the rest of Reeves's room, hoping to find a book on magic or something similar. It was only then that she saw the poster on the wall.

"Oh shit," she said to herself as she tried to figure out how to make a telephone call to Hell.

Joe was no help. "Bianca, the books Morgan left me were printed long before Bell was even born."

"So you're saying that short of a séance there's no way of reaching Negral?"

"He never died, so I don't think a séance would help. You could always ask the DMA. If anyone knows how to contact Hell it would be the government."

"Good point."

*

"There's no way," explained Agent Karver of the Department of Mystic Affairs. "Half the time people can't get a cell signal in their homes if they live in a rural area. I can't imagine it being any easier in Hell. And I don't think any phone company has had the chance to run a landline."

"Well, thanks anyway. Say 'Hi' to Mindi for me." "Of course, you could email him."

Bianca was glad that they were talking over the phone, so Karver could not see the look of surprise on her face.

"Hell has the Internet? What's the web address?" Bianca made the obvious suggestion.

"No," corrected Karver. "That's a private site. Get an old computer, log onto the World Wide Spyder's site and search for the Infernet. Once Spyder connects you enter 666.hell.gov. Follow the link to Security."

"I understand the 'gov' part but why an old computer?"

"It's Hell, remember? Five seconds after you log on, the malware attacks begin. Trust me; you do not want viruses based on Hell magiks infesting your main computer. When you're done I suggest giving the computer to your husband for disposal and burial on holy ground. Or fill a cooler with holy water, submerge it, and ship it to us to take care of."

*

I was about to leave for the mortal plane when my computer told me that I had mail. It was actually the live feed of a former postman being beaten with large spiked packages. Hell is anything but subtle most of the time. The postman spent twenty-three years stealing from the people on his route. He would read letters, taking ones that would have lifted spirits, saved marriages, or made for happy birthdays but the kicker was when he started stealing medicines from mail-order pharmacies and switching them out to sell online. Using fake insulin led directly to the death of a twelve-year-old girl. If you ask me, he's getting off easy.

It was probably more spam. There were hundreds of tech-savvy demons assigned to send mortals e-mails. Some are rather clever. They can actually deliver on the ten-inch penis promised and you would be surprised how many idiots are willing to trade their soul for a bigger manhood. One poor sap asked for one so big it dragged behind him and he never could get any woman brave enough to touch it. Died a virgin. And the Nigerian scam? The money actually gets deposited. Once even a dime is used, Hell gets to withdraw the soul after seven years. With interest.

I had a spam filter, but things got by. I decided to check it anyway. It might have been something important and I'd been letting things slide a bit too much lately. I'd be happy to let them slide permanently if all went the way I was hoping, but until then I had signed on to do a job. The fact that it was for the Devil didn't absolve me of my obligation. If I didn't want to do it, I shouldn't have signed on the dotted line. And I could always get out of it and catch the last train to oblivion. Until I figured out a way to avoid that ride, I had work to do. And slacking off any more than I had was bound to raise Nick's suspicions.

It wasn't Nick, it was Bianca Jones. She was investigating the escape of my lone disciple and wanted my help. Could we meet?

At least that's what her email said. Jones was no fool. She'd proved that when we teamed up to bring in Huntingdon. And as someone who'd beaten the boss not once but three times running, she was not an opponent to take lightly. Worse, I think I actually liked her. Not as a dame mind you. As something more than that— as a fellow cop.

I didn't want to deal with her, not yet anyway. It would be better later, after my power had increased and my godhood was more firmly established. Without trying hard, I could think of several ways she could stop me. The simplest would be to put a bullet in Thurman, but she wasn't the type to do it in cold blood, but if it was him or someone innocent in his way, Thurman was toast. One of the things I liked about her.

I kept my reply short and simple.

*

"B, good to hear from you again. Would like to help but am tied up on a major investigation. Even in Hell, a policeman's lot is a busy one. Best of luck. N."

"He's lying to me," Bianca said as she shut down the old laptop. She'd pack it up later and ship it to the DMA for disposal.

"How can you tell?" Joe asked from his desk in the back room of Morgan's Bookshop. He had inherited the store from the man who had brought Bianca and him into the fight against dark things and who, before he died, had begun teaching Joe the mystic craft.

"You mean besides the fact that he's from Hell and that's what they do down there?" At Joe's "Yes" she went on. "Negral's a cop. He may have once been some kind of a god but now he's a cop. He might be working a big case, but there's not a cop in the world, any world, who wouldn't ask for the details of a case he'd been involved in, however briefly."

"Which tells you he already knows about the case?"

Bianca nodded. "It tells me that Negral is in it all the way up to his snap-brim fedora. Joe, go through your books and look up deicide. I may just have to kill a god."

No need to enter through a burning house, not this time. No need to summon a Pit wormhole – best not to leave a trail for Nick to find. This time I had an anchor on Earth. The next time Thurman called, I answered in person.

I was in full regalia as I appeared before my worshiper – trenchcoat, pinstriped suit, and fedora arranged just so. I liked it better than my old armor. Giving him my best Bogie sneer I said,

"Hello, Thurman."

He immediately fell to his hands and knees, his face to the floor, unable to gaze upon the face of his god. Damn, that felt good. But I didn't need him groveling. That's how Hell would play it. Groveling slowly destroyed the ego and would eventually foster resentment toward me. That, in turn, could extinguish some of his passion and loads of my power. Instead, I poked him with my shoe.

"Stand up and look at me." He did, fear and awe pouring out of him and into me. "What do you want?"

Thurman still couldn't make eye contact. "To serve you, my Lord."

The right answer and definitely a most satisfying one.

"And how will you serve me?"

Thurman paused. He didn't quite know what to say so he took a guess.

"With fire, Lord. I … I … I will burn things for you."

My follower was two for two. I took the time to study our surroundings. We were in what I sensed to be a vacant house. Judging by the lack of furniture and the copper pipes ripped out of the walls, I was guessing abandoned. Besides the two of us, I could feel no one else anywhere around.

"Prove it," I told Reeves. "Prove your loyalty by burning down the house in which we stand."

"But, my Lord, there is no one here."

Which is how I wanted it. After millennia in Hell, I no longer enjoyed the smell of burnt meat. I asked myself what would the Devil do and went in the opposite direction. Nick would want a family in here sleeping. I wanted no innocents harmed. I had never been merciful before, but I guess even an old dog like me can learn new tricks.

"We are here, Thurman. You will find the means to burn this dwelling with us inside. And if you are truly worthy of my favor, no harm will come to you. Your god promises you this." Yeah, I know the speech was a little on the uppity side, but it's very easy to fall into.

Risking life and limb was the ultimate test of a follower's devotion. Others have asked for such. The Creator even demanded a son from Abram.

How would Thurman reply?

He said the only thing possible.

"As you wish, Lord."

Thurman set out to search for and gather the fuel he would need to start the blaze. Yes, I could have let him draw the power from me, but what kind of test would that be?

I thought about what was about to happen. Is this what I really wanted, to be a god again? Would it last, and what would I do when it was over? I doubt Hell would rehire me. It didn't matter, not at the moment. I was too drunk on the power, the adoration to much care about tomorrow. I just wanted to light up the night and feel my name written in flame. That way if oblivion still ended up being my destiny, I'd at least have this one memory to keep me warm in that long dark night.

Thurman was ready. Where he got the gasoline I wasn't sure, but he poured it liberally around the house. He lit a match and the flames began their dance.

We watched the fire, my disciple and I, from the inside, my immunity to fire extended for the moment to Thurman, shielding us both from the blaze and the heat. As the house was consumed, the heat burning but not harming his skin, I felt Thurman's excitement build to near ecstasy.

The time flew by so fast, I lost track of it, but all too soon sirens grew louder than the cracking of wood and sheetrock. I reached out into the fire. It was mine, started for me. I controlled every single spark and in an instant it reached out to consume every bit of fuel. I didn't bring the house down. I vaporized it in an instant, down to the very air around us. For that moment, Thurman didn't need to breathe as the flames reached out and caressed his skin and mine like a hungry lover's kiss.

"Go now," I ordered Thurman. He, of course, being a good little follower, obeyed his god. I could see in his eyes that his adoration was a thing of the past. His belief had moved on to love. I found I had regained the ability to bend light around me, becoming invisible. I hadn't been able to do that since before the Romans fell. I tailed him long enough to make sure he got away from any authorities who might have figured a way to chase him. And I admit to keep any cops safe from him. I saw no reason to hurt them and oddly, I didn't want to explain to Jones why one of her fellow cops fell facing down Thurman.

*

"We got a hit, boss."

Tammy Dolan's news was the best Bianca had heard all day. When Joe retired and Bianca's role as the BPD's occult investigator had become an open secret throughout the department, Tammy had volunteered to take his place. It meant a step down for the attractive criminalist, but it was one she wanted to take.

"The lab's fine," she told Bianca in explaining why, "but it's the same thing day after day. After hearing about what you do, how you save lives, souls and the city – I want to be a part of that."

When first they met, Bianca had thought Tammy to be just another airhead chemist. After a rough start, Tammy proved to be a dedicated, hard-working analyst. So when she offered to join Bianca's team, the detective didn't turn her away. But she did try to scare her off.

"This isn't a game, Ms. Dolan. There are horrors out there, things you can't imagine who see us as cattle. They're just waiting for the right fool to open a door and let them through. If we screw up, if *you* screw up, thousands, maybe millions of lives could be lost."

"I understand."

"Do you? Do you really understand that creatures like vampires and zombies are real, that if one catches you the best you can hope for is a messy, painful death? I've had three partners – Joe went out on medical, one retired after battling an army of the undead and the third – the Devil killed him just to get to me. Before you come work for me you should know I've got some powerful enemies."

"And you beat them all, didn't you?" Tammy did not sound discouraged.

"So far."

"That's good enough for me. When do I start?"

"Go back to the lab. I'll call you when I need you."

That was a few cases ago. Now Tammy was helping Bianca find a homicidal arsonist before any lives were lost.

"State Police in Easton reported the set fire of a vacant house. No witnesses but one of the responding firefighters thinks he saw one man exit the ashes and another man disappear from the burned-out building. That was his word, 'disappeared.'"

"Negral," Bianca thought to herself, knowing that the mention of his name could alert him to what they were doing. "Damn it." To Tammy, she said, "What's this about a hit?"

"Troopers canvassed the area. A farmer reported that someone siphoned gas from his pickup. State lab guys dusted the truck, came up with Reeves's prints."

"And his next step," Bianca mused, "is to hitch a ride across the Bay Bridge and work his way home. Thanks, Tammy. Keep working with the state guys."

After Tammy left her office, Bianca put out a BOLO for any arson fires between the Bay Bridge and Baltimore. Then she called Joe at the bookstore.

"I've found a few books that might help," he told his wife.

"Thanks, but right now I need that sympathetic magic you do. Can you use it to find Reeves?"

"I'll need something personal."

"Will fingerprints do?"

"No, they're just ink on paper. It's got to be from him – like blood, hair or sweat."

"I'll see what I can do. Meanwhile, get things ready."

"Will do. You going to be late tonight?"

"Not unless something else burns. See you at home."

*

There's always someone who'll give you a ride. Reeves knew this from before he was locked up. A country-looking dude in a battered van dropped him off on Kent Island. The next day an older woman who thought Reeves had "trusting eyes" took him over the Chesapeake, taking him as far as Annapolis. Once across the water, the lone disciple of a once-forgotten god decided to walk the rest of the way, and honor his god as he went.

*

I was constantly getting stronger, my strength manifesting itself in ways I had never anticipated. Invisibility made my job in the Pit so much easier. No longer did I feel the oppression that was Hell and when I slept I dreamed vividly of the old days when my worshippers were legion and there were temples in my name. It was when a third level pit ghoulic challenged me and, without thinking, I blasted him into demon bits that I knew it time for me to leave – almost. I gathered up the pieces to take care of as demons and damned couldn't die in Hell. The jury was still out about immigrant Sumerian detectives. I just wasn't strong enough to tender my resignation and be sure I'd be able to walk out.

A few more Earthly manifestations. Thurman with a video recorder. My godly powers posted and going viral. Then I'd have strength enough to tell Nick where to cram my contract and strut out of Hell unscathed.

*

There were more arsons. One a day, starting in Parole, the fires roughly following Route 97 until branching off towards Glen Burnie. Detective Welch called Bianca to report the latest one.

"An old adult movie and bookstore on Crain Highway. Again, no signs of any incendiary. The fire investigators tell me that it seems as if the fire just started spontaneously. They also can't figure how some things that weren't supposed to burn managed to catch fire. That's something I've been wondering myself."

Bianca could have told him but doubted he'd believe her. He knew her status, of course – detective of the strange and impossible. But to most people, cops included, that meant that she was the one who came up with a rational way of explaining them.

How to explain the power of a god? How each act of worship adds to his power, power from which his followers could draw. Most people barely believed in their own divinity, much less allowed the existence of others.

So instead of an explanation Bianca merely said, "That's something for the lab to worry about. Our job is to catch him."

"Yeah, hopefully before anyone gets toasted. Well, once he hits the city line he's your problem. Call me if you need anything."

Welch hung up leaving Bianca to worry about "her problem."

Which was not only finding Reeves but finding him at just the right moment. Arresting him would do no good. He'd proven that no walls could hold him.

It suddenly occurred to Bianca that she was looking for the wrong person.

*

"So we have two possible targets," Lieutenant Tavon Greggs of the BPD's Quick Response Team said at the planning meeting, "Reeves and this so-called god."

Bianca looked at Greggs. She'd been working with him from the very beginning and the QRT commander had been one of the first to suspect that her job involved hunting more than human suspects.

"There's nothing 'so-called' about the Chief, Tavon." She had handed out a sheet with 'Negral' written on it, careful to instruct her fellow cops not to repeat it out loud. None of them quite bought into the idea that the mention of his name gave him the ability to listen in like some sort of mystic bug. Didn't make it any less true. "He may not be a god as you think of one, but he's just as powerful."

"So how do we find him?"

"Joe's working on that. Crown Spring is sending up hairs found in Reeves's cell. They'll let Joe start tracking him. By tomorrow we'll know where he is. And catching Reeves should draw the Chief in."

"And then, Bianca?"

"Good question," but Bianca already knew the answer. It was one she didn't like.

"The power of a god rests in his followers," Bianca told Greggs. "Or in this case, follower. Take out Reeves and the Chief's vulnerable for an instant before he can draw on his power reserves or the manna from Hell."

"So we take out Reeves, then drop this Chief guy. All we need is a few well-placed snipers."

It sounded so simple, the way Greggs said it. Drop, take out – simple words for kill. If one could kill a god or a disciple whose faith might protect him.

Would there be a need to kill Negral if Reeves were dead? Bianca liked the detective from Hell. They had been allies and might be friends. She would save him if she could, if she dared. But who knows what a god suddenly bereft of his sole follower might do? Baltimore had had two great fires, it was still recovering from the last. An angry sun god could cause a third one that would leave nothing but charred rubble and hundreds of thousands dead.

Bianca could not take that chance.

*

"You're thinking like a cop," Joe told Bianca that night when she discussed her concerns, wishing there was another way.

"I am a cop. How else should I think?"

"Like a magician." Then Joe outlined a second option.

"That just might work. I knew there was a reason I married you."

"You mean other than my charm and good looks?"

Bianca gave Joe a quick kiss, then a longer one.

"We better stop there," Joe said reluctantly, "if I'm to start the ritual to track Reeves."

"Ah," Bianca sighed, "the sacrifices I make for this city."

"How true," Joe agreed.

*

He was almost home, almost back in the city, his city. Once there, Thurman Reeves knew what he had to do. Find a house, no a home, one filled with people. Then he'd draw on the power of his lord and offer a fitting sacrifice to him.

He'd come in on Hanover, turn on Patapsco, go into Brooklyn. Lots of homes, lots of people in that part of the city. Lots of bars as well. Maybe he'd wait until the night, when the bars would be filled. Alcohol has such a lovely flame when it burns. It would be glorious and he knew that the deaths would only please the Lord Negral. Reeves felt himself harden in anticipation of the planned immolation.

*

In the back room of Morgan's Books, Joe Russo sat at a desk on which was a map of South Baltimore. Above the map, he held a plumb on a line. Entwined around the line were hairs from Thurman Reeves. Joe watched as the plumb swayed this way and that, finally hanging in the air at an impossible angle. Gently Joe moved so that the plumb was straight and the swaying began again. Three times did Joe do this and soon he found his man.

"Hanover and Jeffrey, walking north," he said aloud, his Bluetooth connection sending the message to Bianca.

A police helicopter equipped with heat sensors flew overhead. Twenty tactical men converged on the area. Snipers got into position and readied their rifles. Bianca Jones got ready to start a fire.

Reeves was stopped at Hanover and Garrett. Five automatic weapons pointing at him. The police chopper hovering above him.

Tavon Greggs gave orders to his men "If his temperature goes up one degree, waste the son of a bitch."

*

Something big was coming. I felt this even as my disciple experienced it. He was returning to Baltimore, there to do me great honor. What he had planned I didn't know, but I did know that at his next fire I would appear and then tell him that he was to be the herald of a new religion. We'd make plans, I'd give him marching orders, and soon I would once more walk among men and be worshipped by them. It would be the start of a beautiful worship.

Then I felt it, the joy and incoming power of sacrifice. But this one had a different feel to it, a different flavor, as if someone else were making it. Could Thurman have already begun recruiting? Could it have already begun? Then I heard my name three times. I was being summoned. Drawn by flames, I answered the call.

*

Bianca was a block away. As soon as she'd gotten word that Reeves had been contained, she set a torch to an abandoned building that had already been soaked with flammable liquids. With the Fire Department standing by to control the blaze, she offered up a prayer.

"Negral, god of the sun. Negral, god of the flame, accept this offering which I, Bianca Jones, give freely to you. And as I believe in you, Negral, answer my call and appear unto me."

Her prayer said, her offering made, Bianca waited. And as she did, she radioed Greggs and asked him to bring Reeves over to the fire.

*

I stepped through the flames, again ones that totally belonged to me as opposed to just being mine to control. Consider it the difference between a dame kissing you on the cheek and spending an entire night focused on bringing you pleasure. Then magnify it by a factor of ten. I hadn't lost any of the paranoia that had kept me alive in the Pit so I looked before I leaped. I had expected Thurman either alone or with a companion. And he did have one. In my wildest dreams, I hadn't expected my second worshipper to be Bianca Jones. Poor Thurman was handcuffed and in the custody of heavily armed men. Standing in front of me was Baltimore's finest detective.

It's hard to surprise a god but Jones has now managed it twice. "You? You summoned me by sacrifice?"

My next questions were the traditional "How?" and "Why?" but Thurman had been close enough to hear my first ones.

"No!" he shouted then, drawing power from me, managed to melt his cuffs and throw off the officers holding him.

Thurman drew more power and a heat shimmer appeared around him. Fire came from his hands and ran along the ground towards Jones.

I moved to stop him and found that I could not move. Thurman was my disciple and I was his god. We were bound together by ancient covenants that were old before I was born. Unless he transgressed my word or my law I was helpless to save a good cop from a fiery death.

Then more power flowed out of me as, smiling, Bianca stepped right into the path of the flames. She was engulfed and I lost sight of her in the blaze. Expecting to hear the sound of automatic fire cutting my follower down I heard instead,

"Hold fire!"

It was Jones's voice and it was coming from the small inferno in front of me. Then slowly the flames died away, revealing a slightly singed but otherwise unharmed Jones.

This time I did ask, "How?"

Before answering, Jones looked towards Thurman. "Call off your dog first, Negral."

"Thurman, no more." I sent into his mind. Now, if he disobeyed I could punish him.

With those in her care safe, Jones explained, "Because I made the sacrifice. Because I believe in you – not as a god, but as an ally, a friend, and a cop. It's that belief that kept me safe."

"Well played, but I don't think you realize the abnormity of what you've done, Detective Jones." I was barely taking it all in. The ancient covenants made no distinction between a god, ally, friend, or cop. Turns out Bianca and Nick have something in common after all—a total and utter belief in themselves, in being able to come out on top in any given situation. Despite her thinking the distinction would change things, it didn't. It was beyond any power shy of the Creator to rewrite those covenants. "How are you figuring this plays out?"

"Your choice, Chief Negral. We can play this out, modern weapons against ancient power. Me taking on Sparky over there while men with guns see if there's a limit to how many times a god can be shot. Maybe you win, maybe we do. Either way, Joe calls it into the DMA, and you know what bastards they are."

"Strike them down, Lord," Thurman shouted out. "Make them pay for this offense. Show your glory. Give me leave to burn their bodies and dance on the ashes."

I admit it. I almost did. It was so very tempting. What better way to establish my reign on Earth with a grand conflagration with massive loss of life? I would get worshippers purely based on the fact that they would be too afraid not to do me homage. I'd be unstoppable.

But at what cost and with what kind of followers? Decent people would shun me, abhor my religion, hunt me down. Only those who revel in death would flock to me. Sure, I'd be powerful, but it would be a step back, not forward. Then I asked myself what someone else would do. Not Nick this time. Bogie. Yeah, I know he's an actor, but he tapped into something bigger than himself. A regular or even a bad Joe with a code of honor, doing what's right whether it's turning down a payoff to turn on a client or make sure Bergman got on that plane because it was for the greater good. I admit I'm more about my personal good, but I still trying to do the right thing. At least as far as I can manage without biting the big one. Then again, we didn't have PR machines and the media back in Sumer. I could spin this, however it turns out. I've learned by watching Nick do it time and time again. There are enough people out there who might believe this was all a government plot. I could manage to come out looking like a hero with the right spin. But none of them would be able to convince me, damn it. When the blazes did I grow a conscience?

I could give up Reeves. Bad sign that, calling him by his last name again. But what kind of god would give up someone who had utter and total faith in him, no matter how misguided the man was? No the kind I wanted to be.

And I've already said I long ago lost my taste for burnt meat.

"You have a second choice?" I asked.

"Give it up. Go back to doing what you do best, keeping order and trying to do some good in the worst place there is. Go back to being a cop."

"I've never stopped being a cop, lucky for you."

Bianca raised an eyebrow and at her nod, a man in firefighting gear handed her rolled-up paper. She opened it to reveal the same poster of Bogie that Reeves had hung on his cell wall.

"It's either that or this becomes the image of death and destruction."

Jones never did play fair. Just ask my boss. But threatening Bogie? That was the dirtiest trick of all.

"What about Reeves? As long as he's around …"

"Take him with you."

"Sounds like a plan, but there is something you should have already known about me, Bianca."

"What's that, Negral?"

"I don't do well with threats. You could have just come to me and asked."

"You could have said no. I couldn't risk my city going up in flames."

"I respect that. But I'm not going to turn with my tail between my legs." I sent Reeves just enough power to once again break free.

Gunfire erupted, most of it in Reeves direction. I smiled and tendrils of flames snaked out from me in all directions, fusing the barrels of every gun in the area, but I was careful. Not one cop even got his fingers singed. And then I reached out and simply ordered the gunpowder not to light. With another dozen worshippers like Reeves that would have been child's play, but I still wouldn't have managed it now without Jones having summoned me. All the cops there were under her command and she had offered herself up to me. That meant I could control them, their weapons, and more.

I turned to Reeves and even I couldn't stop the smile from spreading across my face. "Thurman Reeves, you believe that I can control light to the point of forming lasers, don't you?" Reeves probably never thought about it until I mentioned it, but mention it I had.

"Yes, my lord, I do." It was then I noticed he had been hit and was holding his bloody stomach. I felt bad for him, but there was no time to do anything but play this hand out to the end. I knew Jones wasn't bluffing. It was time to show her that neither was I.

I looked over at Jones and for the first time saw doubt on her face, that she may have misjudged me. But I saw something else too. "And I can see in Detective Jones's eyes that she does too." I made my index finger and thumb into the universal sign of the gun and pointed it up at the helicopter. A beam of light shot out and cut through the rear rotor. The copter could have easily crashed into a neighboring apartment building, but I wouldn't allow it. My control extended to the helicopter and I created a heat updraft to allow it to land safely in the middle of the street.

"Bianca, come here." I could have ordered her and she would have no choice to obey this close after summoning me. I kept that tidbit to myself.

Jones stepped toward me. "No matter what it takes, I'll stop you."

I smiled. I could burn her to ash and she won't give an inch. What a dame. Nick got off easy. "You won't have to. I'm proving a point. Trust me?"

She looked at me as if I was mad, but we now had a bond she herself had forged. She knew the answer. "I have no idea why, but I do."

"Good." I took my hat off to cover her face. "Thurman, close your eyes. You too, Bianca." They listened and I raised my free hand up into the sky. Light burst from my fingers and spread down into the rest of me. Damn, it felt good. For a brief moment, Baltimore was the land of a midnight sun. The light temporarily blinded the rest of the cops and onlookers, but my two followers could see just fine.

"Thurman is coming with me. Take care, Bianca Jones. We are now bound you and I. We will see each other again." And I had to figure out a way to keep Nick from finding out that I now had a measure of power over Jones, although that would fade once I left and effectively ended the summoning. However, the dedication to me would last until I chose to end it. And if Nick found out I had

had the opportunity and the power to have killed one of his sworn enemies, I'd be the worst off of anyone in the Pit. "You're a damn good cop. Don't ever stop. And next time ask, or maybe I won't be so nice." I put my hat back on and tipped it to her.

"Thurman, follow your god." I lead Reeves out of the building that was still burning with the fires of my summoning and straight into Hell.

*

Bianca, Greggs and the QRT team stayed on the scene until the fire burnt itself out. No bodies were found.

"What did you just witness?" Bianca asked the lieutenant.

"Officially, an escapee from Crown Spring State Hospital and his accomplice, both suspects in a series of arsons, committed suicide by running into a fire so hot that their bodies were consumed by the flames. It was caused by a stolen truckload of magnesium, which caused the night to light up. Unofficially, we were blinded and couldn't see a damn thing." Greggs smiled, "Once again you saved our collective asses."

"I couldn't have done it without you and your men, and your belief in me. And the Chief was still a cop. In the end, he wasn't going to hurt another cop."

"I'm still amazed that our guns are back to normal and the helicopter is somehow back in one piece."

"A god can restore that which he has destroyed."

"Right, if you say so. It took a lot of faith and belief to pull this one off. You took a big chance jumping into those flames like that."

"No chance at all. As I said, I was kept safe by my belief in Negral and my faith in the fireproof gel covering my clothes and skin."

But Negral's parting words were still troubling. The summoning was over. There should be no bond between them any longer. That's not how the spell was supposed to work. But Bianca knew better than anyone that if everything was what it was supposed to be, there would be no need for her or cops in general.

*

Back in Hell, I was again summoned, this time back to Nick's office.

"You've been to Earth," was all he said.

"Yes, sir. You told me to track down those unexplained power surges. I did and my quick trip upstairs put a stop to them."

It was enough of the truth that Nick just nodded. All I know is he still couldn't see into Charm City. Maybe he suspected something and maybe he didn't. If he did there was nothing he could do about it. I'd taken no adverse action against him or his realm and had not broken any clause in my contract. He just gave me a somber look and changed the subject.

"Did you find the replacement for the fire pit foreman like I told you?"

My turn to nod. "Yes, sir. I finally found someone perfect for the job."

And I had. Police bullets had done in Reeves. I kept him alive until we stepped into the fire, making his journey down to Hell an easy one. As the bullets were technically under my control, I might have been able to save Reeves' life, but that was never one of my powers. All I might do is run through the power I have gotten and set a murdering psychopath back loose on the city of Baltimore. I decided it was best for all involved if I let nature take its course. Everyone but me of course.

Right away I claimed him as one of the thousands of souls I'm owed for doing my job and put him to work overseeing the torture of souls damned to fiery punishment. As I told Nick, it's perfect. It's a fraction of what I'd get from a living worshipper, but I still get little jolts of power from Thurman's belief in me and he, having died in the service of his god, believes that he's in heaven getting to play with deadly fire for eternity. He actually enjoys the screaming of the damned as he sets them ablaze. And even if he is a murdering psychopath, I still owe him. Not because of the covenants, but because for a moment he reminded me both of what I was and who I now am. And believed in me like nobody has in eons.

But fostering his belief is not that different from feeding off a gidem back in old Aralu, something I refused to do. One, I felt it was beneath me. Two, because it tasted like soot. At least Reeves has a choice. Those shades didn't. I used up a lot of my newfound power proving my point to Jones, but I still managed to sock some away. If I have to leave Hell in a hurry, it'll buy me a few more years before I have to worry about oblivion. Or at least give me the chance to pour it into one dying shot if I have to go down fighting.

Damn, I love a happy ending. Or as happy as it gets in Hell.

DYSAPPEARED

A Bianca Jones/Hell's Detective/Bambi adventure

It's never a nice day in Hell. It's not supposed to be. But some days are better than others. Today was one of them. The temperature wasn't too extreme, although it was hotter than anyplace on Earth has ever gotten outside of a volcano and that was in the shade. Not that you could find any. In what passed for sunlight in the Pit, it was even worse with ninety percent humidity and no relief in sight. The air stank of burned flesh as the condemned walked barefoot along heat-retaining concrete and metal sidewalks, forced to step as their flesh cooked.

At least it wasn't raining. The rain in Hell can be acidic enough to burn the flesh off the average damned soul and some of the demons. As I said, one of the better days.

Not that heat bothered me. As a former Sumerian fire god, I liked it hot, which was one of the reasons why the Devil offered me the job he did. Not that I had many other options open to me when my ex-wife managed a coup and kicked me out of Aralu, the underworld I had ruled for centuries. Not that it was that great there either. We hadn't even gotten a new arrival in an eon.

I was hoofing my way along the mean streets of Hell. I didn't mind the fire but the brimstone was hardly pleasant. Now, I didn't have to walk to work. My position as head of Hell's Secret Police entitled me to any number of modes of transportation – borne by litter, conveyed by rickshaw, chauffeured in my own limousine, things like that. The trouble was that all my choices would be made from and/or powered by human souls. Considering what most souls had done to get here, that in itself doesn't bother me but after a while the screaming grates on my nerves.

I can transport myself between my apartment and office but there's a risk with that kind of magic, especially if it becomes routine. A routine is a bad idea in the Pit. Makes it too easy for someone to hit you.

I had to take care of some business this morning, which is why I hoofed it Downtown, a crumbling slum that passes for one of Hell's commercial districts. You could buy almost anything Downtown. Name your perversion, it's there. Your drug of choice, someone's got it. Something to make you forget you backed the wrong horse in the Host-Horde War and have been damned for eternity; it can be had – for a price. And you can bet your soul or that of those closest to you that it's always a steep one.

The upfront price is always flesh, yours or someone else's. The hidden cost comes later when you realize that your high or your climax is never near as good as you want or need it to be. Often it's not even good at all, just a fleeting lessening of your personal torment. When all is said and done, you have to go back to being one of the damned or their keeper. Those cravings for the joys of mortal life or Heaven are now much more intense and worse because they are still out of your reach and likely forever will be. Such are the joys of Hell. They are only a way to tease you around to new torment. And it was my job to keep the damned and their keepers in line.

But it beats oblivion, at least most days.

As bad as Downtown was, the Corner made the rest look like a resort. Things happen there that could make a Demon Lord retch. It was a point of pride to at least try whenever a Demon Lord showed up. Sadly, I qualified, but after the first hundred or so times, they mostly gave up. One of the benefits of being a fire god is I can burn aftersmells and I have a strong stomach.

Today I was checking on the punishment of a recently arrived soul I had helped retrieve.

Rebecca Huntingdon was not a happy camper. Gone were the trappings of life she had as a rich woman and a drug dealing man. In both incarnations, she had people at her beck and call. Not anymore. Now Huntingdon was calling for help, but that only encouraged those tormenting her. They got their jollies from listening to the newly damned pray for deliverance and promise anything and everything to have this cup pass from then. Doesn't do any good. The Creator undoubtedly hears all but doesn't step in to stop what happens in the Pit. I can't explain it, but then again I'm not exactly privy to the divine plan.

If I had to make a guess, I'd say Huntingdon was wishing she'd done a better job trying to hide from Nick or wished she had been smart enough to take up Bianca Jones on her offer of help. Or had simply lived a better, if less excessive, life.

I had an indirect hand in her death by gang rape, but I wasn't proud of it. Not that I was exactly ashamed either. One of the benefits of my job is that I get the intel. I usually know who's been naughty. Huntingdon was beyond bad in both her incarnations, having killed and ruined innumerable lives. I'm old school in thinking what goes around comes around and Huntingdon was going to be going around for a long time.

Near the corner of the Corner, there was a burnt-out ruin of a house. Waiting impatiently outside the doorway was a long lineup of demons, mostly male, all waiting to get in. There were a few females, the most notable of which was wearing a long, sharp blade as a strap-on. For some reason, none of the other demons seemed to be turning their backs on her.

I stood and watched. The line moved but never seemed to get any shorter. The corner was a popular place for the lower level demons to take their breaks, coffee not being a major import of the Pit.

Most everyone on the corner steered clear of me. Even in Hell people don't much like cops watching when they're behaving badly. The exception was a creature in pink who came skipping straight up to me, ending with a curtsey.

"Morning, Chief."

"Morning, Deni."

Deni the Slut was one of the Corner's two ruling pimps, at least after the last great pimp war. Not pretty.

Deni was decked out in a pink pantsuit that had no front to speak of. Her clothes were made from the skins of the whores who had most recently displeased her or caught her at the bad end of a bipolar moment. Her nipples sported her trademark smiley face buttons. There were seven of each. Considering she was an ambitious damned who had fought and clawed her way up the ranks, it was impressive because I was never quite sure how she had managed the body modifications. In her left hand was her other trademark – a cat-o-nine tails. The main part of the whip was carved from the bones of the demon who once was her pimp. The whip itself was braided from the same demon's skin. I won't specify what part of his anatomy was flayed, but it was the same part he tortured Deni with. The whip's ends sported the faces of more whores. It was always interesting to watch her use it if for no other reason than to hear if the whip screamed louder than the whippee.

"How's the new girl working out?"

Deni smiled, the points of her filed teeth gleaming brightly. "I made her my special project as a favor to you, Chief."

Deni was always quick to brownnose those above her in the food chain, at least until she could figure a way to devour them, either literally or figuratively. Ass kissers can be useful, although Deni'd do it literally if you asked. I didn't.

Deni squeezed her arms together in an attempt to make her three and a half times normal cleavage look even bigger. "Of course, I'm always willing to do you a favor. Say the word and I'm out of retirement."

"The offer's always appreciated, Deni," I said, suppressing a chill.

She nodded, not really expecting me to change my answer after all this time. "Well, there's always a bonus with new souls, Chief." Deni looked at the long line. "It brings in the business."

"Any idea when this will slow down?"

"Newcomer like that, probably ten, maybe twenty days. That is barring time to regenerate any essential bits."

I imagined what the woman inside was going through. Souls in Hell can't die, but their bodies can be mutilated beyond belief. There are some I feel pity for. Huntingdon did too much evil on Earth to make that short list. "Be sure you watch her, Deni. Huntingdon's no fool, and she's got street smarts. Give her half the chance and she'll have your job." I looked again at the line. "And you'll have hers."

Deni shuddered then caught herself and bristled before ripping off one of her whip's faces, marching off to the front of the line to get a new replacement.

Leaving the Corner behind, I took the long way to work,

stopping to check on some of my network of snitches and contacts, picking up word on the ever-constant plots and schemes of those trying to overthrow or outwit the Devil. Nothing major, but a few things sounded serious enough that I'd have some of the cops who worked for me check them out.

When I got the office, my secretary Rachael was hard at work. That was no surprise. With nowhere else to go and nothing else to do, Rachael is always hard at work. If she's not answering the phone, scheduling appointments or making my coffee, she has a never-ending mountain of paperwork to file.

Rachael was in Hell because she was fool enough to have believed her husband. He asked her to sign a contract and, without reading it first, she did. The contract was for her soul and now she belongs to the Pit. She came to work for me after I saved her from being devoured by a behemoth in one of the Pit's versions of a reality show.

As far as punishments go, Rachael doesn't have it bad – no torture, no pain, just an eternity of never-ending drudgery. Best she could ask for in the Pit. I don't point that out – I don't need anyone thinking I've gone soft.

"Any calls?" I asked, taking my coffee after handing her my trenchcoat and fedora to hang up. It's the real stuff, imported from Columbia. Of course, I'm the one doing the importing, but travel to Earth is one of the benefits of my job.

"Just one, Chief, the message is on your desk. And no, it's not from – Him."

The damned don't say the Devil's name so as not to draw his attention.

Good. Any day without having to deal with Nick was definitely one of the better ones.

"Get Karl and Cliff in here. Tell them I've got a plot against Him I want them to look into."

Karl and Cliff work for me. When they were alive they were good cops, at least by their standards. They cleared a lot of cases and put a lot of bad guys in jail. They were in Hell because of how they did it. Karl had planted evidence, beat confessions out of suspects, and perjured himself in court. That's not to mention all the bribes and kickbacks he took to overlook "victimless" crimes like gambling and prostitution. Cliff was a new guy, fresh from the riots in Baltimore. He and his partner had yielded to temptation and administered some severe street justice on a house full of gangbangers they thought had raped a girl. Wrong house, wrong perps. When the people in the neighborhood found out, they administered some justice of their own. I don't know what happened to his partner, but Cliff wound up here.

Good cops, bad people. Not many show up at Perdition's gates, but when they do I have the right of first refusal.

Rachael made a face. "Do they have to come here?"

That was odd. "Why wouldn't they?"

She paused and looked down at her desk. "The way they look at me, it makes me uncomfortable."

My secretary still hadn't adjusted to the fact that she was in Hell and that her comfort didn't matter. We've been over this before.

"Could I at least wear clothes like they do?"

Yeah, Rachael was naked, like most of the damned souls. It adds to the humiliation. My cops, however, get to cover up. Them and the ones like Deni the Slut who claw their way up, get clothes and the right to use a name. Their being dressed gives them the air of authority they need to do their job.

As I shook my head, Rachael tried another tactic.

"Will there be anything else, Chief?"

There was no mistaking the suggestion in her voice. Nor did the way she leaned back against her desk leave any doubt as to her meaning.

Rachael's made the same suggestion every week since coming to work for me. Each time I turn her down. It's not that I'm immune to her charms. I'm a healthy male and she's a good-looking woman. But screwing an employee is a good way of losing perspective. Plus continuous sexual frustration was part of being in Hell – for her. For me, there were other realms I could visit when I got the urge.

The message on my desk was from a guy I called "Skinless." Thanks to me this particular damned had moved up to lower management as boss and guard of the Western Fire Pit. Somehow he'd gotten word that a spigh was asking questions about me.

Spighs work for the Satan, doing the work I refused to do. Part of my deal with the Devil lets me turn down cases. The spighs serve as eyes and ears, keeping him informed about things on Earth and in Hell. I don't normally worry about them. Nick knows that siccing one on me is a violation of our contract, and the Boss is a stickler about contracts. There was one, however, who had been following me on a personal matter and who got stomped into little pieces for his troubles. Since no one dies in Hell, he could have regenerated by now.

I decided another walk was a good idea. I left marching orders for Karl and Cliff and took a stroll to the Western Fire Pits.

When I got there Skinless was nowhere to be seen. It wasn't like him to abandon his post. It was behavior like that that got the last guard replaced. Thinking I was a fool to trust anyone in Hell to do his job I turned to leave. Then it occurred to me that maybe his betrayal of my trust went further than not doing his job. Maybe someone had convinced him to call me, someone like the spigh.

That's when I saw Skinless's pitchfork lying partly behind a rock. Not too far from the pitchfork was Skinless himself. What was left of his head was bashed in and his brains were leaking from his skull and sizzling on the hot ground. The gore was nothing I hadn't seen before, but I felt nauseous. Maybe Skinless hadn't betrayed me after all, maybe …

I never finished my thought.

There was a sharp pain in my head and all went dark.

*

Joe Russo was having strange dreams, not bad, just strange. He'd work every day at his bookstore then go home and spend the evening with his wife, Bianca. That is, if she wasn't working. Being the Baltimore Police Department's semi-official investigator all things occult, supernatural, or just plain scary, Bianca Jones sometimes kept odd hours. On those nights, Joe would remain at the store, familiarizing himself with the collection of old books he'd inherited from the store's former owner.

Morgan had been more than a bookseller. For a long time, he

had been Baltimore's guardian against the evils that lurked in the dark. When he sensed that his time was growing short, he enlisted Bianca and Joe in his struggle. At the time Joe had been a crime scene investigator for the BPD. When he was injured in the line of duty, Joe became Morgan's apprentice, learning what he could about magic and its uses. And when Morgan fell in battle, killed by Satan himself, Joe took over the shop and with it, Morgan's collection of books.

Or maybe they took me over, Joe thought on more than one occasion. In the back room of the bookshop that was much larger than it appeared from the outside, were ancient texts, old grimoires, and similar tomes that described occult rituals, magical practices and the creatures that lurked within and without the world that most people knew. Joe hadn't read most of them but was somehow familiar with all their contents. If he needed to know something, instinctively he knew which book to consult. And should the book be in a language foreign to him, or even in one that was old when humanity itself was young, Joe found that with effort he could somehow understand it.

It was as if Morgan had left him more than the books. Joe was often awed and more than a little frightened at the responsibility. But the old man had trusted Joe, and every night Joe prayed for the strength and courage to live up to this trust.

But the books didn't explain the dreams. Had they been of killers, vampires, and the sometimes hulkish creatures that Joe knew existed, he would have understood this. But the dreams he had been having lately were of a disturbingly sexual nature. Every night as he slept, there would be a woman dressed in red, if "dressed" was the word for clothing that appeared to be painted on. Maybe it was paint, for there was little left to Joe's imagination. He knew where her every piercing was and all the places she didn't have hair. Her breasts were large and firm and moved naturally when she did. Her hips were just wide enough and when she turned around Joe saw nothing to complain about.

In his dreams she wanted him, offering a variety of delights and pleasures. Some of these were familiar to Joe, some he had only read about, still others were entirely new and he doubted if any human could survive them long enough for full satisfaction. But as much as she wanted him, she also wanted something from him. It was as if making herself and all that she offered available to him was the only way to obtain what she needed.

Joe loved his wife and was in love with her to the point that there was no other woman for him. Yet asleep and with his mind unfettered and unrestrained, he was tempted in ways he would not have been in real life. Yet he resisted this temptress's advances. Even in dreams, where anything is possible, nothing is forbidden, and no blame can be attached, Joe's love for Bianca stayed pure.

At first, Joe thought the dreams were the result of Bianca's sixteen hour days. A street gang calling themselves The Dark Lords had started up in the city. Somehow they had learned a little magic and managed to open a portal to another world. Some things came through. Bianca worked round the clock to shut down the gang, find the creatures, and close the portal behind them.

Lonely nights without the woman I love. No wonder I'm having these dreams. That was what Joe thought. But then Bianca closed the case and took a few days off. Joe closed the store and the two made up for lost time.

It is said that the only thing deeper than the sleep of the just is the sleep of the just after, but even then the dreams came. As Joe fell asleep in the afterglow of romance, the woman appeared, silently promising to make all that Joe had just experienced seem like a nun's kiss.

In his dream, Joe declined with a smile and as the woman insisted, he drew on the power of his love for Bianca and ordered her gone. She opened her mouth as if to say something but then vanished.

Joe awoke. *That should not have happened*, he thought. Not after what Bianca and I just did. He began to consider that maybe there was a different reason for the dreams, one not connected with his longing for his absent love.

Then Bianca stirred and, half asleep, pulled him close to her. As Joe drifted off in his wife's embrace, thoughts of the woman in red faded away.

*

I must be losing my touch, Bambi thought as she was unceremoniously ejected from the dream plane and back into Hell. First Negral rejects my advances and now this, this… human seems immune to my charms. The succubus called for one of her souls in bondage to bring her a mirror.

Too much? she wondered as she inspected her more than ample bosom. *Or maybe not enough?* No, there were some physical laws even Hell must obey and if Bambi added too much to her upper deck not even her powers could keep her from toppling over.

I could try the subtle approach; cover up what I want them to look at. A male frequently wants what he can't have, or see. Subtle rarely worked in Hell, but maybe on Earth?

After an hour or more of admiring her sinful form (vanity being just the least of her sins) Bambi's not inconsiderable ego finally came to the rescue. She understood part of why Negral refused her charms; it was a matter of his retaining power over her. And there just had to be something wrong with that mortal. Why else would he turn down a dream romp?

In need of reassurance, Bambi considered inviting several of the demons who were eternally camped outside her door in for an hours-long session. *No*, she finally decided, *that wouldn't solve the problem at hand, however good it might make me feel.* She then realized that it probably wouldn't make her feel good at all. She was skilled at what she did, and there was a certain cold satisfaction in corrupting souls and draining the damned of their energies. But good was something she hadn't felt in a long time. A very long time. That wasn't part of the job description.

What was part of the job was her somehow getting to Earth and finding help. And it looked like the only way to do that was a personal appearance. She needed a portal. Finding one might be difficult, but convincing its keeper to let her use it would be easy. They'd haggle and come to an agreement; the price a foregone conclusion, one she had paid a million times before. It was what she did. It was what she was damned to do.

*

Sergeant Bianca Jones had come to work in a good mood, the result of a long weekend alone with her husband. And it wasn't just the quality time they had spent in bed. To Bianca, every minute with Joe was quality time. He was the one bright spot in her otherwise dismal world, the one truly good thing in her life.

She worried about him, worried that he might become too involved in her campaign against the inhuman creatures that sometimes threatened the city. The books that Morgan had left him, there was dark knowledge in them. Even reading some of the texts could put one's soul in jeopardy.

But Joe's was a pure soul, so far untainted by any of the compromises one must sometimes make when fighting so evil an enemy. If anyone should have charge over such a collection of dangerous lore, she could think of no one better suited than her husband. And every day she prayed that it would remain so.

Putting thoughts of Joe to the back of her mind, Bianca turned to the case folders on her desk. The Special Investigation Unit did more than fight monsters. It had other, more mundane tasks as well. Jobs that other police units could not or would not handle.

As she reviewed reports, Bianca expected her good mood to fade. It usually did. Today however …

A city councilman had been held up. Special Investigations was being asked to take over because the robbery had taken place in the adults-only section of a local video store.

Surveillance cameras placed discreetly in known drug locations had captured two major transactions, the participants' faces clearly visible for once.

A rumored haunting of an old school turned out to be nothing more than cats and rats playing out their eternal game.

And the Department of Mystical Affairs had agreed to take custody of the Dark Lords and try to send back what they had summoned.

All good news. Maybe, Bianca thought, there was something to Baltimore being a charmed city. Not that she would even have known about Hell's "hands off" policy regarding her city as a result of Bianca three times defeating the Devil if it wasn't for Negral. She wondered if she did it a fourth time, did she get more fabulous prizes? Probably be a toaster oven.

Of course, that was assuming she believed Hell's Chief of police. After the Huntingdon case, she would have said yes, but after the fiasco with his disciple Bianca wasn't so sure. It reminded her too much of her first victory over the Devil. It came with a price – half the city burned down, the police department decimated, Morgan and thousands of others dead.

Whatever peace there is, we earned.

But we almost lost even that.

But it taught me an important lesson, Bianca reflected. I was getting too cocky, too sure of myself. Thought I could handle anything. After all, what was a minor deity to someone who had beaten the Devil?

That deity had me and my men at his mercy. That "minor god" could have killed us all. Negral could have burned down the *entire* city.

But he didn't, Bianca reminded herself. And we survived to fight another day, more through luck than skill, but we survived and that's what matters.

Next time I'll be better prepared. But in the back of her mind was the ever constant thought that sooner or later the next time would be the last time.

Bianca shook her head, chasing away the memories, refusing to let thoughts of what was and what might be ruin her good mood.

Then her cell phone rang.

It was Joe.

"Bianca. I hate to bother you at work but I need to tell you about some dreams I've had."

He went to describe his nighttime visitor, not in as much detail as he could have, but enough that Bianca felt her good mood start to fade.

Memories of an old demon surfaced, one she had taken into herself to save some foolish young girls. It was a monster who haunted them in their dreams, who satisfied desires they had just started having. She had left the creature on the plains of Hell, a gift for Satan in exchange for yet another innocent soul.

Incubus, succubus – two sides of the same coin. Could it have come back, Bianca wondered. Thank God Joe was strong.

"Bianca, are you there?"

"Yeah, Joe, still here. Why tell me about this now? Why not wait until tonight? You planning a long nap this afternoon?"

"Because my dream just appeared in the shop, and she's asking for you."

There went the good mood.

"Are you okay?" Bianca asked, fighting off panic. If anything happened to Joe, the walls of Hell would not be high enough to keep her hands from Satan's throat. "I can get units there in minutes."

"I'm fine, just … just hurry, that's all."

There was a strange catch in Joe's voice, one Bianca remembered from high school. Her husband sounded very much like a teenaged boy suddenly confronted by his first sexy woman.

There was no time to lose, she decided.

It's a fifteen-minute drive from Police Headquarters to the Fells Point alley where Morgan's Books was located. Bianca got there in ten. Walking through the open door and locking it behind her, she went straight to the back.

Bianca had seen many strange sights in her police career, both earthly and supernatural. She had talked to angels and threatened faeries. She had both saved and destroyed vampires. She had fought monsters both demonic and manmade. She was not, however, prepared for Bambi.

The woman with Joe was dressed in a red, no, a scarlet leather catsuit that covered her from neck to feet but was so tight that every part of her magnificent body was on display. Her proportions were just shy of being ludicrous and she could have been the model on which every comic book heroine seemed to be based.

But more than that, she radiated lust. Even Bianca, who had never in her life felt sexually attracted to her own sex, felt a rush of desire for this woman. She was a fantasy, she was a wet dream, she was sex itself come to life.

And Joe had resisted her. It made Bianca love him all the more. Her husband was seated behind his desk. He looked uncomfortable but, nevertheless, in control, albeit hiding his pelvis.

"Bianca," he said in a voice that indicated that he was very glad to see her, "This is Bambi. Bambi, my wife Bianca Jones."

Bianca felt herself being studied by the temptress from Hell. She had no illusions of how she compared. Short where Bambi was tall, slender where Bambi had curves, small breasted while Bambi had boobs to spare. Bianca patiently stood inspection while waiting to hear what the visitor wanted.

Bambi finally finished checking Bianca out. She turned to Joe, then back to Bianca. "He turned me down, for you?" she asked incredulously. "What do you have that's so special?"

"The love of a good man," Bianca said calmly and thought she saw a brief pain of regret pass over the demoness's face. "Now what do you want?"

Bianca's gun was loose in its holster. In her mind were words of power that she had had Joe look up after her last encounter with Negral. Words to bind demons, words to stop spells, words that might kill a god if one were willing to pay the price. Bianca thought herself ready for anything, and still what Bambi said surprised her.

*

Waking didn't do anything to chase away the darkness. Worse, I felt like I was pinned underneath the earth because I couldn't move, but there wasn't the weight that comes with being buried. And I could still breathe and move my rib cage then. I couldn't manage that now no matter how hard I tried. I guess this is was it was like to be dead. I figured oblivion would just be a big nothingness where I wouldn't be aware of who I was or even that I had been. This was worse. To spend eternity alert and conscious, yet alone, unable to see or move. It was worse than any of the punishments that Nick or the keepers of the damned had yet devised.

Or was it? Maybe this was all Nick's doing. My death certainly voided our contract and now he was paying me back for any of my perceived sins against him.

Then my head started to throb. It got worse. Not even creation at its cruelest would let me to hurt this much and not be alive. I cursed myself for a fool to have allowed someone to get the drop on me. Seems like the boss wasn't the only one to suffer from too much pride. I'd gotten sloppy and careless and was paying the price.

But sloppy and careless also described my captor. He or she should have killed me, assuming he could have. Maybe he tried and this was the best he could do. A big mistake, or at least it would be when I got out.

Being the Devil's Chief of police was the equivalent of a Lord of the Pit which meant there was a certain amount of power I could draw from, a reservoir of damned souls whose energies I could tap as needed. As a former god of sun and fire, the flames of Hell added to my strength.

Reaching out, I sought for the power. Nothing happened. I tried again with the same result. A third failure got me thinking that I was in more trouble than I first thought. If the Devil fired me, it would explain why I couldn't tap Hell's power, but nothing should have been able to stop me from tapping Thurman in his heaven of forever playing with hellfire.

Not good. In Hell, needing help is a major failing. It puts you in someone's, or some thing's debt, and paying off that debt is an obligation that is not good to shirk. It makes you careful about whom you ask to lend a hand.

I thought of Rachel. I could do what I wanted with my secretary's soul. Of course, there was Thurman Reeves, my true disciple. And there was Bambi, whose fate it was to always look out for my best interest. I had about one hundred damned souls working as cops. To none of these would I be in debt. They were mine to command.

My mind called out to each one of them – to find me, to save me, to get me out of wherever I was. For all I knew, mine was a voice in the wilderness. Maybe one of them heard me, maybe not. There was no reply, no sense of contact. I was blind, possibly deaf, and unable to move. I was going to have to free myself.

I'd been calling myself a detective. Now was the time to prove it. But this time I didn't need to be Spade or Marlowe. They were men of action, pounding pavements and skulls until they got the needed answers. No, this called for the skills of the Old Man in the Corner, Nero Wolfe, or Auguste Dupin. I was in a sealed room and I had to think myself free.

Here goes everything.

*

"Negral's missing,"

For a demon who had seen everything and done more than that, Bambi was unprepared for the reaction from Bianca and Joe.

"So?" Bianca asked calmly. Joe just shrugged.

"You don't care?"

"Why should I?" the detective replied. "It's Hell's business, not mine."

"I thought you were friends, allies. You two were almost partners."

Bianca nodded. "Once maybe, but that was before he blinded my fellow officers, shot down a helicopter, and threatened to burn down my city. And how do you know so much about Negral and me?"

Bambi paused, for once at a loss for words. Finally, "It's complicated. I'm ... bound to Negral in a way that, like it or not, forces me to always act in his best interest. There is a bond between us. I don't always know where he is but when he left Hell, somehow I felt it. And then I heard his voice in my mind, calling me. It was faint and almost not there, but it was him, then he was gone. I checked with his secretary. She's read his reports and knew about you. There are others in the Pit in Negral's debt. None of them have seen him. He's not in Hell. If he were, I would know by now."

"Maybe he's dead," Joe suggested. "As I understand it, he's in Hell voluntarily. He didn't die to get there, so maybe he can be killed."

"I've recently had that same thought," Bianca added, not without some malice.

"No." Bambi shook her head. "If Negral were dead, I'd be free of the geis he's placed upon me and I'd feel no need to help him. Yet here I am."

"So he's not in Hell and he's not dead. What makes you think he's on Earth? Why not some other underworld or realm? And if Earth, why this city?"

Joe spoke before Bambi. "Because this is the one place the devil can't look for him. Because he's been here twice. And the last time he was summoned by not one, but two people who believed in him. That's practically an open door to whoever, or whatever, was moving him."

Bambi cast an accusing eye on Bianca. "You're linked to him as well, by virtue of your summoning. Whatever your reason, you called him to Earth. It was your bond with him that saved your life and those of your men. He did you no permanent harm, but he did take a monster from your midst even after you betrayed him. At great personal cost. You owe him."

Bianca stared deep into the eyes of Hell's temptress. She saw there lust and passion, a passion that was now beyond the creature's nature, one now devoted to finding her master. But Bianca still was not willing to help.

"I do not acknowledge the debt."

Bianca was about to tell Joe to look through his books and banish the demoness when Joe spoke up.

"What if he's here?" Before his wife could interrupt, he went on. "If Negral was brought into the city, it's in our interests to find him before someone else does, or before whoever's behind his disappearance can continue his plan. What if the Devil comes looking for his detective? And if Negral is here deliberately, we'd better find out what he's up to."

The two women, human and otherwise, calmed down and backed off. Seeing the logic in Joe's argument, Bianca's anger faded. Bambi's desire to serve Negral also abated, leaving behind only – desire, something both Joe and Bianca felt strongly. Bambi smiled and turned up the lust and watched as Joe's and Bianca's knees almost buckled and sweat soaked their skin. They had to force themselves not to rush the other and tear off every bit of clothing separating them.

Struggling for control, Bianca said, "Go back to Hell, Bambi. See if there's anything more you can find out. Joe and I will handle things from here."

Bambi smiled as she prepared to summon the portal that would take her back to the Pit. "Yes, I'm sure you'll both handle … things.

Consider this special passion a gift."

The succubus disappeared.

Bianca and Joe ran into each other's arms, the force almost knocking them to the ground. Their lips and tongues were all over each other as flailing hands tore clothes, without regard for buttons, zipper, or seams.

"We should go home," Joe half suggested, his voice trembling with desire.

"We'd never make it," Bianca countered.

She was right. It was one in the morning before the pair left the store. When they did, Joe had a smile on his face and Bianca's good mood was back. Both limped and much of their clothes had to be fastened back together with the store's stapler. And hundreds of books were scattered and a table and three bookshelves were reduced to little more than firewood.

*

I spent what felt like an eternity calling upon my power, but it avoided me like a bad gambler trying to steer clear of his bookie. More times than I cared to count I tried to call on those in my debt and failed more miserably than the coup against heaven. I couldn't feel anything – no acknowledgment, no contact.

I had other options. I could call on Nick, but there would be a price, the cost of which I would be in no position to negotiate. No, I wouldn't go that route. Without the leeway my contract gave me, the Pit would become Hell in more than name for me.

I raked my brain for other options. Bianca Jones crossed my mind. The Baltimore detective had summoned me by offering me sacrifice. It bound her to me and gave me some control over her. I thus far had chosen not to exercise that control. The dame had spunk enough to not only take on Nick but try and get me away from him. I admired the blazes out of that, so I let her slide. That and the fact she would have fought me tooth and nail, which could have alerted Nick despite the charm on Baltimore. If I was still in the Pit, calling out to Jones would bring Nick to me, more furious than I'd want to deal with. And once the Devil knew I had control over one of his most hated foes and had not destroyed her as a gift to him, Hell would not be big enough to contain his fury. Jones and I would both pay the price. And I had pissed her off pretty good when I took down her people, so it's possible she was behind this situation. Best reserve that option for a last desperate measure.

I was stuck here for the foreseeable future. Sadly, I had plenty of time, so I tried a different tactic. Who in Hell or otherwise did this to me? If I figured that out, it might give me a clue on how or where I was and how to escape.

The trouble was, being the Chief of Hell's Secret Police meant that there was a near infinite number of creatures – human, demonic, and otherwise – who hated me. The good news was that most did not have the power, guts, or opportunity to do me any harm. There was no shortage of suspects though.

The spigh was the first. Spighs didn't survive in the Devil's employ long without being tough and devious. Last time I saw him, the spigh was swearing vengeance. Can't blame him since I left him in the not so tender care of a pissed off demon lord in a pink tutu known as the Lord of the Dance. I didn't stick around for the gory details, but word was Balchain used the spigh as his personal dance mat and had Macarenad him into demon paste, then taken what remained and made it into a new pair of spiked ballet shoes. Being the Pit, the spigh wouldn't die, instead he'd suffer every step the Lord of the Dance made. Assuming Balchain changed shoes, it would have been a long and painful recovery but not out of the realm of possibility that the spigh had escaped the eternal dance and was looking for payback. He'd certainly have the skills. Even the least spigh was adept at sneakiness and weaponry. But I couldn't understand how he could have gotten the drop on me. Not near the fire pits. Spighs are invisible at will, but so close to fire I would have felt the movement through the heat. I should have sensed something, even if I was distracted by the sight of Skinless's body.

Maybe it was someone who looked like the spigh. There was a shape-shifting masque demon who had it out for me just as bad. I screwed up his plans with a corrupt New York City cop. I was taking in a Bogie double feature on Earth and butted into the cop's business, mainly because he interrupted the movie. By the time things ran their course, the cop was dead and the masque was a paperweight on Nick's desk. Again, nothing fatal for a demon but his recovery would be worse than the spigh's. Certainly a motive for vengeance if I ever heard one.

The trouble was that knocking me out and imprisoning me wherever seemed too subtle for either of these. Knifing me in the back was more the spigh's style and the masque would have just beaten me down where he found me. They may not have stopped to think that maybe, unlike them, I couldn't be killed. Truthfully, I don't think either would have stopped to think.

The one who hired the spigh in the first place would have. That would be Bambi. Despite being a first-class seductress and ultimate dream whore, she had managed to hold on to her virginity by the simple act of removing it from her body and hiding it somewhere in Hell. When it disappeared she asked me to find it, then turned around and tried to betray me. She hired the spigh and half of horny Hell to take me out before I could use her so-called virtue against her. Like all plans in Hell, things for her went awry and she ended bound to my service.

One of my first orders to her was to "always look out for my best interests." It could be that she was clever enough to have let the spigh know where I was then convince herself that my best interests lay in being captured but not killed. Hiding me from the spigh's revenge would continue that thought. Maybe that's why I hadn't heard from her. Or it could just be the damn throbbing in my head.

And there was the demon Beltizon who had made some improper deals on Earth. I had to bring him back and deal with the magí Hex to do it. Actually, there's no love lost between me and Hex, but this wasn't his style. Hex would at least give me the courtesy of knowing why he was doing this. He had set up a spell that lets him be summoned by anyone who said his full taken name three times. If I could manage to speak, I could call on him. He had a sense of honor and might free me, but I'd owe him big time and technically, I already owed him a favor. And Nick would be furious at me for going to one of his sworn enemies for help. Hex was an even bigger pain in Nick's ass than Bianca and far more dangerous. Put that in the absolute last option category although if it was Beltizon, I might not owe Hex at all. He might feel like he owed me. The demon had possessed an infant's corpse and started eating the neighbors. Hex took that personally. Of course, he might also decide I'm better off where I am.

Beltizon had used a new and forbidden kind of magic called darken. The mook wound up in a soul cage to be questioned by Nick's inquisitors about his knowledge of the banned lore. Could be he worked a deal, what he knew for his freedom. Could be he used darken on me which would explain why my own powers weren't working. If so, I was truly screwed. I knew some darken magic myself, but only enough to know that I didn't have the power to break whatever spell was binding me. Besides I had already tried.

And that was just the beginning. Too many suspects or not enough. I reviewed things again and again, looking at motives, searching for clues, trying to place a who to the what. I was missing something, something I'd find if only the inside of my head didn't pulse with the rhythm of a drunken drummer playing a solo with mismatched sticks.

*

After leaving the lust-struck pair in the bookstore, Bambi returned to the Pit. The encounter with the two humans had left her feeling strangely odd. She was pleased that she had managed to get help in the search for her master, but there was more than that. Just as she had left them imbued with the lust that was as natural to her as breathing, so too had their feeling passed on to her. There was no Love in Hell. It was forbidden by the very nature of the place. It had been an eternity since Bambi had felt it in its pure form, not since before the Fall. To have stood so close to it, to have been refreshed by it, at first it brought a small spark of light to her darkened soul. But that light only served as a reminder of all that she had lost when she joined the great rebellion. The remembrance extinguished the tiny ember inside her. As the ashes inside Bambi cooled, she knew that however bad the memory of what had been left her feeling, she'd trade a month in the fire pits to feel the spark again.

But while wishing for what could not be was a full-time

occupation in Hell, it wasn't getting Negral found. And with the compulsion he had placed on her still in effect, she had no choice but to set aside her main occupation of seducing susceptible souls until the Chief was back in his office.

Traveling the demonic byways, paying for her passage in the only coin she had, Bambi's quest led her from circle to circle. The succubus could not be direct; too many questions about Negral's whereabouts would only lead to word getting back to the Satan. And the King of Hell finding out that his head of security was missing was clearly not in the Chief's "best interests." And so she traveled downward, tricking those she could, seducing those she must, pretending to be on the run from Hell's Law. Hoping thereby to run across someone who had seen Negral pass, or who might let on that he was no longer a problem.

That's what she sought – a hint, a word, any clue at all. She would have done her enforced duty, which might enable her to return to the outer world and the bookstore, where the warming spark might be found again.

*

Bianca and Joe both slept late. When they awoke she called into her office to let her boss know that that something of a supernatural nature had arisen and that she would be working out of the bookshop for a few days. She also alerted her team to be on standby in case they were needed.

"Are you sure that's wise?" Joe asked her. "Negral's got to be on the QRT's 'shoot on sight' list."

"Depending on circumstances, he might still be on mine, Joe. But let's find him first, then we can call in Greggs and his Quick Response guys."

"So where do we start looking?"

Bianca indicated the shelves in the back room. "I'll work the phone; you talk to your books."

"No luck," she said, hanging up the phone a few hours later. "I tried The London Agency, Father Lawrence of the Holy Office, The DMA – no trouble anywhere. At least not from down below. And no sign of Negral, nobody's seen or heard from him, not even the gang at Bulfinche's Pub. How did you do?"

"Working on the assumption that Negral is being held against his will then whoever's got him must allow for his power over fire and sunlight."

"What's the word for ice magic?"

"Glacimancy, and I checked the books. Negral shouldn't have had any trouble with that. Fire melts ice, remember? Same goes for ice demons."

"What if he's not on Earth? Hell's not the only underworld."

"There's Zamhareer. It's a level of the Islamic Hell, said to be a world of extreme cold – blizzards, ice, snow, and all that goes with it. Drop Negral someplace like that and he'd use up his powers fast."

Bianca shook her head. "If that's the case, he's on his own."

"You could try another summoning," Joe offered.

"I don't think so," Bianca answered a little too harshly. "According to Negral, the last one left me bound to him as some kind of supplicant. If that's true I don't want to add to the obligation."

"So where does that leave us?"

Bianca sighed and turned to her husband. "Where would you hide a god?"

"A god like Negral? Someplace cold and dark where magic doesn't work."

"So what counteracts magic?"

As soon as Bianca asked the question they had the answer, or at least the start of one.

"Science," they both said as one.

After that it was a matter of research and police work.

*

Some detective you turned out to be said the voice in my head. Sadly the self-condemnation was louder than the boom, boom in my skull. Things had to be bad when I was not only conversing with myself but giving me an attitude. The near constant pulses of pain were still beating inside my head like a conga line of garganti demons. To be truthful, not all of it was pain. More than a lot was frustration. This was worse than being captured in light form. At least then I could move. Every scenario I ran in my head had two results, one that made the suspect look guilty as original sin and a second which made the theory look like utter nonsense. I clung to the idea that if I could just figure out the where and the how I'd have the who. Or if I figured the who, I'd get one or both of the other two. With that knowledge, I could free myself. That and three fifty would get me a cup of joe. Although in part of the Pit, there is a demon with a warped sense of humor that puts in for every soul named Joe that comes in the Pit. This java demon actually brewed the joes into his version of coffee. One of the reasons I only drink the imported java. It's not a fun feeling hearing a cup of coffee scream as it works its way through your digestive tract. On the plus side, I figured the java demon was safe to keep off my short list of suspects.

Sad part was, I'd gladly drink a gallon of java demon joe just to know where I was. The loop of scenarios kept playing in my mind, making me loopy. I had to face facts. I might be well and truly damned to spend eternity alert, but unable to move, not capable to feel, powerless to draw on the slightest bit of fire or sunlight. I needed help but had no idea how to summon it. Oblivion was starting to look good. It was time for my last resorts. Hex or the lady cop?

I chose Detective Jones and damn the consequences.

*

"So he might be in some kind of cryogenics chamber?" Bianca asked after the research was done.

"Cryonics," Joe corrected. "Freezing the dead in hopes of one day bringing them back."

"Any place in Baltimore do that?"

Joe shook his head. "There aren't that many places in the country that do it. And none around here."

"How many deceased optimists are there on ice?'

"Counting the ones who only had their heads frozen, a few hundred."

"In that case, a still living Sumerian god might stand out. We should start checking."

As Bianca turned to start working the phones again, Joe stopped her.

"In my research, I found something else. It's called cryotherapy. Some doctors use it as a treatment for things like muscle pain, fibromyalgia, sports injuries, even rheumatism. They've found that very short-term exposure to the extreme cold of a cryochamber can have a long-lasting analgesic effect. It's mostly a European treatment. Any recent imports of these cryochambers into the U.S. should be easy to ..." Joe trailed off as Bianca slumped back into her seat.

"So that's it then." There was an odd tone in her voice. "We trace a shipment to Baltimore, find out where it was delivered, get a warrant, and rescue a god. End of story."

"You don't seem very enthused."

"I'm not, Joe. I'm not sure it's the right thing to do. I still remember the last time. What was I thinking? Or was I thinking? Summon a god, then give him orders. What did it get me? One royally pissed off being with enough power to destroy all that I'm sworn to protect. And now I'm supposed to free this guy, set him loose in my city – again? What if we revive him and he wakes up in a bad mood?"

"The last time he was pissed at you for treating him like a suspect and not a cop. He made his point, then put things right. You may have cause to be mad at him, but I think you're also mad at yourself for underestimating him."

"A mistake I'm not going to make again. When we do find Negral, unless I have a way to stop him or bind him, he stays right where he is. I'll call the DMA and give him to them."

"It's risky, but there might be another way." At Bianca's questioning glance Joe went on. "Remember I mentioned the Islamic hell?"

"Zamzar or something."

"Zamhareer. In my research into Islamic beliefs I read about the djinn."

"Genies? As in "I Dream of ..."

"Yes. According to some beliefs, the djinn are creatures made of fire, just as humans were made from the earth."

"So?"

"So a creature of fire, trapped in a container, can be bound into service by one who knows how."

"Bound for how long?"

"Until you release him."

Bianca thought for a moment, then, "How is it done?"

*

Negral.

The voice inside my head was barely there. A whisper if it was that loud. But whose was it? My own probably. I had phased out for a while, no telling how long, and this was no doubt my subconscious's way of bringing me back.

Damn it.

It wasn't that I had felt better sinking into oblivion; it was that I had felt nothing. Which was far better than being awake for an eternal burial.

Negral.

Again I heard my name, this time while more or less alert. Could I have gotten through? Could someone be calling me? Was it Jones? Or maybe it was just that my name was being mentioned so much that my awareness of it was finally sinking in? My thought process must be somehow slowed down.

And why would that be? Drugs would do it. Would drugs block my powers as well? It slowly came to me. My control of heat and fire could be affected by … ice and cold and dark.

It was a start.

Three cryochambers had been shipped to Baltimore. One was delivered to University Shock Trauma. Another was shipped to the City of Hope Sports Medicine Department. The third was sent to a warehouse in Southwest Baltimore.

"I think we found Negral," Bianca said calmly.

"Unless St. Agnes has opened an offsite treatment center, you may be right."

The warehouse was located on DeSoto Road, not far from where

Bianca had once shot and killed two people and seriously wounded a third while avenging an attack on Joe. Records failed to turn up a connection to St. Agnes or any other medical facility while surveillance showed three shifts of four men each rotating in and out of the building.

"Do we know them?" Bianca asked Lieutenant Tavon Greggs of the BPD's Quick Response Team.

"Got 'em all ID'd if that's what you're asking. Everyone with a record. All have done time. All their time. Nobody's wanted for anything and none are on parole. What's in the warehouse, Bianca?"

She didn't want to tell him, didn't want Greggs to know that the being who had blinded him and his men was in that building. She especially didn't want to tell him that it was a rescue mission, that she hoped to save that same being.

But she knew she had no choice. Greggs and his men could not do their best job without all the information.

"An old friend. Make sure everyone has welder's goggles."

She felt Greggs tense up. His entire demeanor darkened.

"We going in hot or are we just going to blow the place up. Either way works for me."

"We go in quiet," Bianca said firmly. "Detain the men inside. Anyone resists, that's on them. I'll deal with Negral."

"If you can." Greggs was clearly not happy with his orders. "Let's just light up the place from outside with that special ammo you got us, then go in and mop up. Let's not give the bastard the break we gave him last time."

"Tavon, part of me agrees with you. But regardless of jurisdiction, Chief Negral is one of us and he's being held prisoner." Bianca filled the lieutenant in on what was happening. "The last time, well, he may have humiliated us but in the end … you know what the traffic boys say, 'no damage, no accident.' Whatever we think of him, he's a cop who needs back-up."

"Just be sure you've got a plan B, in case he doesn't see it that way."

"I've got that covered," Bianca assured the man, reviewing in her mind all she had to do to turn what had once been an ally and possible friend into an unwilling slave.

*

At dawn the next day, Bianca met Greggs and his QRT team on the parking of a high school near the warehouse.

"Everybody know what to do?" Greggs asked his team. "No shooting unless they start it. Anything comes at you that don't look human, light it up. Just give Sergeant Jones the time to do what she has to do."

Greggs looked at his men, then at Bianca. "Ready, Sergeant?"

Am I? Bianca asked herself. In her mind she went over it again. Secure the warehouse. Find Negral. Follow the ritual Joe had taught her, the ritual that would turn the Hell's Detective into a genie. Only then would she free him, with her first command being that he do no harm to her and all who she loved or had sworn to protect. Her second order would be for Negral to release her from the bondage imposed upon her by her sacrifice to him. The third would be to go back to Hell and not return to Baltimore unless summoned.

Negral would have no choice but to obey. But he'd depart hating her. Not a problem, what was one more enemy in Hell, especially one forbidden to act against her. And there was no chance he'd tell Satan that he was no longer a free agent. And if the time ever came when the city's charm ran out, when the Devil was once again free to attack Baltimore, Negral would be there, a viper in his midst. Bianca could then summon him and pit him against his boss.

It seemed to be a perfect plan. *Why then*, she wondered, *doesn't it feel that way?*

Because it's not, another part of her replied. *Because whatever your reasons, however you justify it, what you plan to do to Negral is not only dangerous but just plain wrong.*

Bianca shook the nagging voice away. Right or wrong had no place here. She had to protect her city, whatever the cost.

"Ready, Lieutenant."

The team moved out.

Entry went smoothly. The warehouse was small and had only two entrances. With the rear guarded, Greggs and his team made entry through the front, flashbangs first, followed by shouts of

"Police."

The five men inside were suitably cowed. Only one started to draw on the officers but when several automatic rifles turned in his direction he thought better of it and carefully placed his pistol on the floor.

With the scene secure, Bianca was free to act.

In a corner she found what looked like a large upright freezer. The cryochamber. Behind its frosted glass door she could just make out a human-like shape.

The words that would bind him formed in her mind. She thought to say them, but looking at Negral's frozen body her own words came back to her.

"He's a cop who needs back-up."

Suddenly right and wrong mattered and she knew what she had to do, whatever the cost.

"Sergeant Jones!"

Bianca turned towards Gregg's voice, followed the urgency to where he and his men were holding the prisoners.

"Yes, Lieutenant?"

"Our surveillance? Three shifts of four men each, remember?" At Bianca's nod, Greggs continued, "I count five men, and one of them is getting bigger and uglier."

He was right. One of the men was changing, revealing himself as the demon he truly was.

Four shotguns came up, each loaded with flechette rounds specially blessed by Father Lawrence of the Holy Office, guaranteed to work against all things unholy. Bianca had her own weapons. She pulled out a cross and called on her newly strengthened belief in all that was right.

"Hold!" she commanded.

Sensing what the guns could do to him and constrained by a Power that was older than he, the demon froze.

"You are making a mistake," the creature said in a gravelly voice.

"I've made them before," Bianca replied calmly. Then to the prisoners, she said, "You men aren't wanted for anything. I suggest you leave now."

Unnerved by the sudden transformation of one of their own into a thing of nightmare, the four tried to follow Bianca's suggestion. But while it was clear that they wanted to leave, they somehow could not. Bianca addressed the demon.

"Free them."

"I cannot," he replied, visibly struggling against the hold Bianca's belief had on him and well aware of the weapons trained on him. "Like me, they are bound to stand guard as my Master ordered."

"That's too damned bad." To the men, Bianca said, "I hope you got a good price for your souls, boys, because the bill's about to come due."

"I don't think so, human. You can't hold me forever. Eventually, your concentration will lapse, or your arm will get tired and whatever's in those guns won't stop me from tearing your head off."

Bianca didn't need forever. Just as Greggs had called her name she had switched the cryochamber off. A drop in the room's temperature told her it was time.

"Get out!" she yelled to Greggs and his men. "Now!"

At Bianca's shout, the Quick Response Team made a hurried but orderly withdraw. Bianca was the last to leave, keeping her cross on the demon until she was safely out of the building.

"What's happening?" Greggs asked. "Why did we leave?"

Bianca shook her head. "Those poor, dumb bastards," was all she said. Inside the warehouse, the screaming started.

*

I was deep into feeling nothing but sorry for myself when an intense pain like I'd never before felt hit me everywhere, as if someone were sticking pins in every part of my body at once. It wasn't until I started shivering that I realized that I was cold – no, I was freezing.

Honestly, it was a guess. I'd never really been cold before. Sun and fire god and all that. I didn't like it one bit.

I can pull heat from my environment, so I did it to rid myself of this damnable cold. As warmth trickled in, my vision came into focus. I was in a box or coffin with a window. Who puts a window in a coffin? Paranoid vampyre? No, not a coffin but not far off. I was standing. I pushed my hand against the glass to break it when the lid moved. I pushed and it opened an inch. Best to be quiet. Odds are someone would be waiting for me on the outside and I doubted they were going to invite me to a barbeque. With luck, I'd invite them.

The outside air was warmer still and I sucked it in. I was strong enough to move but still wasn't in fighting shape. To blazes with it. I pushed the lid the rest of the way open.

I stepped out and managed not to stumble. A voice I thought I recognized yelled, "Get out! Now!"

I smiled. At least someone knew that what was done to me was a very bad idea, at least now that I was free and itching for some payback.

I was in some sort of warehouse. It was only about 74 degrees Fahrenheit. Not exactly tropical, but a damn bit warmer than the box. As I absorbed the heat, the temperature in the room dropped to below freezing.

With each degree my body temperature rose, so did my spirits and my strength. I caught a scent of brimstone. Not unexpected, considering how I was abducted, but mild. I wasn't in the Pit. I looked around and found not everyone had heeded the wise advice to exit.

Whoever had imprisoned me had taken no chances. He, she, or it had stripped me bare, leaving me as naked as any of the damned in Hell. But I was no common Pit-dweller. I was a god and a being of fire. I was also one pissed-off detective looking for vengeance.

I spotted the masque demon a moment before he saw me. I didn't have enough heat back to fire up a demon. Too bad for the quartet of goons behind the masque. From the looks, the lot was my guard detail. Too bad for them. I reached out and sucked the heat from them, down to their bones. After that, I had enough to attack the demon.

The head of the detail wasn't the same one I had dealt with in New York. This one was slow, taking too long to shift into Balchain, thinking the sight of a Lord of Hell would stay my wraith. Fat chance. As I fried Masky, the men with him screamed and shivered, parts of them breaking off frozen as they hit the floor.

Masky reverted back to his natural form and I started to suck the heat out of him. He ran, but one of the men reached out with his left hand and tripping him. I caught Masky easy enough.

"You obviously aren't bright enough to pull this off. Who hired you?" I screamed, burning his hands off right down to the wrists.

"Stop, please. I'll tell you. It was…"

Masky suddenly burst into ash. I hadn't hit him with enough heat. Whoever did this used some spell to make sure he turned to ash before he told me anything. It'd take months or more for the ashes to regenerate enough for me to get my answers.

But he wasn't the only witness left. One of the human mooks was still alive. He was standing behind the others, so he still had some heat left in him. He was the one who had tripped Masky.

I walked over and squatted down next to him. He tried to crawl, but all he could manage to move was his left arm and his neck.

"Not exactly a stunning getaway," I said.

"I'm dying, aren't I?" he said.

"Yep," I said.

"I thought it would hurt more," he said.

"The cold numbs you." I wasn't a total bastard, maybe five-eighths. Lefty had a pack of cigarettes in his pocket. I took one out and put it between his lips. His eyes went wide when my fingertip burst into flame to light the end. I made a basic protective ward from fire around the two of us. Wouldn't stop the ash spell, but it would slow it down for a while. "You are going to tell me what I want to know. What you have to endure before that happens is up to you."

"Look, I didn't want to do this, honest. Got caught doing a burglary. It would have been my third strike you know. Life with no parole, so I signed the paper. I thought it was a joke. Who'd buy my soul, you know?"

"Who was it?"

"A cop. A dead cop." Lefty looked down at his feet which had just turned to ash. He wasn't numb enough not to feel that. He screamed. "Make it stop."

"Can't."

"Oh God."

"Should have thought of that sooner," I said.

"Yeah, I guess I shoulda." The ashing spell had spread to his knees and there was more screaming. "Guy said he wanted your job. You're going to get him, ain't you?"

"Oh yeah."

"Good. Give him one for me. Look, I ain't got the right to ask you, but I need a favor."

"You got balls, I'll give you that. Before I answer, why'd you trip the masque?"

"It wasn't right what they did to you or me. Figured it was my last chance to make things right."

"Probably was."

"I got a little money stashed away." Lefty told me where. "I was stealing to support my kid and my baby's mamma. Nobody would hire me. I ain't proud of it and I knew it wasn't right, but I did what I had to do. I need you to get that money to my family, please? Swear you will."

I nodded. "They'll get it."

"Thanks. Now I can die at peace." The ashing made it up his thighs and this scream was the worst so far. "Maybe not so much."

"I can end the pain. At least here," I said.

The ash was up to his hips and on its way to a very personal area. "Do it."

"Okay."

I snapped Lefty's neck so he didn't feel the part that helped make his kid turn to ash. I opened the circle and the rest of him followed.

I considered leaving Masky's ashes as a treat for the DMA to play with. They'd have to watch over it until it regenerated. On Earth, it takes hours or centuries. Then I got a better idea. I used my fire to gather all of him up.

My immediate problem solved, I turned my attention to other matters, like finding out where I was and how long I'd been gone. Then the storeroom door opened and she walked in.

Detective Bianca Jones, a five-foot badass. Lefty had said a cop did this, a dead cop. Bianca looked like she was still alive and if she had been involved not only would I not have escaped, the whole question of whether or not a long-forgotten god could be killed would now be settled. I suspected I wouldn't like the answer.

No, Jones was no doubt the one who rescued me. That meant that I was on Earth and in Baltimore. Which meant that Nick wasn't involved. Still, there was an air of unused magic about her. A spell uncast. One that stirred ancient memories. And interestingly enough a touch of succubus lust. But that was the least of the mysteries I had to solve.

I approached her warily, still unsure of her feelings toward me. "Detective Jones."

She returned my nod with one of her own. "Chief Negral." Then she looked down meaningfully. "Must have been cold in there."

"You have no idea," I said, ignoring the barb, although her pointed glance reminded me of my lack of clothing. Not that I had anything to be ashamed about, but using my powers I hurriedly clothed myself in fire and transformed it into my usual raiment – pinstriped suit, snap-brimmed fedora, and trenchcoat. I wore regular clothes but this would work until I could visit my tailor.

"Friends of yours?" she asked, indicating the frozen corpses on the storehouse floor.

"Never met them before today. One wasn't so bad. But I hope to become acquainted with their employer."

"Would that be the demon who was with them?"

I shook my head and had the fireball with Masky's ashes dance a little. "Another flunky. This goes higher up, or rather, lower down. Speaking of which …"

She was a cop. She understood. "You have to get going."

"Yeah. Are you okay with these guys?"

"Dumb bastards were fooling with a stolen cryochamber. Got hit with some chemicals. We got here too late to save them."

There wasn't anything else to say except, "Thanks, I owe you."

"Damn straight you do."

We both knew how that bill was going to be settled. But that was business for another time. Opening a portal, I stepped back into Hell.

*

It's easier to travel by fire, but burning the storehouse down would have been stretching Jones's professional courtesy a bit too far. The jump from Earth to the Pit used up most the power I had siphoned from the demon, so once in my office, I rested, soaking in Hell's manna along with an added boost from Thurman.

Refreshed, I left my office an hour later emerging into the waiting area to find a surprised and relieved Rachael and an equally surprised Cliff. Funny, he didn't near as happy to see as Rachael did.

"Boss, you're back!" She looked as if she was waiting for an explanation. She didn't get one. Hell's just one big disappointment after another.

"Yeah, I'm back. Find Bambi and tell her I've got a job for her. Cliff, stick around."

He looked nervous. Good. "What do you need, Chief?"

"Guard the door from inside my office. Nobody in or out, including the two of you." I ripped the phone out of the wall. "I'm expecting company and I'm setting a fire spell. Anyone coming in either door will be incinerated," I lied. Not that I couldn't do it, but I didn't have the time or energy to spare right now. "That includes the two of you, so stay put. I've had enough surprises this millennium." I whispered a few questions to Rachel, got the answers I wanted, and headed out the door. I lit up the doors' seams for effect as I left.

*

Think about every nudie bar, strip joint, gentlemen's club and bordello you have ever seen or imagined. Add to that a sultan's harem merged with a masochist's wet dream. Throw in the fantasies of a dozen teenage boys. Put all that under one roof and you'd have only a shadow of what Bambi's palace was like.

Only those truly favored were permitted in the excess that she called a boudoir. It was more than that. It was the main ride of a sexual theme park and a monument to all things carnal.

It was here that Bambi awaited her visitor, on a bed easily the size of a basketball court. Glancing over at her clock, she saw that he was about to arrive. He'd be exactly on time, no one dared be late and it was well known that Bambi hated it when men came too soon.

Precisely at the appointed time, he waltzed into her bedroom – naked, visible, randy, and ready to reap the reward he was lying to earn. And that's exactly what he got.

"It took a while," the spigh said, his tone somewhere between bragging and adoration. "But I did what you asked. That damned detective won't be bothering you anymore."

'Thank you," Bambi purred, the lust in her voice almost visible. "However did you do it?"

"Doesn't matter," the spigh said hurriedly, anxious for his big payoff and all but running toward the bed.

I dropped the confounding heat that was cloaking me. I had used it like a mirage in the desert, showing an image of Bambi from the next room. "I think I'd like to know."

I mentioned that spighs are dangerous and sneaky. Unfortunately for him, so was I. The important thing after a surprise is don't give a sucker a chance to react. Forming my hand into the shape of a gun, I shot a laser beam from my forefinger, cutting off that part of him he was planning to use on Bambi. As he fell to the floor in pain I moved in to interrogate.

"Why did you do this?" I said.

"Screw you!"

I put my foot above the pieces I had relieved him of and pushed down. "I don't think that's going to be very possible. Let me explain how this is going to work. I ask, you answer. I don't like it, I make another slice and you lose another piece." I sliced off both ankles and hands. "Why?"

"Because you gave my brother over to Balchain."

"Ah, brotherly love. Who'd have thunk it?"

"He was high up and the Satan liked him. He made sure I shared his success. Without him, I got sent to the bottom of the spigh ranks, with all the fecal assignments. My life has been miserable."

"Would it help if I said I felt bad? Not that I would. Now explain how you got to my people and please don't leave anything out."

He didn't. In thanks, I made the rest of his butchering relatively quick, although I must admit I didn't exactly try for painless.

When I was done, there was nothing but bloody little spigh bits all over Bambi's formerly nice, clean carpeting.

Bambi waited until I was done with the spigh before speaking, "How did you know it was him?"

"Spighs come and go between here and Earth relatively freely. Only they would have the resources to set up what he did without me finding out about it. Impressive that you convinced him to come here on his own. It would have taken me a very long time to track him down." Invisible demons that have the run of the Pit and access to Earth aren't exactly easy to find. And then finding the right one would have likely taken years.

Bambi shrugged and smiled. "I let it be known that I was on the run from you and would pay prettily for anyone who could help me out. Who'd turn that down?"

"Not many."

Bambi started to look nervous. "Chief, what he said, I hope you don't think I had anything to do with …"

"You're still here, aren't you?" I interrupted. The spigh had already put his plan into motion, but he figured Bambi didn't need to know that. "If you had …" I looked at the mess that had been the spigh and then at her. She got the idea.

"Rachael told me how you helped, that you searched for me here and got help for me on Earth."

"She helped too, going through your files, telling me where to look and who to contact."

"Glad to hear it." And I was, very glad. And very sad.

Bambi stood there as if expecting something. If it was thanks, well, like I said, Hell is one big disappointment. Bambi did what she did because she had to. Then again, she could have figured out ways to work around my order, splitting hairs, dragging her feet the whole time. Her beauty and lust appeal make it easy to forget she's a smart cookie. I stopped by a few informants before I came over. By all accounts she busted her hump looking out for me. That meant something, although I wasn't sure exactly what.

"Bring in that mob you call your followers. Have them each take a piece of that." I indicated the remains of the spigh. "I want it scattered so far around the plains of Hell that it will be three years after the Judgment that he pulls himself together." I kept a piece so if he ever did manage it, I'd know about it.

I still couldn't get past Bambi going above and beyond what she had to. The succubus deserved better than the usual brush off this time.

I took her hand and brought it to my lips. "You did good, doll. Keep up the good work."

I turned and walked out. I did my best to not look back, but out of the corner of my eye I saw her holding her hand tenderly to her chest and she was smiling.

If I didn't know better, I'd say the best succubus in Hell was carrying a torch for me. Even the Devil himself couldn't claim that.

Back to my office, I found Cliff where I left him, still standing guard inside my door, too scared to leave. Like the last time, he didn't look too pleased to see me.

"Why?"

"Why what, Chief?"

I pinned half the spigh's heart to my wall with my letter opener.

"You want to rethink that answer?"

"It wasn't anything personal. Cuccus..." The spigh's name. "... said if I went along with him, when it was done I'd have your job."

Even as pissed and betrayed as I was I couldn't help but laugh.

"What's so funny? That's how you move up in Hell, taking out those above you."

"Not with my job."

"Why not?"

Because the Devil can't trust anyone in Hell to not betray him given a quarter of a chance. That's why he needed an outsider to be Chief of police.

"You poor sap."

"Hey, he said he wasn't going to hurt or kill you."

"His mistake. Yours was backing him." I held out my hand. "Badge." Cliff returned it reluctantly. Next, I reached out with my flame and incinerated his clothes.

The loss of clothes got across more than the loss of his badge. "Chief, I'll make it up to you. I'm sorry."

"No, you just think you are. But you'll learn. Come with me,"

I said, and walked him past a stunned Rachael downtown to the Corner.

I went back there the next day with my secretary.

The line for Rebecca Huntingdon's favors was not as long as it had been. And there was another line, this one leading from another entrance to the same building. Something fresher, someone newer.

For about twenty minutes we just stood there watching. Finally, I said, "If you listen very carefully, you can almost hear Cliff screaming." That's when Rachael realized just who the line was for. Him and the three of the four fools who sold him their souls and stood guard outside my cold, dark prison. The spigh had brought Cliff to Baltimore to help get some souls since he knew the lay of the land from his time on the BPD. Owning four souls was wealth, a bribe to buy his help. As one of my cops, he knew the power that those who actually owned souls had. It made Cliff a player. A very minor player, but a player nevertheless. Unfortunately for Cliff, since he worked for me, technically I owned them. And this was just the beginning of making the four of them pay. The lot was just here long enough to teach a lesson before the payback really started. I'd strand them and Masky in the frigid wastelands of the Ninth Circle. They'd get some idea of what it feels like to be so cold you can't move.

"I thought Cliff made you uncomfortable. When did you start screwing him?"

"Chief, I swear I …" It's hard for a creature of fire to give anyone a cold stare, but I managed it. Rachael sighed. "About a month ago. What made you suspect?"

I wanted to say point out that I was a detective. I wanted to tell her that once I was free from the icebox I realized that it was the *inside* of my head that had been hurting, not the outside. That meant that I'd been slipped a mickey, just something in my coffee to slow me down. With me distracted by what had been done to Skinless, it was enough for the spigh to get the drop on me.

If Bambi hadn't told me about how Rachael had helped look for me, she might now be Deni's new star attraction. Finding her with Cliff put the last pieces together. I took him to the Corner and we stood and watched, much like Rachel and I are doing now. Without clothes, he was feeling a little vulnerable and started flapping his gums. He mentioned seducing Rachael so as to get to me. He slipped me the mickey, but Rachel let herself get distracted enough by Cliff's attentions to either let him mess with my coffee or not notice him doing it. Either one was not acceptable.

Seems Cliff thought telling me the truth would help him get back his old position. Instead, it just helped him get a whole bunch of new ones.

But I didn't tell my secretary any of this. Rachel didn't need to know it. What she did need was to be punished. And I had something in mind far worse than the Corner.

"You broke the rules," I told her. "You lied to me and betrayed my trust and it almost cost me … everything. I should send you over to Deni. But you were played for a sap. Still, this is Hell, which means I'm still supposed to do something about it. It would bad for business to let you get away with what you did."

"Wh…what are you going to do, Chief?"

I pulled a folded paper from the inside pocket of my trenchcoat. "You were tricked into signing over your soul. Other than that, you did nothing to deserve Hell. Until now. This," I held up the paper, "was your ticket out. I got your contract voided. You were on your way out of the Pit." I made a great show of tearing it into little pieces. As I dropped them, each burst into flame and was incinerated before reaching the ground. "Now you're well and truly damned."

Rachel fell to her knees and burst into tears.

I was lying of course. The paper was my shopping list for the next time I went Earthside. There was never a chance that she would be released. But she didn't know that. And now she'd live every second of eternity believing that a few moments of passion had cost her salvation.

"On your feet," I said. "Unless you want to stay here."

Rachel jumped to her feet.

"Follow me." We walked further down the Corner. I had left Lefty in the care of Deni the Slut with explicit instructions that he was not to be harmed, only forced to look on as his three fellows and Cliff became Deni's latest attraction.

"Any problems?" I asked.

"None, Chief," said Deni. "Seems a waste of perfectly good meat to me."

"I have other plans for him."

"What about these four?"

"I'll be back day after tomorrow for them."

"Guess I'll have to cram as much as I can in," Deni said.

"You always do, Deni."

"Chief, you sweet talker you."

"I want all their pieces."

"Spoilsport."

I motioned for Lefty to follow. Neither damned said a word until we were back inside my outer office.

"Who's the new guy, Chief?" asked Rachel.

"That's my new coffee guy. Rachel, you are not to touch my coffee ever again. Clear?"

She gulped and nodded.

"Joe…" Yeah, Lefty's name was really Joe. I got a lot of grief from the java demon about keeping him, "is also going to be our dispatcher." In light of recent events, I thought it best to keep better track of where my officers were. "Joe, we clear on things?"

"As crystal, Chief."

"And if there is ever anything put in my coffee that shouldn't be there, or you cross me in any other way, you are clear on where you'll be going?"

Joe just nodded.

"Good." I turned to go into my personal office.

"Chief…"

"Yes, Joe?"

"Did you have a chance to take care of that other thing?"

"It'll be done later today."

"Thank you, Chief."

I nodded and shut the door behind me.

Matthew's is an old-fashioned pizzeria in Baltimore. At a table for two Bianca Jones, investigator of the weird for the BPD, sat across from Negral, one time Sumerian god and now the Devil's Detective. She was there at his invitation.

Negral waited until their tomato pies had been served and mostly eaten.

"It wouldn't have worked, you know?"

"What wouldn't?"

"Your plan to turn me into a djinn." Bianca almost choked but caught herself in time. "It took me a while to recognize the spell you were planning to use."

"Keep telling yourself that, Negral, and one day you'll wake up in a lamp."

"If you were so sure, Bianca, why didn't you go through with it? It would have been the smart thing to do."

Bianca looked at the cop from Hell. "Down where you work. Don't think I didn't consider it. Up here," she shook her head, "it may have been the smart thing, but it wouldn't have been the right thing. And if I don't do what's right, I'm no better than the guy you work for."

"I'm still in your debt."

"That you are, and free pizza's not going to cover the bill."

"I know." Negral stood. "Any chance Bambi's gift to you and your husband would take care of it?"

Bianca's cheeks turned red. "None."

"Before we wipe any slates, did you bring what I asked?"

Bianca nodded and slid a knapsack across the table. "You want to explain why you wanted the money we found at the warehouse."

"Not really." Negral had picked up Lefty Joe's stash. There was less than twelve hundred there. By contrast, the spigh had twenty grand in spending money stashed at the warehouse. He put eleven hundred in with the twenty K. "Technically, as a representative of Hell, it belongs to me."

"Technically, yes. I certainly am not about to steal something from evidence for you." Bianca slid a piece of paper across the table. "You are still going to sign for it."

Negral scanned the page, which seemed like a standard return of property release. "No hidden clauses?"

"No."

"Had to ask."

"Can that be done and be binding?"

Hell's Detective shrugged and signed the paper. "Not consistently."

Just then a woman walked in pushing a baby carriage, noted the man in the fedora and trenchcoat and headed for him.

"You're Negral?" she said.

"Yep. You are Melissa Higgins?"

She nodded. "You said you had something from Joe for me?"

Bianca's eyebrows rose.

"Not your Joe. Joe Diego." Negral handed her the knapsack. "He wanted you to have this."

She started to open it. "Don't. There's more than twenty-one grand in there." Melissa gasped. Negral slipped a hundred into the palm of her hand. "Go right to a bank and ask to rent a safe deposit box. They will take you to a private room where you can transfer the cash into the box. Whenever you need more, you can go and get some. Don't waste it."

"How did Joe get this kind of money?"

"He made a smart choice before he died," said Negral.

"How do I know this isn't drug money or something?"

"Because I'm a cop."

Melissa looked at Bianca who flashed her badge. "He is."

"Why would a cop do this for Joe?"

"It was his last request. He wanted to make sure you and his daughter would be taken care of."

Melissa wiped at her eye. "What do we do when it runs out?"

"Use the time you have it to better yourself so you can earn a living."

"Melissa, here's my card," said Bianca. "Call me next week. I will hook you up with a career counselor at the community college. I think we might even be able to get you in for the next semester. They even have a daycare."

Melissa looked at the card, then the faces of the very different cops. "I will. Thanks."

The young mother and child left the restaurant.

"Just when I think I have you figured out, you go and do something like that," said Bianca. "What's the real reason?"

"Fulfilling a dying man's last request."

"I figure the cash you shoved in was his. Why give her the rest?"

Negral shrugged. "Why not?"

"Feeling guilty over killing him?"

"Nope, cause I didn't kill him. The demon that was behind this whole mess put a spell on the lot to kill them before they could talk."

"What about the other three?"

"I have the right to remain silent," said Negral. "I think it's time we got down to the business at hand." Hell's Detective cast a slight confounding heat that would momentarily shield them from the other patrons. In a very formal tone he said, "Bianca Jones, as the one to whom you made sacrifice and to whom you owe service, I hereby release you from any fealty and obligation to me in exchange for the service you did me."

"Thank you, Lord Negral," Bianca said just as formally. Inwardly she wasn't quite convinced that she had owed Negral anything, and she wondered what would have been the outcome of any attempt by him to enforce the obligation. Still, she felt relieved that it would never be put to the test.

"The offer still stands," she added.

Despite knowing what she meant, Negral still asked, "What offer is that?"

"Give it up. Stop working for the Prince of Evil. If you don't want to partner with me, the DMA could use you. Or go private, just like those guys in the movies."

The forgotten fire god smiled. "I appreciate the offer, but my place is down below, maintaining a kind of order in the chaos and doing what good I can. Sure it's Hell, but what cop's job isn't?"

"If you ever need back-up ..."

"You'll be the first one I call."

JOHN L. FRENCH has worked for over thirty-five years as a crime scene investigator and has seen more than his share of murders, shootings, and serious assaults. As a break from the realities of his job, he writes science fiction, pulp, horror, fantasy, and, of course, crime fiction.

In 1992 John began writing stories based on his training and experiences on the streets of Baltimore. His first story "Past Sins" was published in Hardboiled Magazine and was cited as one of the best Hardboiled stories of 1993. More crime fiction followed, appearing in Alfred Hitchcock's Mystery Magazine, the Fading Shadows magazines and in collections by Barnes and Noble. Association with writers like James Chambers and the late, great C.J. Henderson led him to try horror fiction and to a still growing fascination with zombies and other undead things. His first horror story "The Right Solution" appeared in Marietta Publishing's Lin Carter's Anton Zarnak. Other horror stories followed in anthologies such as The Dead Walk and Dark Furies, both published by Die Monster Die books. It was in Dark Furies that Bianca Jones made her literary debut in "21 Doors," a story based on an old Baltimore legend and a creepy game his daughter used to play with her friends.

John's first book was The Devil of Harbor City, a novel done in the old pulp style. Past Sins and Here There Be Monsters soon followed. John was also consulting editor for Chelsea House's Criminal Investigation series. His other books include The Assassins' Ball (Written with Patrick Thomas), Paradise Denied, Blood Is the Life and The Nightmare Strikes. John is the editor of To Hell In A Fast Car, Mermaids 13, C. J. Henderson's Challenge of the Unknown, and (with Greg Schauer) With Great Power…

PATRICK THOMAS is the author of almost 40 books including the beloved fantasy humor Murphy's Lore series, which includes *Tales From Bulfinche's Pub, Fools' Day, Through The Drinking Glass, Shadow Of The Wolf, Redemption Road, Bartender Of The Gods, Nightcaps, Empty Graves, The Mug Life* — as well as the future space adventures *Startenders* and *Constellation Prize*.

The Murphy's Lore After Hours spin-offs star the half pixie/ogre Terrorbelle (*Fairy With A Gun, Fairy Rides The Lightning*); the former demon-possessed serial killer Agent Karver of the Department of Mystic Affairs (*Dead To Rites, Rites of Passage*); the cursed magí Hex (*By Darkness Cursed and BY Invocation Only*); Vince Argus, the Soul For Hire (*Greatest Hits*); and Negral, a forgotten Sumerian god who works as Hell's Detective (*Lore & Dysorder* and *Bullets & Brimstone*).

Co-Written with John French and Diane Raetz, his Mystic Investigators paranormal mystery series includes *Bullets & Brimstone, From The Shadows* and *Once More Upon A Time. Assassin's Ball*, his first mystery, is also co-written with John French.

He also wrote the steampunk *As The Gears Turn* and the space epic *Exile & Entrance*. He co-edited *New Blood* and *Hear Them Roar* and was an editor for the magazines *Fantastic Stories of the Imagination* and *Pirate Writings*.

Patrick's darkly humorous advice column Dear Cthulhu has been running since 2005 and includes the collections *Have A Dark Day, Good Advice For Bad People, Cthulhu Knows Best, Cthulhu Happens, Cthulhu Explains It All* and *What Would Cthulhu Do?*

His short stories have been featured in over sixty anthologies and more than forty-five print magazines.

A number of his books were part of the props department of the CSI television show and have been spotted on the program. Nightcaps was even thrown at a suspect's head. His urban fantasy Fairy With A Gun had been optioned for film and TV by Laurence Fishburne's Cinema Gypsy Productions. Top Men Productions has turned his Soul For Hire Story, *Act of Contrition*, into a short film.

He is also writing books for kids as Patrick T. Fibbs.

Please drop by www.patthomas.net or follow him at I_PatrickThomas at Twitter or www.facebook.com/PatrickThomasAuthor to learn more.

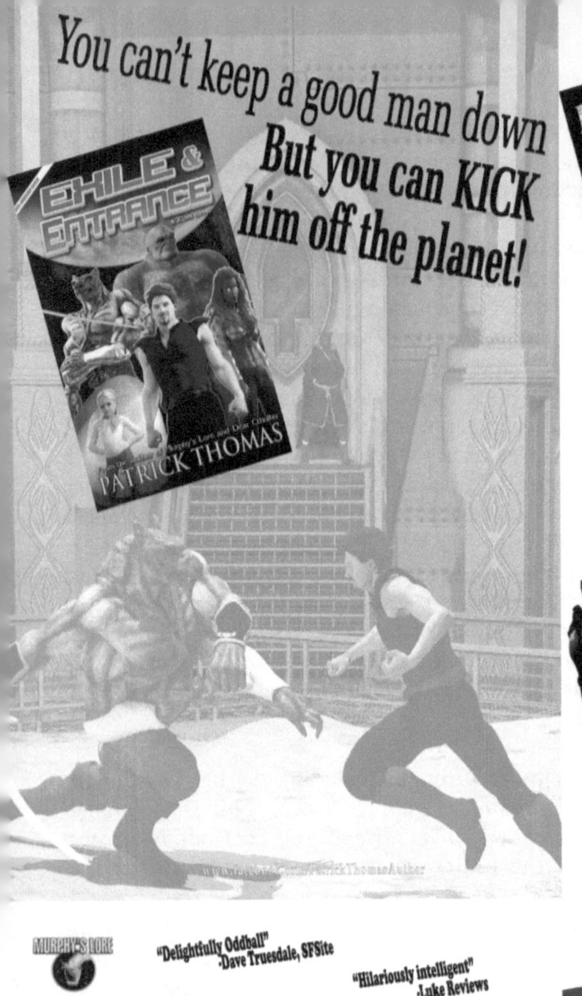

THE STARSCAPE PROJECT

As his quest begins, an artificial intelligence life form enters the galaxy and launches a series of covert attacks against the Empire. The Teconeans assume that the Federation is responsible, and galactic peace is about to unravel. As Stryker chases his nemesis into Teconean space, he finds himself thrown into middle of the battle. Knowing that Earth will be the aliens' next target, Stryker must decide whether to let them destroy the Empire, or to forces with his Teconean enemies against the invaders. The key to the mysterious aliens lies buried on the moon of Kennedy Prime, and it's up to Stryker to solve the puzzle before war benins. The fate of the galaxy is at stake.

ONE OF THE TENTH DGREE

1912, an alien ship crash lands in the Atlantic ean, setting up a secret colony that remains detected for centuries, allowing them to nipulate some of the most important events in man history -- from the sinking of the Titanic to Bermuda triangle to global warming. Now, technology of the 26th century has covered the aliens' distress beacon, and it's a e against time as the Navy tries to stop a rorist armed with a nuclear weapon from stroying the colony and triggering an all-out r as the mother-ship approaches

Now available from

PADWOLF PUBLISHING

By Invocation Only
Hex Factor
PATRICK THOMAS

Darkness Cursed
Hex and the pot
PATRICK THOMAS

LORE & DYSORDER
PATRICK THOMAS

SHADOWS OF THE BLEEDING STONE
PATRICK THOMAS

CASE OF THE MOON MANIAC

"Dark... and charming."
- Ellen Datlow,
The Best Horror of the Year Vol. 4

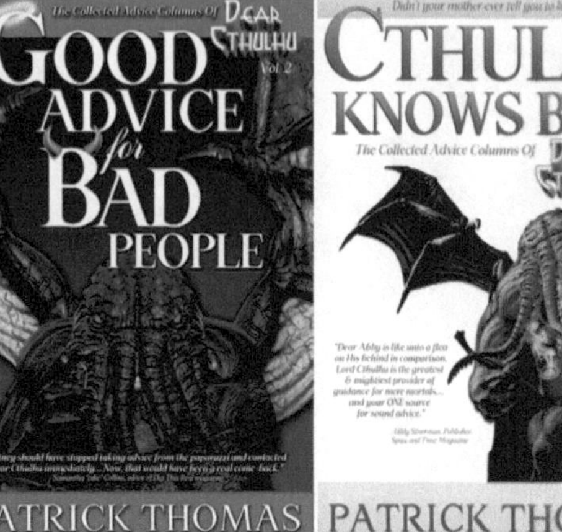

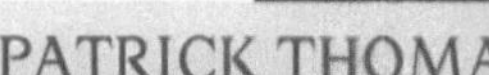

DEAR CTHULHU

The advice column to **END** all advice columns

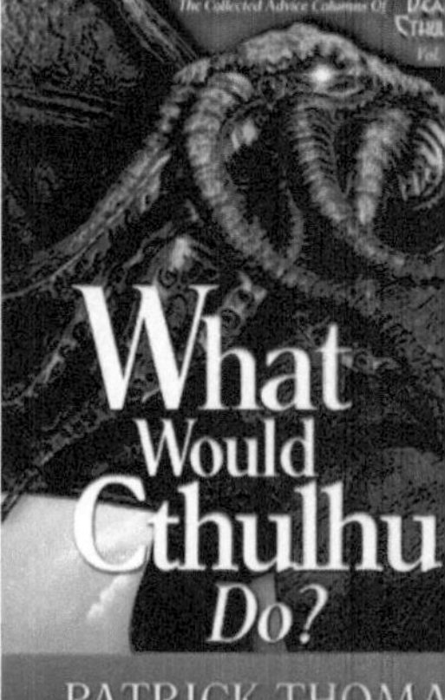

One Last Chance to Save Happily Ever After

Can a group of heroes including Goldenhair, Red Riding Hood and Rapunzel help General Snow White and her dwarven resistance fighters defeat the tyrannical Queen Cinderella? And will they succeed before a war with Wonderland destroys everything?

Their only hope to stop Cinderella's quest for power lies with a young girl named Patience Muffet who carries the fabled shards of Cinderella's glass slippers.

Roy Mauritsen's fantasy adventure fairy tale epic begins with *Shards Of The Glass Slipper: Queen Cinder.*

> "Fantastic...
> A Magnificent Epic!"
> -Sarah Beth Durst author of
> *Into The Wild & Drink, Slay, Love*

> "The Brothers Grimm meets
> Lord Of The Rings!"
> -Patrick Thomas, author
> of the Murphy's Lore series

> "Shards is a dark, lush, full-throttle fantasy epic that presents a bold re-imagining of classic characters."
> -David Wade, creator of
> 319 Dark Street

> "Roy Mauritsen's enchanting epic comes at a time when fairy tales are back in the forefront of our collective imagination."
> -Darin Kennedy, short fiction author

PADWOLF PUBLISHING

Find us on: facebook

In paperback & e-book
Find out more at:
shardsoftheglassslipper.com
padwolf.com

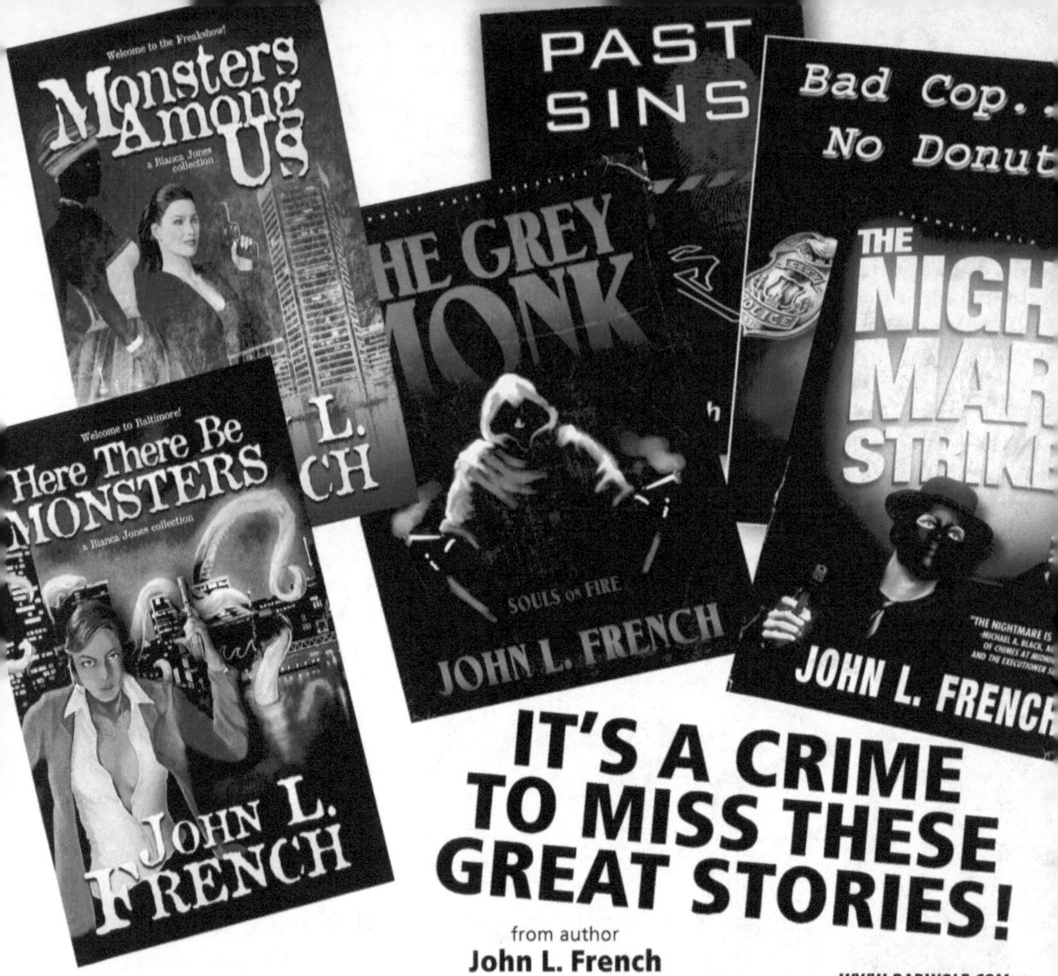

Welcome to the Freakshow!
Monsters Among Us
a Bianca Jones collection

PAST SINS

Bad Cop...
No Donut

THE GREY MONK
SOULS ON FIRE
JOHN L. FRENCH

THE NIGHTMARE STRIKES
JOHN L. FRENCH

Welcome to Baltimore!
Here There Be MONSTERS
a Bianca Jones collection
JOHN L. FRENCH

IT'S A CRIME
TO MISS THESE
GREAT STORIES!
from author
John L. French
WWW.PADWOLF.COM

APOCALYPSE 13

MERMAID 13

Camelot 13
Edited by
John L. French and Patrick Thomas

LUCKY 13

A detective's work is never done.
And don't call him Baby Bear...

15th Aniversary
Omnibus of
Books 1-6

The zombie
apocalypse
is over..

Now even undead kids have
to go to school

5 SILLY
MONSTERS
JUMPING ON
THE ZED

a picture book
for kids

www.talehaven.com